Dragon Home

DRAGON HOME

LEGION OF RIDERS: BOOK ONE

J.D. Hallowell

SMITHCRAFT
PRESS

Smithcraft Press
110 San Paulo Circle
West Melbourne, FL 32904

ISBN 978-1-62927-027-2

CONTENTS

DEDICATION

DRAGON HOME is dedicated to all who feel the magic and rise up on dragons' wings with fire in your hearts.

Acknowledgements

WHILE SPACE DOES not permit me to acknowledge everyone I owe a debt of gratitude to regarding this book, I am especially grateful to my wife, Jennie, my son, Connor, my brother, Jim, and my friends Matt DuPree, Craig Janssen, and Craig Lloyd-Smith, who have been endlessly patient, encouraging, and helpful. Lori B. of Dragon's Edge in the Melbourne Square Mall, who keeps me supplied with dragons and connected with local readers, definitely merits a mention. Special thanks are due to several authors who have given generously of either their general or specific advice and support, especially Michael J. Sullivan, Leeland Artra, Cheryl Matthynssens, Brian D. Anderson, T. Jackson King, Cheryllyn Dyess, and everyone at the Fantasy Science-Fiction Network, as well as Jaimie Engle, whose tireless energy and enthusiasm along with the wealth of knowledge and insight that she shares so freely makes her a treasure, and last, but certainly not least, the incredible and inspiring Kerry Hall. No thanks would be complete without mentioning Taylor Rogers of Double R Danes, who donated a Great Dane puppy as the successor to Indie, my service dog partner of twelve years who passed to shadow in the summer of 2017. Of course, my deepest gratitude is reserved for my readers and fans, without whom I am simply talking to myself.

PROLOGUE

"I WONDER WHATALL of this is about," Wanda asked, flexing her wings restlessly. "I know that any Lineage Holder can call for such a meeting, and no one is actually obligated to attend. However, if the meeting is open, as she has claimed, why did she exclude us?"

"I'm not sure," Geneva replied. "She stopped speaking to me before we even finished in Horne. I had to go through the other dragons most of the time to coordinate our combat tactics. She claimed she was simply too busy to talk with every individual involved, but since my bond-mate was the overall commander, as was agreed by everyone including the non-bonded dragons, it seemed there was more getting in the way of communication than her duties. If Delno or I needed those dragons under her command to do something specific, I had to go through one of her subordinates even when she and I were close enough to converse in actual spoken words, as you and I are doing now."

"Yes, Nassari and I had the same trouble with her after the first major skirmish when we burned those beast-men before they could ambush our soldiers. She spoke with Saadia and Pena readily enough when they needed to coordinate with her, but she acted as if she had no time to deal with you or me." Wanda said.

"Whatever the reason, she has called for a meeting of Lineage Holders a month from now, but she has specifically avoided inviting the two of us, or even pinning down the exact time and date. Delno and Rita have to return to Bourne in the morning, which means that Fahwn and I will have to go with them. She may be hoping that I will be occupied in the north and unable to attend," Geneva stated. "However, that still does not explain her reasoning for the meeting, or for leaving us out."

"I may be able to shed some light on that," Saadia interjected.

Both Geneva and Wanda turned toward the smaller blue dragon expectantly but waited patiently for her to collect her thoughts rather than prompting her to continue.

Finally, she said, "I have been talking to my mother, and she is very concerned with the number of non-bonded dragons who have come forward and found bond-mates. She is making noises that men are trying to enslave us as a species. She has told several of her friends that she believes the riders may have an ultimate goal of putting all of us under their control."

Fahwn blew a raspberry and said, "She has no idea what is happening with that. The dragons who have come forward have done so of their own free will! No one is being coerced into this, and it is certainly not some plot set in motion by the humans involved. Hmmph! It could be argued that the dragons are seeking out and enslaving their human companions, if you use that logic, since it is our people who have come searching for partners."

"That may be," Pina responded, "but there are those who have voiced similar fears. Her arguments won't fall only on deaf ears. A few of the dragons who were too old to fight with us in Horne have heard that many have bonded, and that, coupled to the tales of that compelling stone and how it was used on our own kind, have them worried. Some of the oldest dragons alive are not so far removed from the beginnings of our race, and the thought of humans enslaving dragons is all too real to them."

"Well, be that as it may," Geneva spoke up, "we can only do what we are doing. It is not as though Sheila can force us to give up our bond with our partners." The other dragons all nodded. "We will have to watch this situation very carefully. I still do not know what her problem is in this concern, but the answer will present itself soon enough. This meeting will obviously take place, and I intend to be present for it."

"As do I," Wanda added.

"Well, then," Geneva said, "since we have discussed this all we can, and we all have an early day tomorrow, I suggest we get some sleep. Wanda and I will stay abreast of what is going on with our own people, and all of us will do everything we can to help our bond-mates get their business here in Corice finished so that we can move back to Horne and settle our new home. So for now, I bid you all good night."

The other dragons all said their good nights as well, and one by one they settled down to sleep.

Geneva was the last to close her eyes. "*We will get our home in the south settled,*" she thought to herself and smiled. "*Of course, it may be settled more to the liking of the bonded dragons than to that of anyone else.*"

Then, still smiling, she, too, drifted off to sleep.

CHAPTER 1

"REALLY, CAPTAIN, YOU are being totally unreasonable. I am simply asking for the supplies that have already been authorized by both the ruling council and the King himself," Nassari said for the third time. He closed his eyes and rubbed his temples with his fingertips.

The captain, a balding man of about fifty, waited for the rider to compose himself.

Nadia watched the exchange but said nothing.

Putting on his most winning smile, Nassari looked the man in the eyes and said, "It has been just over a month since the war between Corice and Bourne ended, and the King has authorized funds to help the Riders outfit the new Legion Headquarters. The council may take a dim view of having to fund our endeavors, but His Majesty does not."

"His Majesty may be behind you on this Rider, but the paperwork you have here makes my job clear. I do apologize, but I can only give you what is on the order. I can't provide what isn't authorized," the man replied.

"Well, I am trying to understand your problem," Nadia interjected, "but perhaps you don't understand ours. We have twenty-seven newly bonded pairs to outfit before we push on to Horne. The king, with the council's approval, has said that all of the new Riders are to be given basic equipment so they can begin training. Some of the poorer candidates, especially from Bourne, don't even own a belt knife or any personal bedding. All we're asking for are the simple necessities that were promised."

"Again I'm sorry, Rider," the captain responded, "despite all of their promises to honor the dragons and their Riders for all that they have done, the politicians are sore about spending Corice's money on people who, considering that riders are neutral, aren't even actually loyal citizens of Crown. Now that the council members can operate behind closed doors, they are looking for ways to thwart that decree. Enough of them know about the military to understand how to write the purchase orders in such a way as to frustrate your attempts to outfit the newly bonded riders."

"What exactly are you saying?" Nasssari asked.

"The authorization doesn't say anything about having thirty dragon saddles made, and the signed decree says that Corice will fund the Legion Headquarters, not those individuals who will travel there," the captain replied.

"No," Nassari responded as reasonably as he could, "it says 'foodstuffs and other supplies as needed.' The saddles are part of the other supplies we need. Without them how are we expected to leave Corice and establish our headquarters?"

"Saddles are equipment, not supplies, Sir. Supplies are things like clothing, footwear, and stuff used for personal hygiene, you know, general consumables. Livery, weapons, tents, and even personal bedding can be cleaned and reissued, so such things are equipment, and your purchase order is for supplies only. I know it seems like we're arguing semantics, but army regulations are clear on nomenclature."

"Fine, if clothing is deemed to be 'supplies,' then consider the saddles to be clothing for the dragons, and get the saddlers to make the damn things," Nassari's exasperation came through despite his best efforts to hide it.

"Dragons don't wear clothes, and saddles aren't clothes anyway," the captain said tiredly. "Look, Rider, I'd like to help you out in this, but the council has made it crystal clear that all supplies are to be for the Legion headquarters, not for the personal use of individuals. You are to get only what's been authorized, and it was made especially clear you were to be given no weapons, no shields, and no livery. Myself, I think it stinks, especially since it was you Riders who did the bulk of the work getting all of that mess with Bourne sorted out. I've bent the rules and slipped in the blankets you wanted by diverting some of the newly repaired stuff before it could be checked in and added to my inventory, but I can't hide having saddles made. I'm close to retirement, and if I give you what you're asking for, I will lose my rank and my pension. I may be of noble birth, but I'm not independently wealthy and I need to think of how I'll feed myself and my missus. I'm sorry."

Nadia, who had been going over the list of supplies they'd already been given, said, "What about that bulk leather over there. Is that supplies, or equipment?"

"Bulk leather is considered to be general consumables, ma'am" the captain replied.

"Fine," Nadia said, "We'll take all of that you have on hand, and that heavy thread on the shelves above it, too."

The captain looked thoughtful for a moment and then shrugged his shoulders and added the supplies Nadia requested to the list.

Nassari looked at her and raised his eyebrow.

"Two of the new Riders are leather workers. One is a journeyman and served part of his apprenticeship in a saddlery in Karne," she said. "We'll just make our own and use any money that saves us on the labor costs for other supplies."

Nassari looked at her and grinned. "No task is too daunting for you, is it, dear?"

"I don't know," she replied, "I haven't tried everything." Then she smiled mischievously and added, "Yet."

Chapter 2

"IT'S GOING TO take more than a month for Ben and Robin to get those saddles done," Nassari complained. "I wish we had more in the coffers. I'd like to hire some outside people to work on this so that we can get underway. I am going to miss my homeland, but I won't miss this bickering and begging we have to go through every time we want anything."

"Well, I have to agree with you," Nadia said as she toweled dry. "I am getting tired of the politicians also. They talk of the Riders as heroes and saviors to,the public because the people like us. Then, when they are behind closed doors, they try to restrict our funding to the point that we are lucky to have enough bread and cheese to feed ourselves. We aren't exactly eating high on the hog here. It's not like we've asked for gourmet foodstuffs and chefs to prepare them."

She stopped speaking while she dried the top of her head and the towel fell in front of her face. Nassari thought about their relationship as he watched her. He liked watching her. He was a bit surprised to find that he found her so attractive. Before he had bonded to Wanda and become a "responsible" Rider, he had liked his women comfortably rounded and somewhat less capable than Nadia intellectually. He hadn't taken advantage of half-wits, but he'd preferred his female companions to be of less than stellar intelligence since conversation hadn't even been on his list of priorities.

Nadia was definitely not one of the slower-witted buxom beauties he had dallied with in the past. She was shorter even than Rita by at least an inch, and she had a youngish-looking face that at first gave the impression she wasn't any more than about fourteen or fifteen. Some of that was compounded by the fact that she wore her hair short for convenience. Also, she tended to wear boys' clothing rather than girls', which hid her natural curves and accentuated her small stature.

The one thing she didn't seem to be good at was making clothes, so she had to buy them. The Corisians tended to be very pragmatic people and most mothers made their children's everyday garments. The problem with girls' clothing in sizes that Nadia could buy and wear was that it was usually frilly and not made to stand up to the rigors of normal daily activity, much less heavy work and physical training. Boys' clothes that were available at shops also tended to be for dress, but dress clothing for boys simply meant white shirts and dyed pants rather than typical light brown unbleached linen.

Nadia was nicely curved, but since it was proportional to her petite size it usually didn't show through the loose shirts and pants she wore. That, added to the fact that she could outfight most of the men she sparred with in both hand-to-hand and sword practice, tended to make people think that she didn't have a feminine side.

Because of the manner of dress, and her sometimes gruff mannerisms, she was mistaken for being a tom-boy. She was definitely a woman though. Nassari had found that out soon after they had begun associating. While she was one of the most capable people he knew, she could be soft and vulnerable when she was alone with him and comfortable in her surroundings. When she let her guard down, she was perhaps the most feminine woman he had ever known, and completely capable of holding up her end of an intelligent conversation, and he was thoroughly enchanted with her. Sometime during the development of their relationship, she had become one of his best friends as well as his lover.

He realized she had been talking and shook himself to break the spell. "I'm sorry, Nadia, I was paying more attention to watching you than listening to what you were saying. Could you repeat that?"

She smiled and shook her head, "You'd think that as long as we've been together the novelty of seeing me naked would have worn off."

"I don't think that will ever happen, Darling. At least I hope it doesn't." He took her hand in his and kissed it.

Her smile broadened and she pulled him to her and kissed him on the lips. When she let him go, she said, "What I was saying was that Ben is not just making those saddles. He is teaching the new Riders to make their own. This way he can supervise half a dozen or so at a time for a couple of hours each day with each group. It will take longer to get the saddles this way than it would if we had them made by outsiders, but the new Riders will get valuable experience and will be better able to care for and repair their own gear." Before he could comment, she added, "I know that you, Delno, and Brock want the Riders to be somewhat reliant on those they are to protect, but I see no reason for them to be so dependent that they become helpless when it comes to basic necessities." Then she wrinkled her nose slightly and said, "Especially if they find themselves at the mercy of people like our own politicians. Besides, we won't even have that miserly bunch to provide us with funds once we move to the Fort."

"Well, I can see your point," he responded, "but the reason I wanted to have those saddles made was to get these people in the air and out of here as soon as possible. I am eager to get back to the Fort and put everything in order there, but I am also simply anxious to quit this place. I have had all of these scheming politicians I can handle for the time being." At her somewhat shocked look, he said, "I know, I used to be one of them. I left here to try and change my life and ended up embroiled in the politics of another country. Then I returned and found more of the same. I probably would have been fine with it all if I hadn't bonded with Wanda, but being bonded with a dragon, especially a Lineage Holder, has given me a new perspective on things. I want nothing more now than to get the Legion Headquarters set up and then have a holiday so that we can take Walker up on his offer to show us the Elven lands. What

I desire most, besides being with you, is to learn more about the world at large."

"Well, Nae-sah-rae," she used the name Walker Longleaf had given him back in Horne when he felt that his good friend Nassa-ri should have a name that at least sounded Elvish, and changed it accordingly, "I would like nothing better than to get out of these mountains and into lower, more temperate climes myself, but Delno and Rita are still helping his mother get the Duchy of Bourne situated, and that leaves you and me to make sure these new Riders are settled and ready to travel to Horne."

"Fine, but once those saddles are made they can continue training on the fly," he responded. "I don't care how cold it is, or how hard the snow might blow, we are leaving as soon as I can be sure the new Riders can fly southwest without falling off their dragons."

He poured a glass of spiced wine and sat down. She moved close and sat on his lap facing him. As he finished taking a sip of the wine, she took the glass and drank a bit herself. Then she kissed him again before she got up and moved back to the large polished metal mirror on the dresser to comb her hair.

"We also have to make arrangements to visit both of our families. I'm sure that your mother will be as interested in meeting the woman you have taken up with as my father and brothers will be in meeting my man."

"I am somewhat dreading that encounter," he replied. "I am not unknown in this town and my reputation won't exactly lend itself to instilling confidence in the family of a young woman."

"Well, Dear, while most of the people, especially the men, we meet in our day to day activities underestimate me…"

"Often to their chagrin," he quickly added.

She raised her eyebrows and smiled before continuing. "I can assure you that my father and brothers have known me long enough to have no such false misconceptions. They will take our relationship at face value because they know that I am a fully mature and capable woman." Then she frowned slightly and added, "What terrifies me is meeting your mother."

He laughed and said, "Darling, my mother is just a simple woman with a wonderful disposition. She will love you."

"So you have said, but I am taking her only son away from her. I can see the situation from that point of view. I just hope she is as sweet and understanding as you think she is."

"I could say the same thing about your family. There are five boys; however, I am not only taking away the youngest child, but your father's only little girl." Then he smiled and said jokingly, "I think we should have both families get together at one big party, and then serve nothing but finger foods, and make sure that the only silverware in evidence is no sharper than the spoons in the condiment dishes."

She laughed but nodded in agreement. Then she began pulling on a long heavy nightgown. At his look of inquiry, she said, "I'm going to look in on the new Riders before I go to sleep. Many of the kids in this batch are barely into adolescence, and I don't trust any of them to keep their urges in check. I am going to make absolutely sure that the boys are in the boys' dorm and the girls are alone in their beds. I know that we have adults between the two sets of rooms, but I just want to see for myself. We are having enough trouble with the council as it is; I don't want them to start berating us because we can't even control the youngsters in our own quarters."

"That's a good idea," he responded. "I've already asked Wanda to get their own draconic partners to watch for any nonsense. They might slip past us, but they can't do anything without their dragons knowing about it. Of course, this wouldn't be necessary if the council hadn't vetoed the King's suggestion of giving us the use of another building."

She shook her head and replied, "The way they hold on to the purse strings you'd think the money was coming from their own pockets. The other building we were looking at is used for nothing more than storage of carnival decorations for the harvest celebration. That junk could easily be moved to an empty warehouse in the dock district."

"I know, Darling," he replied, "I pointed that out to them. They still claimed they were afraid that such a move, once made, would make it difficult to move the stuff back due to the bureaucracy involved and that could make the dockside building unavailable once trade barges start moving again in the spring. Then I asked about using one of the empty warehouses ourselves. Even though I assured them that we plan to vacate any structure we use long before spring, they vetoed that under the pretense that the storage space might become vital if 'something comes up'; as if there might be another war soon, or some such."

"Well, they seem to be looking for anything they can use against us. They talk about us, and even Delno and Rita, as if we are doing something immoral. I don't even want to repeat some of the insults that have been whispered about the relationship that Craig and Adamus share. In a world of such uncertainties, you'd think anyone would be happy for people who have come together in an honest bond of love and friendship, but old prejudices and ingrained customs run deep no matter how outdated and invalid they are."

She paused for a moment before adding, "I think they would love to have one of our younger girls come up pregnant so that they can use that as an excuse to cut our funding." She angrily shoved her foot into one of her house-boots so hard she tore the stitching at the top seam. "Damn."

"Careful, Nadia, those boots may be warm and comfortable, but they are little more than house slippers and not made for rough treatment by people who have magically-enhanced strength."

The look she gave him would have made some grown men cower. "My strength isn't enhanced that much; these slippers weren't made with quality in mind."

"No, they weren't," he said thoughtfully. "We seem to be getting seconds on everything that is given; then the council finds fault with everything we do."

She thrust her arm into one sleeve of her robe and said angrily, "Besides the fact Riders are not usually held to their narrow-minded moral code, it's not like we are doing anything wrong; you can't expect human beings to make solemn vows of commitment for three millennia or more; we just aren't built that way as a species. You and I are as committed as any two people can be, but who can say for sure whether or not we might grow apart after one or two thousand years? Human beings just aren't designed to deal with such things on that kind of timescale."

She paused for a moment, and then added, "Besides, our culture is mixed and there are different customs concerning committed relationships from household to household. Among the mountain folks that my family calls kin, a couple is considered married when they move in together and start commingling their property, so by my family's way of thinking, we are already," she raised both hands and made quote marks in the air with her fingers, "properly married!" She paused long enough to draw breath before continuing her train of thought, "Among others, simply introducing your prospective mate to your parents is enough to confirm the wedlock. The very idea of a formal ceremony after a lengthy courtship is a left-over that migrated north with the Exiled Kings, but these people are using our relationship in an attempt to impugn the moral standards of all Dragon Riders."

"I didn't know that they had been doing that so blatantly," he replied. "I have been spending so much of my time trying to get our supplies and get ready to move that I have been, mercifully, unable to attend court very often since we returned from Bourne."

"Yes, well, I have been attending in your place, and I have suffered the brunt of it. I have held my tongue until now because I didn't want to burden you with such asinine nonsense."

"I will have to take a more active interest in our dealings with them then."

She stopped and looked at him, and then said, "I may not have known you as long as Delno has, but I have come to recognize that look. What do have in mind?"

"Oh, nothing much, Darling," he replied. "Just remember though, I have been deeply involved with the politics and politicians in this city for most of my adult life. I know all of them." He smiled and added, "I not only know them professionally, but I know who is sleeping with whom, and where all of the 'political' bodies are buried. I will talk with certain people and see if we can't curtail this rubbish," his smile broadened, "and see about loosening a few purse strings."

She paused with her hand on the doorknob. "Nassari," she said sharply, "you can't jeopardize our position by blackmailing the council."

"I have no intention of jeopardizing our position, Nadia. You go and check on the kids. I'll bank the fire and turn down the linens so that all you will have to do when you get back is come to bed."

She opened the door and left the room to go and check the younger Riders. She did notice, however, that while Nassari had assured her that he wouldn't compromise their situation, he hadn't said specifically that he wouldn't blackmail any members of the council.

Chapter 3

"**I** JOINED THE DRAGON-HUMAN coalition because the beast-men had become such a threat, and to stop that madman who was using those monsters in his bid for power, not so that the Dragon Riders could put so many of our people under their direct control!" Sheila said hotly.

"We are not 'under their control', Mother," Saadia stated flatly. "We have chosen to put a life of utter loneliness behind us and bond to these men and women. I, as one of the 'controlled' dragons you mention, am happy with the arrangement. I will say again in front of everyone present that, while I agree with you that those who do not wish to bond shouldn't be forced into the company of humans, you have no right to try and stop those of us who want to spend our lives with human partners from doing so." At Sheila's harsh stare she added, "Don't look at me that way. If you simply wished to hold me out as an example of an enslaved dragon you should have had me stay away, not called me to this meeting as a witness."

A murmur that could be felt throughout the Dream State circulated as groups of those interested parties who were not taking a direct part in the discussion *talked* among themselves.

Before Sheila could say anything, Wanda spoke up. "I, like Saadia and the others here in Corice, have chosen to bond of my own free will. No one coerced me into this, and I am quite content with the arrangement. As a Lineage Holder, I see no reason that dragons who wish to find bond-mates should be prevented from visiting cities and searching for the companionship they crave."

Sheila made a rude noise and replied, "Lineage Holder, your lineage has been scattered and much was lost. You can no longer legitimately trace your ancestry back to the forty-three original dragons who freed themselves from slavery at the hands of humans and established the first Council of Dragons, and ultimately our whole society. Your inclusion in the Council has more to do with respect for your great-grandmother than with your knowledge and ability as a Lineage Holder."

"Mother!" Saadia shouted so violently that the fabric of the Dream State wavered. "You have no right to speak to Wanda that way."

Sheila puffed up to reply but didn't get the chance. There was a bellow that would have gotten them all ejected if it hadn't come from Geneva herself, even though many of those participating in the discussion were members of the Council of Dragons.

"I will not listen to slurs against one who has distinguished herself so well in battle against our ancestral enemies. Also, I may be young, but I too am a member of the Council, and while I am not old enough to have had the honor of personally knowing Wanda's great grandmother, I do know Wanda quite well. She is an important member of our leadership and her knowledge and wisdom are not in question despite her youth. Her lineage lore is only scattered because while your line chose to flee our ancestral home in the mountains east of Horne, her family and mine chose to stay and fight the beast-men. It is only by chance that my own many times removed grandmother survived and became the first bonded dragon rather than dying in that ancient war against the Roracks along with Wanda's ancestor thousands of years ago."

"Are you saying I'm descended from a line of cowards?" Sheila hissed.

"No," Geneva stated flatly. "Many chose to leave their territories to the beast-men rather than fight, including members of my own family. But Wanda and Geneva chose to stay and fight for all dragons, and because of that Wanda's lineage became scattered as some of her matriarchs over the millennia were killed in the ongoing struggles. You are not only insulting her and her ancestors but me and mine as well. Many in both our families died. It is only by luck that it was the youngest daughter of the line who found my many times removed great-grandmother after she was attacked and badly wounded so many thousands of years ago; she was the last of our line to live and die un-bonded. It is a minor miracle she had enough strength to give over the family lore when she was found dying by the one who would carry her name after she passed to shadow."

Sheila opened her mouth to speak but Geneva didn't give her the opportunity.

"Wanda's family was not so fortunate, and they lost more than one Lineage Holder over the long interval, and her lineage was diminished because youngest daughters had to reconstruct the lore from the memories of siblings," she continued before the older dragon could interrupt. "However, what was lost or got confused happened because they were fighting for all of us, and such deeds should be acknowledged with reverence. However, rather than honor that line's sacrifice you choose to give insult in order to cloud the agenda because you have no real argument other than your own racial prejudice. You hate humans because the mages who created our species tried to enslave us. That was thousands of years ago; those men are long dead, and your enmity toward the species should be buried with them."

"It's easy for you to accept this new plague of bonding Geneva, members of your line have been the beasts of burden to men for eight generations," Sheila said, refusing to address Geneva's accusation about her motives. "However, for my line, unbonded since the beginning, there have only been four generations, and we fully remember. You make pretty speeches, but the point remains that it was humans who tried to enslave our entire race, and that is a fact that is still strong in the memories of the lines that have remained pure and true to our own species' needs."

Wanda growled and Geneva faced Sheila as if she might actually lunge at her. Dragons began leaving the Dream State at such a rate that the fabric of the whole place started to come apart, and the scenery wavered wildly.

"The first dragons to bond were adults," Sheila shouted, "but it has always been custom since then that men should only bond to those born into such servitude, not taking their 'candidates' from those of us born in freedom."

Suddenly a dragon appeared right in the middle of the three antagonists. "Oh, 'custom' my cloaca," Carina cried out. "I am nearly half again your age, Sheila, and there is no formal agreement regarding the 'custom' you mentioned. Men have simply not sought us out before now, and we have kept to ourselves. My own daughter, Dina, has, of her own free will, found a young human to bond with. She is pleased beyond measure by the arrangement, and I am happy for her."

"That one of your daughters has done this thing is no surprise," Sheila spat back causing the surroundings to actually blur, "You have cried about your perceived lack of companionship to anyone who will listen for centuries. Why you don't get fitted for one of those saddles and become a beast of burden for some human is beyond me."

Carina made a dangerous growl.

"Beasts of burden?" Geneva said incredulously, "We wear those saddles so that our bond-mates can travel with us safely and not slow us down. Without those devices, we must either risk injury or death to our partners or walk alongside them like some plodding beast. Again your words are inflammatory and insulting, not spoken to make a clear argument."

"Enough!" Kalah, another Lineage Holder shouted. "I, as the oldest living dragon, am final mediator at these meetings, and I have the deciding vote in formal council in case of a tie. My word carries much weight as to the direction these assemblies take and when such a conference should end. We have no more than two dozen Lineage Holders here tonight. Many of the others simply don't see any problem in this matter and are not interested in attending. Since there can be no real resolution because all six cells of Lineage Holders aren't present, I am putting a stop to this before it gets any further out of hand."

"I have brought a real concern before you all," Sheila stated hotly.

Kalah cut her off before she could get further wound up. "I'll not have you tearing the Dream State apart with your bickering tonight. It can be rebuilt easily enough, but you are upsetting most of our kind with this nonsense. Many of those who have fled this place hope to mate and become pregnant next spring and only came here this evening for companionship. I won't allow anyone, even a Lineage Holder," she glared at all of them, but her gazed settled longest and hardest on Sheila, "to do anything that so upsets our people that it might cause distress for our next generation."

Sheila lowered her head but refused to further acknowledge the rebuke.

"Sheila," Kalah said, "you called this meeting to alert us to what you claim is clear evidence that humans are once again attempting to enslave our species. Instead of evidence, you present us with prejudiced conjecture. Your own witness, indeed, your own daughter, has clearly stated that she was not coerced into bonding and that she is quite happy with the relationship." Sheila looked as though she was about to say something in her defense but Kalah didn't give her the chance. "When it became obvious that the meeting wasn't going your way, you chose to cloud the issue by giving insult to three Lineage Holders. Two of them are very young, but they have proven themselves to be not only brave but wise. The third is your elder by more than a millennia. They have all earned their places here, and should be heard, not shouted down because you don't like what they have to say."

She paused and looked around for a moment. "There are many dragons who do not wish to be bonded, and, as young Saadia has pointed out, those dragons should not be forced into close proximity with humans, and no one has made any attempt to do so. Indeed, as I understand it, some of the humans who have bonded were not looking for such and could claim, if they wished, that it is we dragons who have committed a crime. What is happening appears to be that some part of the magic over which neither side has control is causing this, and neither side is responsible." She paused again before adding, "Sheila, you have not made your case. Despite our desire for companionship we are an independent people and have always held that each person should choose her own path, provided it does not harm the common good. Therefore, there is no custom that prevents a dragon from seeking out a bond-mate. Those dragons who want to be bonded to end their loneliness should be allowed to do as they wish, not forced to stay clear of humans and be miserable."

Kalah paused and glared at Sheila, almost daring her to argue. "This meeting is adjourned; if any Lineage Holders disagree with my thoughts on this matter, they should contact me directly and we can set a time to convene in person so that we don't disrupt the Dream State with such an emotionally charged issue."

*　　*　　*

"My mother will settle down with time," Saadia said later when she, Wanda and Geneva held a private conversation outside the Dream State after the meeting ended. "She isn't a bad person, but the slavery issue was always more real to her. She will come to see reason eventually. After all, she is more than three thousand years old and remembers when there were more than five hundred bonded dragons, and none of them felt as though they were enslaved."

"Perhaps when the Legion is established and we have pushed the beast-men back enough that some of our ancestral lands can be reclaimed, she will see the good in all of this," Geneva remarked.

"Yes, that should allay much of her fear," Wanda replied, "providing, of course, we can keep that damned King of Horne from trying to annex those lands."

"Do you think he would try that?" Saadia asked.

"Yes, he would," Geneva stated flatly. "You've never had dealings with the court in the capital city of Roahn. But Wanda and I were there with our bond-mates when Nassari and Delno worked out the agreement that gave us full use of the old fort and surrounding plain. The man tried hard to place the Legion under the direct control of the military of Horne, and thus under the control of the King himself. Delno was carefully watching for just such trickery, and Nassari is much too clever at politics to lose a battle of wits against one such as the dullard who sits on the throne of Horne. The agreement makes it clear that we are a private entity, but that agreement is only binding until Thomas changes his mind. Our position is a bit tenuous, but I have confidence in our bond-mates, and if they fail, we will have to take a more active role in the negotiations. Thomas may be a bit of a megalomaniac, but he hasn't the power that Warrick had to control either the beasts or us. If it comes down to that, he can be forced to see reason. Our ancestral lands will once again be in the hands of dragons; however, those dragons may all be bonded."

Saadia and Wanda both nodded in agreement as the three bid each other a good night.

CHAPTER 4

"**D**EL, IT'S GOOD to have you back in Larimar," Nassari said as he greeted his friend. Then he turned to the woman who accompanied Delno and added, "Where are my manners? Momma Laura, it is always a pleasure to see you." He leaned forward and kissed Laura Okonan on the cheek and she hugged him.

Delno's mother laughed and said, "Nassari, did you think I would let little things like affairs of state stop me from coming to this gathering? I have known you since Delno beat you up and then brought you home for me to doctor when the two of you first met at the ripe old age of five."

"He was five," Nassari said, "I was much older and more mature: I was seven."

Laura smiled and added, "My husband wanted very much to be here, but someone who actually speaks with my authority needed to stay, so he opted to remain in Bourne and handle the day to day chores of running the Duchy while I attend to matters here in the capital. He sends his best wishes, and his deepest regrets."

Quite a few men in the room stopped what they were doing and looked at the doorway. While Laura Okonan was lovely, and even in her mid-forties still turned heads, Rita had just entered, and she was radiant. She was wearing the same tight red tunic with the golden embroidery, and form-hugging black silk pants she had been given by Missus Gentry in Orlean so many months ago. She even had the mother of pearl comb with the cloisonné flower in her hair.

"Rita," Nassari said, "it's always a pleasure to see you." He extended his hand and she simply moved closer and hugged him briefly.

"We have missed your company in the last month, Nassari. Perhaps now that Bourne is nearly settled we will be able to see you and Nadia more often."

"Speaking of whom," Laura Okonan said, "where is she? I greatly wish to meet the young lady who is grand enough to make an honest man of Nassari Orrin."

Nassari briefly feigned indignation and then said with a smile, "She will be down shortly. We got caught up in some details concerning Rider business this afternoon, and so got a late start on dressing. I was barely able to get changed out of my work clothes in time to greet our guests: her preparations were progressing well when I left our quarters."

Laura Okonan looked around and could see a group of people she took to be Nadia's family standing off to one side. They had arrived nearly a quarter of an hour earlier, but as was the custom among some of the mountain folk, were politely waiting for Nadia to introduce them to Nassari and his family. Then she saw Nassari's mother standing about ten feet away talking with one of the Dragon Riders.

"Well, I will console myself with talking to your mother for the time being." She moved off to speak to Helen Orrin.

Delno looked thoughtful and Wanda said, *"Geneva has relayed that Delno would like to know if you are still having problems with the Council concerning funds and supplies."*

Nassari got a somewhat mischievous smile on his face and his eyes lit up. *"Tell her to tell Delno that all of those types of problems have been handled. What cropped up today were simply the logistical difficulties that can occur when we have thirty new Riders to train all at once and there is a blizzard blowing outside, especially when well over half of those Riders are below the age of sixteen, and would rather be doing anything other than training."*

Delno nodded, and Wanda said, *"He says that he understands, Love. He also says that he apologizes for not being here to help you. Now that things are settled in Bourne, he expects to move back to Larimar and assist you in getting everything sorted out so that the business of getting the Legion Headquarters set up can be attended to."*

Nassari nodded in return, but before he could relay any further communication, everyone turned to look at a side door at the head of a short flight of stairs. The doorway was the portal to an enclosed passage from the Riders' quarters in the next building. Nassari looked too, and there was Nadia, looking more beautiful than even he had ever seen her. She was wearing a long green dress that was an exact match for the color of her draconic partner, Pina. The dark, malachite fabric offset Nadia's green eyes wonderfully. The neckline dipped deeply, and the dress was also slit up the left side halfway between her knee and her hip and showed just enough of her leg to get attention without revealing too much as she walked down the stairs to join them. The dress hugged her curves nicely, so as to show her figure off without being overtly provocative.

Nassari moved forward quickly and met Nadia at the foot of the steps. She took his arm, and he proudly escorted her into the room. Since it was not the custom of Nadia's family to present the partners to both sets of parents at once, and Nassari and his mother originally came from Southern Trent where wedding customs were entirely different, it had been decided he would first introduce Nadia to his mother, and then they would introduce him to her father, followed by introducing the parents to each other.

Nassari led his spouse to where his mother was standing with Laura Okonan. "Nadia," he said, "this is my mother, Helen Orrin. Mother, this beautiful young lady is the love of my life, Nadia Cutter."

Helen Orrin smiled and extended her hand. "I am so very pleased to meet you, Dear. I have longed for the day that my son would bring such a nice young lady to me and say those words," she said as the two of them shook hands.

Nadia smiled, "Nassari has told me so much about you, Ma'am. I'm happy that I have finally met you."

Nadia's father, with his sons following respectfully behind him, had moved close enough that she only had to turn around to introduce him to her husband.

"Nassari," she said, "this is my father, William Cutter. Father, this is the man to whom I have given my heart, Nassari Orrin."

Nassari took William's hand and said, "It is an honor to meet you, Sir."

He had expected Nadia's father to have questions or comments, but the man simply shook his hand and replied, "It's good to meet you, Son. Welcome to the family."

Nassari realized that Delno's brother Will had snuck in at some point and was standing with the rest of them. The man had the sometimes disturbing talent of being able to magically hide from those around him. He could suddenly appear, as if out of nowhere, nearly any place he chose. This time, though, he had simply been coming in the main door as Nadia had made her entrance, and no one had noticed, even though he wasn't magically "cloaked."

Will smiled at Nassari and Wanda said, *"Saadia has relayed that Will says that while all of the younger Riders are not in bed at this early hour, they are settled for the night."*

Nassari grinned at Will and nodded almost imperceptibly in acknowledgment of the report.

Will wasn't as strikingly handsome as his older half-brother Delno, but he certainly wasn't homely either. It was easy to see from his chiseled features that he had the mountain people's blood of his father running in his veins, but that was softened by his mother's finer features. Eleven of the new Riders were young women ranging in age from thirteen to eighteen, and nearly every one of them vied with the others for Will's attention. It was enough to drive the poor man to practice his talent on a regular basis, but it also gave him some measure of influence over the girls, so he could usually get them to settle down and behave themselves. Tonight, with the party being held in the adjacent building and Nadia and Nassari both occupied, he had been left to see to it that both boys and girls retired to their own quarters before he joined the festivities. The other adult riders who were on duty this evening would then keep watch.

Wanda would, of course, see that the "kids'" draconic partners reported directly to her if that situation changed at any time throughout the night. Normally, even with a Lineage Holder asking them to do it, dragons wouldn't report on their partner's behavior like that. However, these dragons were not hatchlings. They were fully mature, most more than two decades old, and they understood that not only were the humans to whom they had bonded little more than children, such sneaking about could cause great problems for them all with the people who still controlled the money needed to fund the Legion. The dragons, even though fully mature, had bowed to Rita's sentiment, backed up by two Lineage Holders, that the children were not to be considered adults with adult responsibilities and privileges until at least sixteen years of age. The new Riders complained that the adults had turned their own partners into nannies, but the objections weren't serious, and everyone took it as a good-natured game. So far the adults were still ahead about a dozen to zero, and Nassari fervently hoped that they could keep it that way; at least until he could get his charges safely out of Larimar, and away from the scrutiny of the local politicians.

Nassari again smiled and nodded to Will before turning back to the guests and playing the good host. Once the parents had each been presented to their offspring's partner, they were introduced to each other. Then it was time for introductions all around. Since Nadia had five older brothers, and Nassari considered the Okonans to be part of his family, the remainder of the procedure took the next quarter of an hour.

As the two families began to intermingle and talk, Delno pulled Nassari aside so that they could have a semi-private conversation. "I've known you for a long time, my friend," Delno said. "What was that look on your face when I asked you about funding and the council?"

"Del," Nassari said, smiling like a kid who had just gotten away with an extra helping of dessert, "I told you, the council has been handled. We had some miscommunication initially, but that was weeks ago. I was able to make them see reason. Now they are behind me one hundred percent and are as anxious to get the new Riders geared up and ready to travel with me as I am to be traveling. We will be ready to move everything, including ourselves, to the Fort by the Winter Solstice. Once there, I hope to have everything set in place and routine established by late spring."

"Nassari," Delno said sternly, "I know that there is more in what you don't say than there is in what you do say. Have you actually managed to negotiate with them, or have you somehow extorted the funds you need?"

"'Extortion' is such a harsh word; it implies crude methods of persuasion," Nassari replied in a whisper. "I greatly prefer the term 'blackmail'. It is so much more subtle, and implies that the ones being compelled are at least as guilty as the person doing the coercing."

"Nassari, I need these people to stay favorably disposed toward us until we can get everything and be on our way. I also don't want to end up alienating my uncle, the King. It's only been about seven weeks since we brought Bourne under Corisian rule. I don't want the goodwill we garnered from that to be tainted by threatening the council members."

"Relax, Del. Blackmail is nothing new on the Corisian political scene. It is used all the time, though seldom does one have to use it on as many people in one instance as I have done in the past three weeks. Since the council members I have spoken with don't want my information to come to light, they have decided that the best way to ensure that is to see me quickly on my way. Therefore, they have authorized the funding needed to accomplish the task. I will soon take the new Riders and all of the equipment that hasn't already been shipped, and I will leave this city, more or less for good, and the King will not be bothered with the details."

A small bell chimed and Nassari said, "Ah, dinner is served. Come, Del, let us gather our ladies and find seats at the table."

William Cutter was exercising his prerogative as a father and escorting his daughter to the table. Nassari simply extended one arm to his own mother and one to Laura Okonan and showed both women to their seats.

As he escorted Rita to her chair and held it for her, Delno watched his friend Nassari play the room. One thing became abundantly clear: He, Delno, might be the Rider of Geneva and holder of a Dragon Blade, but when it came to playing politics, Nassari was the master, and he was no more than an advanced apprentice.

CHAPTER 5

ONCE THE MAIN course had been finished and the meal had settled down to polite conversation and nibbling while sipping spiced wine, Nadia's brother, Sidney, spoke up. "I've been traveling with caravans as a guard for three seasons now. We winter over here, but we travel as far south as Iondar. I've met three fellows with the name Nassari, and I have to say they were all nice enough, but they were also all dark-skinned men of Iondar. How did a light-skinned fellow from Larimar come by such a name?"

"Brock asked the same question of me before he even met you in Palamore. I told him it was your story to tell and that he would have to ask you if he wanted to know," Delno said from across the table.

"Well," Nadia said, with a bit of annoyance in her voice, "my brother is prying. Perhaps Nassari doesn't want to talk about it." Nadia herself had never asked that question, but she knew that he had never talked about his father. She assumed that his mother had spent time in the company of a Vanner or hired caravan guard, and Nassari was born out of wedlock. She didn't want Helen Orrin embarrassed, especially at the wedding party.

"I have to agree with my daughter on this," William Cutter said, sensing her discomfort. "It's getting late and we still have a fair bit to walk tonight, so if you don't wish to talk about it no one will mind," he added as he glared at his youngest son.

"No, it's all right," Nassari said. "My family has no secrets in this matter. However, it is more my mother's story than mine, so I will allow her to tell it if she chooses."

Everyone looked to Helen Orrin and waited. Laura Okonan placed her hand on Helen's hand and smiled, "You don't have to if you'd rather not," she said.

Helen returned Laura's grip, "I don't mind. I got over any shame I felt about this a long time ago." Then she looked around at everyone and continued, "Here in the north it is still the norm for young women to take a husband before they become pregnant, but they aren't shamed and shunned by their families if they find themselves surprised. Where I come from in the south of Trent, though, is a different story, especially among the common folk of the far south. A young woman who gets pregnant out of wedlock is looked on as no better than a common whore, and her family bears the brunt of her disgrace. Often when it happens the girl will be spurned and driven from her home, and her family will simply tell everyone she's dead. There have even been times that young girls in such a circumstance have been killed in suspicious accidents, but no one investigates those 'mishaps' very well."

"That's barbaric," William Cutter said. "I wouldn't have been happy if Nadia had turned up pregnant, and I would have chided her for not being more careful, but I wouldn't have been willing to lose my daughter over it, and I certainly can't imagine doing anything so outrageous as taking the lass's life for an adolescent indiscretion."

"Well," Helen replied, "many of the southerners would disagree with you. The young man involved, himself little more than a boy, really, denied being the father when I told him. He swore it wasn't him. When I pointed out to him that he was the only one I had ever laid with he promised that he would get five or six of his friends to claim differently and increase my shame if he were brought into it. I went to my mother and told her everything. Unfortunately, either my father overheard us, or, more likely, she told him what I had confessed to her. In fifteen years, I had never seen him so furious. He beat me for it, and he swore he'd kill me. My mother convinced him to leave the house to think about it, and she left with him, pleading for him to reconsider."

Rita drew a breath sharply and said, "Men and women have been killed in my homeland for such treatment of children."

"Such abuse isn't unheard of in this country," William said, "but once discovered, the offending party is usually taken on a hunting trip by several of the men from the community so they can 'talk with him,'" Then he added somberly, "and none have ever returned from a second trip if it was deemed necessary."

Helen smiled at Nadia's father and continued, "My mother finally came back alone a short time later. She barely spoke to me as she cleaned the sores that my father had left with his belt. Then she sent me to my bed and told me to stay there until I was called. It was nearly midnight when my father came home. He had another man with him; he said that this man would be my new husband and that I would be leaving with him in the morning. The man was older than my father and smelled of body odor and distilled wine. I tried to say no, but my father made it plain that I would either leave with this man or die. He said I had dishonored the family, and the only way to right that was to either take a husband immediately or forfeit my life."

William squeezed the small dessert fork in his hand so hard it bent.

Helen paused as she took a sip of her wine. Sidney, who had instigated the telling of the story, looked very uncomfortable. Everyone else who had not heard the story listened intently. The emotions playing across the faces of both Rita and Nadia made it clear that, while they wanted to save Helen the ordeal of telling the story, they were fully engrossed and wanted to hear it all.

Finally, Helen continued, "The man, his name was Jon Simons, was just as bad as I thought he would be. He was traveling with a caravan out of Iondar. He was abusive, and he didn't care that I was a young girl, and pregnant. He used me any way he liked, and if I struggled, he would beat me. I was too strong-willed to yield to him without a fight, and beating me was his downfall."

"He should have been killed outright," William said forcefully, and all of the men present nodded in agreement.

Again Helen smiled before she continued.

Speaking loud enough to be heard by all, but looking directly at William, she went on. "We had been underway for about ten days when the caravan master heard my cries while Simons was whipping me. He charged into the tent and took the rope the man was using and put a stop to it. Simons made the fatal mistake of attacking the caravan master, and the man, already enraged by what he had interrupted, killed Simons with his bare hands. I remember lying there naked amid the filth of the tent and Caravan Master Orrin standing there looking around for something clean to wrap me in. He couldn't find anything he thought suitable for the purpose, so he used his own over-shirt. He picked me up as if I didn't weigh anything and carried me to his wife. He laid me on their bed, and had her tend to my flesh while he got some other men and took care of Simons' body."

Again, she stopped for a moment while she sipped her drink and gathered her thoughts. No one asked any questions or tried to prompt her to continue, though William smiled at her encouragingly and reached across the narrow table and grasped her hand briefly.

After a few more moments, she went on. "The caravan master was gone for some time. When he returned, my wounds were cleaned, and I was nearly asleep. He took one look inside the wagon, and then nodded once to his wife, grabbed a blanket, and closed the canvas flap as he left to find a place to sleep outside on the ground. His wife stayed with me, and even held me when I began to cry uncontrollably during the night. The next morning she gave me some clothes and said I could join them for breakfast or stay in the wagon and she would bring me something to eat."

"They sound like good people," Nadia said quietly.

Helen nodded to her, before going on. "I opted to join them by the fire. When I finally dressed and went out, I had made up my mind that I had to tell them my whole story; I was sure they would then want nothing more to do with me. After I had told them everything, the man, Nassari Orrin, looked at me and said, 'So you're pregnant, huh? Well, I guess it's a good thing the Missus is a midwife.' They never looked down on me for what I had done. Once my body had healed, they did expect me to work for my keep, though they kept the tasks light because of my condition. They treated me as a member of their own family from day one, and when my son was born, I named him after Nassari. If I had had a daughter, she would have been named Mara, after his wife. I stayed with them for more than three years, traveling on their route and wintering over at their home in Iondar. My son and I took their last name as our own, and I put my old life completely behind me."

She paused for a moment and William, despite his earlier objection to prying, couldn't help but ask, "So how is that you settled here in Corice and not Iondar?"

She smiled sweetly at him and answered, "Well, even though I loved the Orrins and had come to think of them as my mother and father, I also came to realize that I didn't want to raise my son as Vanner. They understood; it's a hard life and not everyone is suited to it. They knew that a woman on her own could make a life for herself here in Larimar, so on our next trip north, when my son had not yet reached his third birthday, my adopted father used his influence with a local merchant he traded with to get me a job, and then helped me get set up in an apartment of my own. I saw them regularly for a long time after that on their annual trading trips north, but they retired to their homeland of Iondar nearly ten years ago, and I have lost contact with them. Wherever they are, I hope they are happy, healthy, and prosperous. They are such good people they deserve only the best."

When she finished, no one else spoke for a long time. Laura Okonan held her friend's hand and smiled encouragingly at her. Both Nadia and Rita had tears running unchecked down their cheeks, and the men were blinking and wiping away the water that had sprung up in their eyes as well.

Finally, Sidney said, "I apologize for prying, and I thank you for trusting us enough to tell your story. You're a strong and wonderful lady, and Nassari is lucky to have you as a mother."

"That was quite tale you told," William Cutter said. "I can only second my son's sentiment; you are an extraordinary woman, and I applaud what you've accomplished, especially now that I know the whole of the matter." He paused for a moment before adding, "However, as I said earlier, it's late, and we still have to walk home through the snow. I hate to leave such good company after what feels like such a short time, but we must be on our way."

Nassari and Nadia got up and saw her father and brothers to the door. The good-byes took several minutes. When they returned to the table, Nassari said, "So, Del, are you and Rita staying at the palace, or should we find you quarters for the night?"

"They have a room at the palace," Laura spoke up. "In fact," she turned to Nassari's mother, "I'd like you to join us, Helen. I have a proposition for you. I'm looking for some key people to help me in Bourne, and I have need of someone with your organizational skills. If you'd like, you can sleep at the palace tonight, and we can discuss the whole thing with my uncle in the morning."

Helen looked at Laura for a moment and then said, "I never would have dreamed of leaving Larimar, even if it was only to go to Bourne. However, now that Nassari is compelled by his duties to move to Horne, I find that being close to my best friend might take some of the loneliness away, especially if I can also find meaningful employment. Your offer intrigues me, Laura, I will definitely come to the palace with you and discuss this with your uncle tomorrow."

"Well, then," Delno said, "that only leaves one thing before we adjourn."

Everyone looked at him expectantly.

"We have been so busy, first with the war, and then with everything else, I had almost forgotten about it completely, but now that I have you and your son together in the same place, I have to ask. Whatever happened to Chester? He obviously didn't travel to Palamore with Nassari. I had assumed that he had stayed with you. Is he all right?"

Helen laughed and said, "He's fine. However, he had always spent more time at our neighbor's house than at ours. The old man, Gary Timmons, loves that animal, and fed and cared for him more than we did, and he would never even let us pay for the food. He insisted the animal was no bother. So when Nassari left for Palamore, he gave Gary the dog outright. He is now living in the lap of luxury. Gary not only feeds him the best food money can buy, Chester has his own couch near the fire to sleep on."

On that note, they all got up and began preparing to go to their respective quarters.

CHAPTER 6

"**N**OW THAT WE have saddles for all of them, the training should progress more smoothly," Will said to Nassari and Nadia as they waited for the new Riders to assemble for flight training. "Will you two be joining us in the air today?"

Nassari shook his head, "She has to see to the remaining provisions that are being shipped downriver by boat, and I have to visit Elom and ascertain if there are any last minute supplies he wants to send by either boat or dragon. There's some room still on the barge, but I figure that with over thirty of us flying, even our good mastersmith can't send so much as to overburden us now that the bulk of the goods are already loaded."

"Only if he should decide to come along himself," Will quipped, and they all laughed.

"I don't think there is much danger of that happening. He gets around just fine, but he hasn't felt the need to travel since he got out of the army." Nassari shook his head and added, "I actually wouldn't mind if he did come to Horne, at least long enough to set up the metal shop at the Fort. We will negotiate for some things from Horne in payment for keeping the borders safe. After all, there are still Roracks out there, and we can be reasonably sure they will band into small groups and make raids again. However, I would like everything set up as well as it can be to ensure that we are as self-sufficient as possible; I can think of no one who could do a better job of establishing the metal shop than Elom."

Will nodded in agreement just as a girlish voice behind him said, "We're here, Will. Are you ready for all of us?"

That question was accompanied by the giggling of all of the young female Riders, as well as groans, and even a couple of raspberries from the boys. Adamus, who had remained quiet up to this point, laughed out loud. Adamus had no inclinations toward any female, and he found Will's predicament with the girls to be quite funny.

"It's all well and good for you and Craig to sit back and laugh at all of this; the two of you are so close no one but your dragons would dream of trying to get between you."

Though Will's tone might have been mistaken as anger by someone who didn't know them, it was just good-natured jibing between friends.

"Yes," Nassari said looking directly at Adamus, "the two of you are good for each other. Before you met Craig, you didn't have any particular interest in scholarly pursuits, and Craig had shown even less interest in the more physical aspects of being a Rider. Now you are more prone to study, and Craig can regularly be found doing calisthenics and sword practice with the others, as well as flying maneuvers. I believe that riders tend to find what they need. I think it's part of the magic that surrounds and seems to protect our bondmates."

"Of course, that does nothing for Will's predicament with the girls," Nadia pointed out.

Everyone, including Will, laughed a little.

"Youth has always been controlled more by impulse than by the ability to reason," Nassari stated flatly, "but our city council members are quick to use any perceived impropriety, real or imagined, against us when doling out funds."

"Get them in the air, and work them as long as you think the dragons are up to it," Nadia added. "Let the cold weather and exercise wear them out. The kids may complain, but we still have enough nights between now and our departure that they have plenty of time to get into trouble. I'd prefer they be well-trained and exhausted rather than have them save their strength and run us ragged keeping them from to sneaking into each other's rooms at night. If they can't control their urges, we'll have to keep them too tired to do more than sleep until they develop some common sense."

"Oh, don't worry on that account," Will replied, "I have every intention of working them until they are ready to drop. I want to get few a moments' peace after dinner tonight, myself."

He and Adamus both saluted, and then headed off to get the Riders mounted up.

"I'll walk with you as far as the gates," Nadia said to Nassari, "then I, too, will have to be about my task."

"Hopefully, I will get finished with Elom quickly and be able to join you by lunchtime. I'll have Wanda relay to you through Pina if it works out."

They watched until all of the Riders who were flying had taken off and were little more than specks in the sky. Then he took her hand in his, and together they walked back to the city.

CHAPTER 7

"Elom," NASSARI CALLED out as he walked into the metalsmith's shop.

Instead of Elom, a man, who looked to be in his mid-forties, turned and greeted him. "Nassari, I haven't seen you since you helped me and those doctors get together to make those braces for my son."

"Nathan!" Nassari said in surprise as he smiled at Elom's father. "I thought you had retired. What are you doing standing over a forge wielding a hammer?"

"I still like to keep my hand in things around here," he replied as he strode forward and reached out to shake.

Nathan wasn't quite as tall or broad as his son, but it was still easy to see where Elom got his size from. Nassari's hand, even though not small by any standards, was dwarfed by that of the smith.

"I found those drawings you wanted, Dad," Elom said as he came in through a side door. He noticed Nassari and smiled. "I'm glad you're here earlier than you said you would be. I was hoping we would have time to talk this morning while we get the last of the stuff off to Horne."

"I was up early getting the new Riders into the air, so I was able to get here sooner than I expected. Thank you for your help with all of that, by the way. Those buckles and fittings you sent over allowed our own leather workers to finish the saddles without having to go back to the Council and beg for more funds."

"Thank my father: he heard you were having trouble with the Council and had a fit. Then he and several of the journeymen worked nearly round the clock to get the things made. I was just the delivery boy this time."

Nathan Riley waved Nassari's thanks aside. "I heard you were havin' trouble with those skin-flints over in the government offices and just got fed up. Elom's mother was dying of that damned plague, and then you showed up with that Elf healer who cured her and everyone else. As if that wasn't enough, you brought those dragons to fight our war for us, and then made sure that Bourne and Corice will remain at peace for all time. Listening to those idiots bickering over the few coins you needed was enough to drive me out of retirement to try and pay back some of the debt that this country owes you and yours."

"Well, I am still grateful," Nassari replied. "As for you coming out of retirement, though, I hope we haven't put you to too much trouble."

"It just so happens," Elom spoke up, "that that brings me to what I wanted to talk to you about."

Nassari first looked to Nathan to see if he objected to the interruption. Since Elom's father didn't appear to mind, he nodded for Elom to continue.

"Well, I've given it a lot of thought. The journeyman who has opted to go with you is good, but he's just finished his tenure here. If you're going to be setting up a new operation, you'll need a mastersmith to put it in order. Since my father has returned to work, he's realized that he's sorry he ever retired in the first place; after all, he's only fifty-three. With him here to run this shop, I can come with you for a time and see to it that you get set up proper in Horne."

Nassari stared blankly for a moment, unsure he had actually heard those words come out of Elom's mouth. He had been joking with Will about Elom coming along, but he hadn't dared hope it was even possible.

"Are you absolutely certain of this?" he asked the big man.

"Aye, as certain as I've ever been of anything. I thought that I had done so well since I was injured, but I've come to realize that there's a big world out there I've always wanted to see, and I've been hiding here in this shop because deep down I'm scared that I'm a cripple. I realize that I have to move out and get around to finally put all of that behind me. I will probably come back before too long, but for now, I want to travel a bit and feel useful. Since two men I owe more to than I can ever repay are going to Horne to set up headquarters for this new Legion of Riders, the least I can do is go along and help in some small way." He paused and looked at his father, who only nodded for him to finish his thought. "This way I can repay some of what you and Delno Okonan have done for me, and I can stop hiding in this shop and prove to myself that even though my legs don't work as well as they used to, I'm still a whole man."

Elom then crossed his massive arms over his chest in what Nassari knew was his classic pose that meant all discussion on the matter was over.

"Very well, my friend, I learned a long time ago that there's no arguing with you once you've made up your mind. Will you be traveling with the last of your equipment by barge and then by wagon, or would you like to shorten your trip and fly with us when the Riders leave?"

"Well, I don't like barges; they're too slow. I haven't even gotten close to your dragons yet, but the idea intrigues me, if they can handle the extra weight."

Nassari laughed and said, "Dragons are capable of carrying a rider and passenger quite a ways before tiring. I'm sure, if we have you fly with the lighter Riders and change off frequently, we can accommodate you."

Nathan spoke up, "Well, I will say that I will miss you, son, but I reckon this'll be good for you. I'm happy to be back in the shop, and, while your mother loves you dearly, we can use a break on the grocery bills."

Elom threw back his head and laughed heartily. It had long been a running joke in his family that since he was as large as two normal men, he also ate accordingly. Elom always took the joke good-naturedly. While the big man seemed a bit taciturn at times, especially when his mind was occupied with some intricate project, Nassari had known him long enough to know that he was actually slow to anger, and had a wonderful sense of humor.

Elom sobered a bit and said, "I'd like to meet some dragons, if that would be all right."

"Do you have time to do so today?"

"Aye, I've just got a few things to get sent off to the docks to be loaded on the last shipment, and then I can catch up to you. Do you want to meet in the city, or should I just look for you on the field outside the gates?"

"I'm meeting Nadia at the docks, and then the two of us are going to lunch. Once we finish that, we will go to the field. If you would like, you can find us there. You know Delno's brother, Will?" At Elom's nod of assent, he continued, "If Nadia and I aren't there, look for Will. He can introduce you to some of the dragons while you wait for us. Then, if you like, as a preview of what you're in for, one of us can probably take you on a short flight."

"Might as well get started then," Elom replied. "The wagon is loaded, and the lads who are helping are just waiting for me to check it over and sign off on the manifest."

He clapped Nassari on the shoulder and strode away with that peculiar rolling gait of his. Nassari noticed that, while Elom's gait was different than other people, he still moved along at a good pace. His legs might be somewhat bent, but it didn't slow him down much, and his spirit was still mostly intact.

CHAPTER 8

NASSARI HAD BEEN preoccupied with his conversation with Elom as he walked to meet Nadia. Having the mastersmith along would ensure that the Fort had the best metal shop available. He noticed Nadia and waved as she got closer. She started to wave back, but the smile on her face turned to a look of horror, and she quickly changed her gesture of greeting to the sign for "danger, move now" that Walker Longleaf had taught them. Nassari knew she wouldn't use such a sign as some kind of frivolous joke, so he quickly threw himself forward and rolled out of the way.

The move saved his life. The large axe that had been aimed at his head bit empty air, and the wielder, expecting to contact flesh, overbalanced and nearly lost his footing. It had been a clumsy overhand swing, and the battle-axe bit deeply into the hard-packed limestone street of the dock district. Unfortunately, it didn't bite so deeply that it stuck. The assailant quickly pulled the two-handed weapon up to high port arms and moved to close some of the distance that Nassari's roll had put between them.

His attacker, though not as massive as Elom, was still huge. The man was more than a full head taller than Nassari himself. The assassin handled the great-axe as if it weighed no more than the average sword. Nassari was sure that if the first blow had connected, it would have literally split him in two down the middle. Pulling his own sword and *main gauche*, he readied himself for another strike.

His attacker was big, but he moved with some speed. The man jabbed with the small spike on top of the weapon and then quickly made a swinging attack that caught Nassari's winter coat and tore a large slash across it. The guy wasn't slow, but he wasn't particularly well-trained either: his movements were clumsy.

As the stranger was trying to cut him down like a tree, Nassari quickly lashed out with his own blade and got the giant across the face. The cut opened a gash from the assailant's left ear all the way to his chin and exposed the bone of his lower jaw. Delno Okonan might be the best swordsman in Corice, but Nassari had trained under some of the same masters as his friend. He was good.

The axe-man was obviously used to fighting against others who weren't so capable. When he felt the pain of the cut and saw the blood dripping onto his arm, it seemed to dumbfound him momentarily.

"What is this about?" Nassari asked while his foe was distracted from the fight. "I don't know you. Why have you attacked me?"

"You'll all pay for what you've done," the man's voice sounded almost like a growl. Then he glanced back down at the blood pouring onto his sleeve from the large open wound on his jaw and actually did growl as he raised his massive weapon in preparation for another overhand swing, as if he were about to split a piece of firewood rather than attack another man. Nassari heard Wanda scream in rage overhead, but he had no time to acknowledge that she had come.

The assailant's reach was amazing; Nassari tried to step back, but he barely got his sword and *main gauche* up in time to catch the blow. The force nearly broke his wrists as the axe impacted both of his blades. Something flew at high speed and hit him in the face. There was a sharp pain in Nassari's right cheek and a look of triumph on the face of the giant as the man began to push the cutting edge of that enormous axe toward the right side of Nassari's neck. Even with dragon-enhanced strength, Nassari was no match for the colossus. He was forced to his knees as the cutting edge inched closer and closer to his jugular vein. Just then, his attacker's eyes flew open wide and his lips parted to scream as his face contorted in agony. There was no accompanying sound, though, and he fell to the ground with his back arched forward, his body completely rigid. The great-axe seemed to fall to the limestone in a kind of slow-motion dance. It wobbled on the blade edges almost like a coin before settling. Nassari had an odd feeling as if the seemingly muffled sound of the axe clanging to the pavement was coming down a long tunnel and not actually emanating from the object itself.

At first, Nassari was completely confused. The man had nearly had him, and then, as far as he could tell, suffered some type of seizure and fell. He wondered if Wanda had used magic, but when he looked, however, the cause was apparent. Nadia's belt knife was buried in the giant's back up to the hilt, just under the man's floating rib. She had angled the ten-inch-long blade up perfectly and stabbed him in the right kidney. Nassari couldn't help but feel a pang of sorrow for his assailant. Being stabbed like that is so painful that the victim's diaphragm freezes, and he can't move air in or out of his lungs. He would have liked to have asked his attacker some questions, but his skill as a healer was nowhere near that of Nat or Delno. By this point, it was a toss-up whether the giant would bleed to death first, or die of asphyxiation. Either way, the man would not be able to supply any answers.

To Nassari, still riding the adrenaline rush, it seemed as though time was passing slowly. It also felt as if several minutes had passed, even though it had only been seconds since the attack had been thwarted. Then he remembered to widen his field of vision, and time began to behave itself and flow at a more normal rate.

The first thing he realized was that he was still on his knees. The second was that Nadia was reaching for him and her hands were trembling. The third thing he noticed, as she gently touched his face with her shaky fingers, was that he had been wounded. His cheek hurt where her fingertips brushed against his skin, even though she was trying to be gentle.

He reached up and felt his cheek. Nadia was actually crying, and telling him to let her get it. He had never seen her so upset. He gently pushed her hands down and smiled at her. Smiling, of course, sent a lance of pain through the whole right side of his face. He felt the piece of metal that had struck so deeply that it sliced his upper gum and the inside of his cheek from his canine to his wisdom tooth, and it now grated against his teeth. He steeled himself and pulled the thing out. Fresh blood washed into his mouth as he looked around to see if there was another assailant hiding nearby who had used a ranged weapon on him. There were no obvious threats, so, as he spit out the blood, he examined the unlikely dart. It was single-edged and looked as if it had broken away from something. Then he noticed his sword, which he realized he had dropped when the giant fell. The "dart" was a shard from his own blade that had broken free when he had caught the axe with it. The force of the blow had been such that the broken piece had been driven deep into the side of his face. He looked at the great axe. It, too, had been badly notched, but fortunately, the metal that had broken away from it had taken a harmless trajectory.

"Nassari, I have no room to land without the danger of inadvertently harming some bystander, but if you don't tell me what is going on I will do so anyway!" Wanda said.

"Don't land, Love, I was attacked, but I am fine."

"You are bleeding profusely; I should come down."

"Injuries to the face and head always bleed profusely. I will be all right. Please stay aloft and watch out in case there are more of them."

Wanda didn't like not being able to come to him, but she understood that there could be other assassins near in case the first one was unable to complete the job. She had been joined by Pina, and they both circled while thoroughly scanning the crowd and the surrounding buildings with their magical senses, as well as their eyes. They were flying so low that people unused to seeing dragons were ducking their heads, and everyone could feel the wind as they both beat down with their wings to stay aloft.

Nadia shook her head to clear it. Then she forcefully drew several deep breaths to calm herself before saying, "Here, let me heal that." She quickly examined the wound and then drew the energy she needed. As Nadia healed Nassari, he watched the man who had tried so hard to kill him shudder one last time and then go completely slack. He died without making a sound.

The city guards came running up with weapons drawn. They hurriedly surveyed the scene and then asked Nassari what happened. As Nadia retrieved her knife, almost a short sword that she carried as a back-up, he told them everything he knew about the whole event, which was no more than an account of the attack itself. When they pressed him for answers about why it had happened, all he could do was plead ignorance.

Nadia listened to the guards repeat the same questions several times until she had had enough. "We have told you everything we know. We have no idea who that man is or why he attacked a Dragon Rider. Perhaps you could get some answers if you went and asked your own ruling Council about this."

Nassari stepped between Nadia and the guardsmen and said, "She isn't serious, of course. We have had some trouble dealing with the politicians—everyone knows that—but if we have ever called them backstabbing, it was just a figure of speech. I'm sure that no one on the Council would have any more knowledge of this than we do." He tried to put his sword into his scabbard but the broken section caught annoyingly. He finally managed to sheath the blade and then added, "Since we can be of no further assistance, and we have pressing Dragon Rider business elsewhere, we will bid you goodbye."

Nadia started to protest, but he used the Elven sign for silence, and she allowed him to lead her away.

Once they were out of earshot of the guards, she said, "Why did you hush me? It very well could have been one of the Council who sent that assassin."

"It could have been," he admitted, "though I doubt it." At the look she gave him he said, "The Council members have never stooped to such tactics. They might attempt to ruin us financially if we stayed around, and they certainly would try and beat us to a bloody pulp with their bare hands if the opportunity arose, but they have always drawn the line at cold-blooded murder. Besides, that giant did say one thing to me."

"What did he say?" she pressed as Nassari paused for breath.

"I asked him why he was attacking me. He said, and I quote, 'You'll all pay for what you've done.'"

"So you think that he was simply out to kill Dragon Riders and not you in particular?"

"Perhaps he was out to kill politicians. After all, I was active in politics long before I bonded with Wanda."

The look she gave him could have frozen water, and left no doubt that the incident was still too fresh for her to appreciate a joke.

"All right," he said, "I don't know if the man was specifically looking for me, or just out to kill any Rider he found at the docks, but if he had been sent to assassinate me specifically, he wouldn't have said that we will all pay."

"So, on that slim bit of deductive reasoning, you are simply going to dismiss the possibility that the assassin could have been sent by one of the council members to ensure that you actually do remain silent? Personally, I don't think, at this point, that we should ignore any possibility."

"I have no intention of ignoring anything, which is why I made light of your suggestion to the guards, and then motioned for silence."

"How do you expect them to investigate if they don't know that someone on the Council could be guilty in the first place?"

"I don't expect the guards to investigate."

She stopped walking and just stared at him. He quickly took her by the arm and got her moving again.

"My darling, you are the most capable woman I know, and I am extremely grateful that it was you backing me up against that troll.

However, when it comes to politics and politicians, you are a complete novice. First, the city guards are here to keep the peace: they are not here to investigate crimes. Even if one of them did go and ask the council members if they had anything to do with that attack, do you believe that the guilty party would simply admit to it?"

"I hadn't thought about that," she replied.

"Now, the first thing you need to realize is that the council members rarely know anything about the day-to-day happenings in this city unless such happenings directly involve them, or their own business interests. Since most of them should, therefore, be totally unaware of the attack, I intend to go and talk to all of them and see if anyone is surprised to see me alive. That will tell me much more in one evening than the city guards could find out if they investigated for a year."

Nadia smiled and said, "I should have realized that you would know what you are doing. I'm sorry, my love, I ought to have held my temper and let you handle it."

"No harm done," he replied. "Even if the guards are inclined to take your suggestion seriously, they won't be able to actually go and ask any questions before I have a chance to speak with everyone who could possibly be involved." He stopped and shook his head. "I know we were going to have lunch, but talking with the city guard has cost us time, and I still have to meet Elom outside the gates. Besides, that whole incident has taken away my appetite, anyway."

"I'm not hungry either, but why are we meeting Elom outside the gates?" she asked.

"Come on, and I'll explain it on the way."

CHAPTER 9

S INCE WANDA HAD been joined by Pina back at the docks, and both dragons had then protectively circled their human partners all the way to the gates, the dragons were so intent on watching for danger in the city that they weren't maintaining contact with Saadia, Beth, or any of the other dragons on the field. Therefore none of them, dragon or human, were prepared for what they found when they reached the northern gates of Larimar.

What Nassari saw first was that there was a new dragon present. She was slightly larger than Wanda. Nassari estimated that she was very nearly a match for Fahwn in size, and Fahwn was the second-largest dragon he knew. This newcomer was red, but not as brilliant a red as Fahwn, and she had a distinctive bright orange flash on her chest.

What he saw next caused him to stop short and be sure that his eyes weren't playing tricks on him. There, standing so close to the new dragon that he was almost leaning against her, stood Elom. The smith's face was turned toward the newcomer, but his eyes were not quite focused. He was obviously in mental contact with her.

As Will walked up to him, Nassari just looked from Will to Elom, and then back. His eyes spoke the unasked question on his mind.

"Elom came out looking for you and found me instead," Will said. "Nora showed up about a quarter of an hour after he did. She had heard that we were willing to help un-bonded dragons find partners, so she came seeking us out. When I went to talk with her, Elom followed me. Before any of us realized what was going on, they were bonded."

Nassari shook his head and said, "Well, I don't know if this is good or bad, but, as your brother would say, there's nothing for it now but to play the tiles we've been dealt."

He started to move toward the newly bonded pair, but Will grabbed him by the elbow and held him back. "There's something you need to know before you go over there."

He stopped and gave Will his full attention. He had lost track of his surroundings once already today, and it had almost cost him his life. Before Will could continue his train of thought, though, a somewhat nasal voice said, "I thought that you said there were no more dragons seeking out partners. And just what are you doing here anyway, Orin?" the speaker said with some surprise, quickly adding, "Shouldn't you be down at the docks making arrangements to get your pack of sorcerers and strays out of Corice?"

Nassari rolled his eyes and turned to face the man. "There were no more dragons seeking partners when I said that, Marvin. However, there are literally hundreds of un-bonded dragons still out there. There is always the possibility that one or more of them will see that many of their kind have found Bond-mates, and wish to do so themselves." He replied to the first question before answering the second, "As to what I am doing here, that is Dragon Rider business, as is the progress of our preparations to leave." Nassari had never allowed any politician to bully him before, and he wasn't about to start now, especially with all that had happened so far this day.

"Well, the Council has given you all of the money you are going to get," Landry shot back. "No more of these new riders will be outfitted with money from Corice, and I don't care what dirt you have on whom."

Marvin Landry was every other politician's nightmare. The man was honest to a fault, and he had no known vices that could be used against him. As far as anyone could tell, he had never cheated on his wife, he didn't drink, and his own personal business was so honest and aboveboard it was a wonder to most that he was able to turn a good profit. He was the one man on the Council that Nassari had not been able to blackmail.

"I want nothing from the Council anyway, Landry," Elom's voice boomed out from twenty yards away. "The day I need to go beggin' at your door is the day I'll fall on my own sword, you skinflint."

Everyone watched as Elom walked toward them. Nora began to follow her new Bond-mate. As she did Will's words came back to Nassari, "There's something you need to know before you go over there." It was immediately apparent that Nora had a deformity. She walked on three legs because her right front leg was a little more than half the size of her left. Still, like Elom and his rolling gait, she covered well and the deformity was more a curiosity than a real impairment. Having fought on dragon back, Nassari was sure the stunted leg would not be a great hindrance in battle; just an inconvenience that she could overcome.

"Elom Riley, what do you think that your father will say when he finds out that you have taken up with these sorcerers and their dragons?"

Nora eyed the man with obvious dislike.

"My father will be happy that I am doing so well, and keeping such good company. As far as any equipment I need, what I can't make myself, I can afford to buy. Therefore, if that's all you came out here to complain about, you can march your arse back to the city and leave us to be about our own business."

Landry looked at Nassari and said, "I won't be spoken to like this. I am an elected official, sworn to not only look out for the best interests of Corice but also the interests of Corisian commerce...."

"I own one of the businesses that you swear you are lookin' out for, you damn fool," Elom said cutting him off. "Now, if you have nothing more to carp about, why don't you go back and count your beans?"

"Rest assured, Nassari Orrin, you haven't heard the last of this," Landry said as he rounded on him. He glared at Nassari for a moment, and then, as a parting shot, he added, "You will not only get no money for supplies for these two, I will personally see that you also get no assistance from the army quartermaster at all. Your giant friend can make his own damn saddle out of metal because he'll get no help from the military leather workers."

As Marvin stomped off, Elom said, "I've never had any use for him. The man is completely honest, and he's never cheated anyone at business that I know of, but he's a pompous ass and bein' in his company just sets my teeth on edge."

"It's because he is so arrogant about it. Honesty is an admirable characteristic, but he flaunts it the way that some rich people flaunt their wealth and act as if no one else could possibly be as good as they are because of it," Nassari replied.

CHAPTER 10

"TWO DRAGONS APPROACH, *Love*," Wanda said. "*They are Geneva and Fahwn, and Geneva says that Delno wants to speak with you.*"

"*Tell them to join the party. We might as well have the whole gang here.*" To Elom he said, "Delno and Rita will be landing in a few moments."

The smith smiled and replied, "I know, Nora was telling me while you were getting the message."

They suddenly found themselves in the shade as Geneva pulled up and settled her hind legs onto the grass. Delno had her land so close that everyone was pelted with dust, snow, and bits of dry grass as she backstroked to cushion her landing. He jumped down from her neck before she even settled.

"You really do have a problem with keeping your rump in that saddle, don't you?" Nassari said with mock severity as Delno trotted up to them.

"Well, I came here this morning to talk with you about the preparations for moving the Riders, and when I found that our good mastersmith here had bonded to a dragon, I just couldn't contain myself." He turned to Elom and said, "I can't say that I am at all displeased, my friend, but this is most unexpected."

"The whole thing was just as startlin' for me," Elom replied. "I came here to see Nassari and meet the dragons. I had decided to accompany the Riders to Horne and see that the new metal shop gets properly set up, so I figured that meeting some of the dragons would be appropriate since they would have to carry me so far. I found your brother, and while we were talking, a new dragon showed up. When Will went to meet her, I just kind of tagged along. When we got close she and I looked at each other for a moment, and then she reached out and touched me. There was a bright flash of light, and the next thing I knew we were talking to each other in our minds." As he reached the part about actually bonding, he grinned broadly.

Never one to sit by and be excluded from a conversation, Rita said. "So, Delno, any more of your friends you want to have meet an un-bonded dragon?" At his look of total innocence, she teased him further, "After all, you've only got about half of Corice bonded now." Everyone, including the dragons, laughed.

Two men Elom didn't recognize joined the group, bringing the number of Riders present, including the newest, up to eight. Delno realized that Elom had never met Craig and Adamus, so he introduced them.

Elom quickly took the opportunity to make sure that everyone was then introduced to Nora. Once that was out of the way, Craig had to hear Nora's story.

"I am nearly a century old," Nora said. "I have always longed to seek out humans and see if the old stories of adult dragons bonding were true, but I never had the courage. I have known Marlo for many years, and she and I even traveled together on rare occasions. She told me in the Dream State that she had met her Bond-mate and encouraged me to seek out Delno Okonan. She said he would help me find a partner, also. It took me months to find the courage to come forward. I was worried that I would be rejected because of my physical deformity. I came here today expecting to be turned away. Then Elom came out, and when I looked at him, I just knew he was for me. The magic passed between us quickly, and now neither of us will ever be alone again."

As she spoke the final words of her narration, she snaked her neck down onto Elom's shoulder and then leaned her head onto his chest. Even as large as Elom was, he was still dwarfed by the dragon. His torso was almost completely hidden by her head. He reached his arm up around her neck as far as he could and held her tenderly. His eyes glistened with moisture, and a single tear trickled down Nora's cheek.

Delno gave them a moment, and then said, "All we need to do now, then, is to go to the quartermaster and have a saddle made." As both Nassari, and Elom, shook their heads he looked at Nassari and asked, "Are you having trouble with the Council again?"

"Nope. He's not; I am," Elom replied. When Delno looked at him with one eyebrow raised, he said, "That jackass, Marvin Landry, decided to come out here and personally tell the world that the Council wouldn't buy any more equipment for any new Riders. I've never liked that arrogant little twerp, so I told him to go about his business and leave us to ours. I'm afraid I put my foot in it. Now the man has said he will personally see to it that I get nothing from the quartermaster even if I'm willing to pay for it myself."

"Damn!" Delno swore. "Well, I didn't want to do it, but I suppose I will have to go to my uncle and see if he will directly order the quartermaster to deal with us against the Council's wishes. Even my uncle's generosity has limits, and we are getting close to them."

"There's no need to bother the King because I haven't learned when to keep my big mouth shut," Elom said. "I got myself into this mess, and I'll get myself out of it. All I need from anyone is a set of plans for a general purpose saddle. It'll have to be modified to fit my bulk, and still make accommodations for my braces, so anything I have made will have to be completely custom anyway."

"That's all true enough," Nassari said, "but we need to leave in a few days, and saddles take time even with several skilled workers doing the job."

Delno was nodding in agreement to Nassari's observation but Elom said to him, "The man who made those scabbards hanging at your side is the best there is. He moved up this way from Trent. The way I hear it, he had a problem with keeping his pants buttoned when he was younger, and he left Trent because some minor nobleman took offense at him dallying with the man's wife. He came to Larimar with little more than the clothes on his back and took a job in my father's shop so he could feed himself. It wasn't long before my dad found out how good he was at leatherwork. Dad helped him get his whole business set up and we've used no one else since. The man makes fine scabbards, and he makes other typical leather goods as well, but he produces the best saddles you can find. The reason he isn't more well-known for his saddle making skills is that the rigs he makes are so expensive he only gets a half dozen or so commissions a year from nobility and high-ranking military, but people travel from as far off as Iondar to have him make a custom saddle for 'em." Then he smiled and added, "Rupert owes me and my family. He won't have any trouble working overtime to get me set up. Get me those plans, and then you and Nassari do what you need to do and leave my gear to me. I'll be ready to travel when the time comes."

Rita suddenly spoke up, "Nassari, your coat is ripped as though it's been sliced with a blade, and that looks suspiciously like dried blood on it. What happened, and are you hurt?"

"I'm fine," Nassari replied.

"You're fine now," Nadia retorted, "but you were nearly killed by that assassin down near the docks." She turned to Delno and added, "He was attacked by a man who was nearly a match in stature for our good mastersmith here."

Everyone stared at Nassari waiting for an explanation. Finally, he said, "I went to meet Nadia down by the docks when she had finished seeing to the last shipment being sent out. The man attacked me from behind, but Nadia saw him and warned me in time. His first swing missed completely, and his second only got my coat."

"So, that's his blood then?" Rita asked, still concerned.

Nassari shook his head, "No, It's mine. I caught his third strike with both my sword and *main gauche*. He was a lot faster than I anticipated he would be considering his size, and I didn't have time or presence of mind to get a magical shield in place." he paused while he pulled his sword from the scabbard and showed them the blade.

"That piece broke out of the blade and went through my cheek. With our blades locked, he forced me down and was moving the cutting edge of his axe to my neck when Nadia buried that leaf blade of hers up to the hilt in his back and skewered his right kidney."

Elom took the weapon from Nassari and said, "I'm sorry my friend, I thought I had supplied you with a quality blade. It must have been flawed."

"Don't fault the blade, Elom," Nassari responded. "Nadia wasn't exaggerating when she estimated the man's size. He was an inch or two taller than you, and nearly as broad. That axe he carried weighed a good two stone, maybe a wee bit more, and he put all of his force in an overhand swing. If that sword hadn't been made of your finest steel, it would have shattered completely and I wouldn't be standing here telling my side of the story. That blade saved my life!" Then he added, "If it's any consolation to you, the sword did more damage to the axe than was done to it."

"Well, it's weakened, and not to be trusted now," Elom said. Then he looked at the *main gauche* and found the guard on that weapon had also been compromised. "This one's done in, too. Come with me to the shop and we'll find you something that's serviceable to use until I can get the forge going in Horne, and then I'll make two new ones to your liking."

"I'll stop by later; Delno and I have to make the final arrangements for this excursion."

Everyone present, including several of the dragons, shouted, "No!" in unison.

Then Delno said, "If you have been attacked by an assassin, I don't want you walking around with nothing but a damaged knife in one hand, and a weakened sword in the other. You'll go with Elom and get new blades. We can talk on the way."

Nassari shook his head and then told the rest of the story of the attack. "So you see, I don't think the man was after me specifically. It's no secret that we had one barge still loading that would push off today. He most likely waited down there and attacked the first Dragon Rider he found."

Nadia spoke up before Delno could get the chance. "If that is the case, dear, why didn't the man simply cut me down before you arrived? I remember seeing him while I was waiting for the bill of lading for the last wagon coming from Elom's shop. That was at least ten minutes before you got there. A man of that size is hard to miss, even in a crowd."

Nassari looked thoughtful for a minute and then said, "You have a good point, Nadia. Although, it's still possible that he wasn't targeting me specifically, but was after any of the leaders of the Riders. And there is the always the chance that, if he saw you, he thought you were nothing more than a young girl and dismissed you," Then he rubbed his chin and said, "This is an interesting puzzle, and I really do need to go and check on a few things at the Council House."

"Nassari," Delno said in a voice that left no room for argument, "You are not going off anywhere alone! You and I can talk on the way to Elom's shop, and then we can go from there."

"Del..." Nassari started to protest but Elom cut him off.

"Oh, he'll go to the shop with us," the big man said with a somewhat mischievous grin. "Remember when we were younger, and one of you wouldn't want to come along with the other two of us?"

Nassari looked at him and said, "You wouldn't dare!"

"Oh, wouldn't I," Elom replied in an innocent tone. "If you try and go somewhere alone, I'll toss you over my shoulder like a feed sack and carry you, just like when we were twelve."

Nassari smiled and said, "I didn't have a fully-grown dragon to protect me from you then."

"As far as I am concerned," Wanda interjected, "if you do not do as these men say, I will keep you in this field under my protection until we leave for Horne."

Nassari started to protest and then shrugged his shoulders as he realized that he had been outmaneuvered. He turned to Delno, and said, "I believe I'm beginning to see the advantages of staying together, Del; lead on."

Just then five of the girls ran up to Will. The oldest girl in the group, who was about fourteen, was carrying some rolled up papers, which she handed to him. They were, of course, the plans for a standard dragon saddle. Will had simply had Saadia relay the need for them to one of the girls through her own dragon.

"It takes five of you to bring such a small roll of papers?" Will asked, as he glared at Adamus and Craig, who were both laughing.

The girls only giggled in response. Then they just stood there, showing no inclination to return to the Riders' quarters. Craig and Adamus were having a grand time watching. In fact, everyone was a bit amused at Will's predicament.

"Well, be on your way then," Will said to the girls. "I'm sure that Craig will be along shortly and start your lessons. If you want lunch before magic class starts, you'd best go and get something."

"Oh, it's all right, Will," Craig said solicitously, "I have to finish packing all of my books and supplies, so magic classes have been canceled until we can set up in our new location." Then he smiled broadly and added, "The girls are all yours, if you have need of them."

The look in Will's eyes belied the smile on his face as he said, "That's so kind of you Craig. I'll be sure to return the favor at my first opportunity."

As Will turned to send the girls back to quarters, Delno stopped him. "With what is going on, I think it would be best if Nadia and Rita return with them." The girls looked disappointed as he turned to Rita and said, "We have no idea what all this is about yet. There is still the possibility that the assassin at the docks didn't attack Nadia because she is easily mistaken for a young girl, rather than a mature Rider, however, that could change and the youngsters might become targets as well. Therefore, until we are all safely in the air and out of Larimar completely, I believe that none of the younger Riders should be out and about unless they are accompanied by at least one adult, and I would prefer that we all start traveling in groups of at least three."

Rita simply nodded her agreement and said, "Leave it to the two of us."

Nadia turned to the girls, all of whom were now pouting because they would be sent back to quarters with the women, and said,

"We've had an assassination attempt today, and until we can figure out if it was aimed at one person in particular or at Riders in general, you will be under even stricter adult supervision. So, pull your lower lips in, ladies, and get moving."

She pointed in the direction of the city gates, and she and Rita herded the girls back in the direction from which they had come.

Delno looked around at the men on the field and said, "Now, for the rest of us. I know that there are other adult Riders who aren't here at the moment, and Nassari and I have a great deal to discuss and do. So, Adamus and Craig, I will leave you to help Nadia and Rita get the house organized so that no one is left alone. I would insist that you two find at least one more person to team up with, but I know that Adamus is an excellent swordsman, and the only Rider who might rival Craig at magic is Jhren. Therefore, both of you be careful and watch each other's backs, and don't let any Riders go about alone, especially the youngsters."

Both men nodded and saluted before turning and walking back toward the city.

"Now then, as far as we four go…" Nassari started to say something, but Delno held up his hand for silence. "Nassari, I know that you are also the Rider of a Lineage Holder, but for the time being, especially since you may be the main target, please, for once in your life, just do as I ask." Nassari smiled and nodded, so Delno continued, "Good. Nassari, you and I will be together most of the time during the day; when we separate at night, we will be with our respective human partners, and our dragons will be able to keep watch as well. Will, you stay with Elom."

This time it was Elom who objected. "I can take care of myself. I'd rather not be responsible for your brother's safety."

Again Delno held up his hand to forestall further comment. "Elom, I know that you can still move around just fine. I also know that you are stronger than any two men our enemies might send against you. However, you are not impervious to being shot in the back with a poisoned dart. I am not placing Will under your protection, I am pairing you off with another very capable warrior, who also has magical training that you lack, in the hopes that you will look out for each other."

"I don't think I'll be in much danger in my own home or shop," Elom replied.

"Suppose that an assassin came to your home and missed you and hit your mother with a poisoned dart?" Elom looked at him and then nodded and looked at the ground. "You see, my friend," Delno continued, "as long as there is the slightest danger to any of us, we endanger those around us. That is why you are not only going to stay with Will, but you are also going to sleep in Dragon Rider quarters starting tonight."

Elom continued to stare at the ground for a few seconds before looking Delno in the eye. Then he simply nodded in agreement.

"Good, I will start by giving a bit of background concerning magic." Elom looked at him sharply but said nothing, so he went on. "Nearly everyone has some connection to magic, though it is a very weak connection in most cases. Concerning the dragons, the stronger the connection, the more likely a person is to bond. Though this isn't a prerequisite for being a candidate, in some people the magic is so strong that it manifests in the form of one or more magical talents or abilities. In my case, I can find nearly anything I put mind to finding. I have come to believe that Nassari's gift of the tongue is the outward manifestation of his connection to the magic. Will's talent, or ability, is being able to hide in plain sight. If you aren't extremely careful, he can disappear while you are watching him."

Elom looked at Will and then back at Delno.

"I'd have him give you a demonstration, but we have worked hard at keeping his talent a secret, and I need you to keep it to yourself as well. I don't want him openly displaying that talent here where anyone from the city might be watching. However, you can be sure that we have used his ability to good effect in our past endeavors. It might be an advantage to us now, also, but until we find better use for it in our present situation, you and he will stay teamed up. I don't want any Rider to go anywhere alone, not even a short trip to the privy!"

"All right," Elom responded, "but tell me one thing." As Delno looked at him expectantly he said, "I have never had any magical talent. I can't hide, I'm not a great talker, and as far as locating things, I'm lucky I can find my own stockings when I get dressed in the morning. How is it that I bonded so easily with Nora?"

Delno and Nassari both laughed out loud. At Elom's bewildered look, Delno said, "My friend, you have been working magic for years. When I showed Brock my Dragon Blade, he could appreciate the craftsmanship you put into it; the piece is exquisite. However, the Dragon Blade has so much of its own magic about it that it hides what you instilled into it with your handicraft. When I handed Brock my *main gauche*, he immediately sensed that there was more to that than just a big knife. He said work like that was a kind of magic all its own, and he could sense it in the blade itself. Nassari was right about what he said earlier; if that blade he held this afternoon had been made by someone else, it would have failed, and he'd be dead. I don't know how you've worked the magic into the blades you've made up to this point, and it's obvious that you don't either, but I'm anxious to see what will come out of your forge now that you are bonded to a dragon. When things start to settle down, you'd do well to talk with Craig and Jhren about all of this."

The Riders then assured their draconic partners that they would all be very careful before they turned and headed for the city. Elom walked in total silence all the way to the metal shop.

CHAPTER 11

THE FOUR COMPANIONS were all surprised to find Elom's mother in the shop when they arrived. "Momma Riley," Nassari exclaimed, "it's good to see you out and about."

Pamela Riley had been almost totally housebound for the last ten years. She suffered from painful swellings of the joints, and when the problem was particularly bad, she developed pleurisy. The worst of it, though, was the constant fatigue the poor woman was afflicted with. Nassari had often thought that the real reason Nathan had gone into retirement was to stay home and take care of his beloved wife.

"Oh, I get out much more often now that I've spent some time under the care of the Elven healer you boys brought with you to save our city." As Nassari, Delno, and Will all looked at her in surprise, she continued, "After he had the plague under control, he came back here, and he brought the King's own healer with him. The two of them did a proper examination of me. Then Master Nathaniel, bless the man, taught me how to make an herbal tea to help with my affliction. He also told me what foods not to eat so I won't aggravate the condition, and Master Morran looks in on me now and again. I think he's learning from Master Nathaniel and they are using me as a study subject. At any rate, the Elven healer has said he will be coming back this way to check up on how the King's physician is handling my case." She paused for a moment before adding, "Master Nathaniel is a true wonder and a truly good man."

"To that," Delno responded, "I can only agree. I will tell him of your compliments and thank him personally when I see him next."

Pamela smiled and opened her mouth to speak, but looked at her son and shook her head instead. "How did you get that splotch of dirt under your collar?" She said as she licked her thumb and reached up to wipe at the side of Elom's neck.

Elom winced slightly and responded sharply, "That's not dirt, Mom. It's a permanent mark, and it's a bit tender."

She grabbed his collar and pulled it down revealing what looked to be a wine-colored birthmark. It wasn't fully formed, but it definitely had the shape of the head and neck of a dragon.

Pamela put her hands on her hips and said in her sternest mother's voice, "Off with that shirt then. Let's see the rest of it." As Elom hesitated, looking to Delno and Nassari for support, she added, "Your friends won't save you from me. Get that shirt off, or I'll pull it off of you."

As Elom pulled his tunic over his head, and the full mark came into view, everyone stared in stunned silence, though for different reasons. Elom's mother, not knowing anything about Dragon Marks, thought that her son had gone and gotten a tattoo. It was obviously a dragon. Though it still had a ways to go before it would become a perfect image of his Bond-mate, it was much more pronounced than any fresh Dragon Mark Delno had ever even heard of. Delno's own mark had been little more than a vague abstract of a dragon so soon after bonding and could have been mistaken for a birthmark. Such a mistake could not be made in this case.

Elom's chest was huge and the picture took full advantage of the broad canvass. This dragon, like Rita's, was in flight. The body was positioned to the right side of the smith's breastbone, and the wings spread halfway around his right deltoid on the one side, to nearly where his arm joined his body on the other. The tail extended down to his waist, and the neck snaked up slightly to the left so that the head of the dragon could be seen just above the collar of the man's tunic. Delno surmised that, like its owner, it was one of the most impressive specimens of its kind in existence.

"Elom, you're nearly thirty years old, and I have no right to tell you how to run your life," Pamela Riley said sharply, "But what in the world did you go and get a tattoo for?" Then she shook her head in disgust and added, "If you were dead set on such a thing, you could have at least found a better artist. Look at it, it's fuzzy around the edges and has a half-done quality about it." She shook her head and titched her tongue at him.

Delno came to his rescue, "That's not a tattoo, Momma Riley," he said as he removed his jacket.

"Not a tattoo?" she replied. "Delno Okonan, you've never lied in your life; don't start now."

"I'm not lying, Ma'am," he replied as he began to pull his own shirt over his head. "What your son has on his chest is a Dragon Mark."

Seeing the bronze-colored dragon on Delno's chest, she stared wide-eyed and shook her head.

Before she could accuse Delno of being in collusion with her son on this, he quickly added, "This mark was placed on me by the magic that passed between us when Geneva and I bonded. Nassari has one on his upper left arm and shoulder, and Will has one on his shoulder blade. As for Elom's mark looking unfinished, it will continue to change until it is an exact image of the dragon to whom he has bonded."

"Bonded?" she whispered; her lips continued to move but no further sound came out.

Nathan looked at Elom and said, "I guess you had best tell us all of it, son." He then put his arm around Pamela and the two of them stared at their offspring expectantly.

"All right," Elom responded. "I went out to meet up with Nassari like I had planned. Nassari was a bit late, and I was talking to Will when he told me that a new dragon was landing, and he had to go and speak with her. I followed him out on the field to wait for the dragon to land." He paused for a second and his look became a bit far-off and dreamy, but he continued, "When she landed, I remember thinking how beautiful she was. Her color, the way she moved, the almost shy way she was standing there. Then she looked right at me, and we just stared at each other for a moment. Then tears started to roll down her cheeks, and she leaned over and put her head against my chest. There was a bright flash, and I was so disoriented that I almost fell over. The next thing I knew, I was rubbing my chest with one hand, and hugging Nora's neck with my other arm, and we were both speaking to each other in our minds." His smile faded and he came back to the here and now. Looking at his parents he added, "I didn't set out to bond with a dragon: I never would have believed it was possible for me to do, but now that I have, it seems like the most natural and wonderful thing in the world."

Pamela looked at her son and said, "You speak of this dragon the way I'd like to hear you speak of a wife. I don't understand how a man can be bonded to such a creature."

"The bond between human and dragon goes much deeper than the bond between man and wife," Delno said. "A person who is bonded to a dragon is linked on a level that runs so deep that if either partner dies, the other will lose his or her hold on life entirely. In fact, that bond can only be broken by death."

His words did nothing to reassure Pamela or Nathan so Nassari added, "It's not as though he is now bonded to Nora to the absolute exclusion of all else. Both Delno and I are bonded and we have human partners as well. Delno and Rita are together and have adopted three young children. Nadia and I formally introduced each other to our families a short time ago. Elom would be free to take a wife of his choosing if he becomes so inclined, though he would do well to choose a Rider since his lifespan is now such that he will outlive a non-bonded woman by many centuries."

As the realization of how long he would live suddenly surged to the forefront in Elom's mind, he looked pained.

Delno looked at Elom and said softly, "I'm sorry my friend; that is the curse of the Riders. We will outlive any of our family and friends who aren't also bonded with a dragon."

Pamela, forgetting the discomfort it might cause, reached out and ran her fingers over her son's Dragon Mark, and then, with tears in her eyes, she said, "I don't really know what all of this means, but it can't be a bad thing if such good men as you four are involved with it. I guess all that I can do now is accept that it has happened and deal with it as best I can."

"There's nothing really to deal with," Nassari assured her. "This changes nothing. Elom is still your son, and he still loves you both. He is still going to Horne with the rest of us, as planned. The only thing that has changed is that now when he wants to come back and see you, it will be a shorter trip because he will be flying in a straight line with his draconic partner, rather than taking slower transport around the western mountain range."

Pamela Riley looked at Nassari for a moment and then began to chuckle. "Nassari, you've always been able to see the bright side of everything." Then, as everyone else laughed with her she added, "Even as a boy, you could always make me laugh to help Elom get out of trouble."

They talked for a while longer, and then Delno filled them in on what had happened at the docks. While Pamela didn't want Elom to go off into danger, Nathan was quick to agree that the safest thing for all concerned was for his son to move into the Riders' quarters where he would be surrounded by other warriors, and any trouble that might occur wouldn't be as likely to inadvertently cause harm to innocent bystanders.

In the end, Will and Elom stayed to get Elom's affairs in order and agreed to meet the others back at the Riders' lodgings later that afternoon. Then, after Nassari had chosen two new blades, he and Delno left the shop to attend to their business.

CHAPTER 12

"**I** THOUGHT WE AGREED to go and see the council members," Nassari said, as they walked right by the Council Chambers.

"We did," Delno responded, "and since the council members are at the Palace, that is where we are going."

"Now who's keeping secrets? I didn't know that the Council was meeting with the King. Why didn't you tell me sooner?"

"Mostly because, with everything else that has happened, it had slipped my mind until you asked. The Council isn't meeting with the King, though." At Nassari's perplexed look, Delno added, "The King is holding formal court to publicly decide the fate of a rabble-rousing nobleman from Bourne who was recently convicted of openly recruiting followers to overthrow the legitimate government and sent here to be sentenced, and the Council is required to attend today in accordance with both custom and the law. This particular Bournese has been trying to get his countrymen to rise up and throw off the 'invaders from Corice'. He hasn't been successful, but Dorian is unwilling to give such people a chance to sow the seeds of revolution since we've only taken control so recently. Once people have had a few years to get used to the idea of Bourne being a duchy under the direct control of Corice, men like this one will mostly be a laughing stock anyway. Right now, though, anyone who is facing any hardship might be swayed into thinking that the privation is the result of our conquest of Bourne, rather than the direct result of Torrance bankrupting his country in his efforts to conquer Corice."

"Ah, you are getting more devious in your old age," Nassari replied as they walked up the steps of the Palace. "We will not only see the reactions of the council members to me being alive, but the reaction, if any, of this particular nobleman as well." As Delno nodded, Nassari added, "We may make a politician of you yet, Del."

"There's no reason to be insulting, Nassari."

Once inside, they quickly made their way to the main hall. The space, though not particularly small, was a bit crowded. It seemed that there were many people, besides the council members who were present, who had an interest in the proceedings that were scheduled this day. As the two entered, King Dorian called them by name and asked them to come and stand beside him on the raised dais. Since this not only put them in full view of everyone, but also gave them the best vantage point to see if there were any who were surprised that Nassari was still alive, Delno was quite pleased that his uncle had made the request.

By now, the King's guards had learned not to challenge the Riders, so no one asked that they relinquish their weapons. Delno took a position on the King's right, and Nassari took a similar position on the left. Both Riders immediately began to scan the crowd, judging each person's reaction to their own appearance. Delno did take a second to smile to his mother, who, as the Duchess of Bourne, was in attendance in her official capacity.

A guardsman entered and walked directly up to the King and reported that the dissident from Bourne would be brought in momentarily. The Riders used that distraction to relay their findings about the crowd to each other. Neither had seen any sign that any of the council members present had been involved in the incident at the dock, though three of them were absent and had sent subordinates as representatives.

The doors opened and a very thin man of medium height, with black hair, a black beard, and a large hookbill nose, was led into the hall by a guard. Four more guards followed, carrying spears at high port. They weren't exactly menacing the man with their weapons, but the implication was clear: if the man tried to escape, or made any attempt on the King, he would be run through before he could succeed.

The nobleman carried himself with an air of arrogance, even though he was being brought before the monarch to be judged. He followed the lead guard until that man said "Halt!" about five paces from the dais. The prisoner then gazed up at the King. The haughty gleam in his eye was pure defiance. He glanced to the King's right, knowing that the Monarch's most trusted man would stand there. He glared at Delno in utter contempt. Then he turned his gaze to the left.

His expression when he saw Nassari lasted less than a second, but the wide-eyed look of shock was unmistakable. Nassari starred straight into the man's eyes and simply smiled. Much of the arrogance drained from the noble as did a good deal of his color. He knew that he had given himself away as being part of the assassination attempt at the dock. If he wasn't the mastermind behind it, he was at least in it up to his scrawny neck.

"*Wanda,*" Nassari said, "*I need you to contact Saadia and find out how Will and Elom are coming along.*"

"*Saadia says that they are at the saddler's. Will wants to know why you have asked.*"

Dorian noticed the look on Nassari's face and simply sat looking at the prisoner as if he were actually thinking about the man's fate. In reality, he had seen the subtle interchange between the Bournese and the Rider and was giving Nassari time to complete whatever silent communication he was involved in.

"*If they can get themselves free, I have use for Will's talent.*"

"*I have relayed the message, and they have acknowledged. I could send another Rider to accompany Nora's Bond-mate, and have Will report to you, if you would like.*"

"*Yes, Love, please do that, and tell them to hurry. I will attempt to delay matters here until Will can arrive. Tell Will that it is imperative*

*that he not be seen at all on his way, or once he arrives here. I don't
need to see him, so he can simply relay that he has arrived through Saadia and you."*

A few seconds passed and Wanda said, *"Adamus and Craig were
already on their way to the smith's shop to accompany the pair to quarters. They will stay with Elom, and Will is now on his way to the palace."*

"Thank you, I will relay Will's orders once he gets here."

Nassari, realizing that Dorian was waiting for him, made the
barest of nods to the King and closed his eyes. Dorian correctly in-
terpreted the signal and sat up straighter, ready to begin the proceedings.

"Clarence Bourne Lowell, you are a dissident. That in itself is
not a crime, and We would normally not even take it seriously.
However, We have also found that you are not content to simply
protest, but are actively involved in trying to recruit a rebel army to
overthrow the lawful government in the Duchy of Bourne. Therefore, you have already been tried and convicted of treason in a
Bournese court, and have been brought before Us here to be sentenced."

Lowell looked as if he might speak, but Dorian held up his hand
for silence and the Sergeant of the Escort simply glared, so the man
held his tongue.

"Now then," Dorian continued, "We have decided that keeping
you in Our prison would not only be a waste of funds, but it might
actually help to you by turning you into somewhat of a martyr.
Therefore, it is Our judgment that, even though your crime warrants incarceration or death, you shall be sent into exile, and your
name will be stricken from the Roster of Peers. You will be escorted to the southern border of Corice. Once there, you will be given
the horse you are riding, three day's supply of food, a skin of water,
a tinderbox, one hunting knife, a blanket, and a canvas tarp for shelter. Once you have left this country, you are never to return. If you
are ever again found on Corisian soil, and that now includes the
lands of the Duchy of Bourne, your life will be forfeit: that sentence

to be carried out immediately upon such discovery. Further, anyone in Corice who is found to be in communication with you, either directly or indirectly, once you are in exile, shall also be guilty of treason and shall share your sentence."

The guards started to step forward, but the King again held up his hand.

"There is one last thing before We consign you to your fate. The Signet ring you wear is the property of the Duchy of Bourne, and it is one of the symbols of the steward of the town of Lowell. We, therefore, order you to surrender that ring to us, here and now."

Lowell made a fist of his left hand, displaying the ring as what little color he had left drained from his face, and he shook his head from side to side. Finally, he found his voice. "This ring is the property of my family. It was given to my ancestors by the rightful King of Bourne over a thousand years ago. It has since been handed down from father to son and has been mine for over a decade. You have no right to take it."

Dorian looked at the man the way someone might look at a particularly interesting specimen of bug before he steps on it. "We have every right to take it, and you are hereby ordered to relinquish it."

Lowell actually shook his head and covered the ring with his right hand the way a petulant child who has been caught playing dress up with mother's fine jewelry might do. He stood and continued to shake his head in a feeble attempt to defy the order.

"Will is in the Great Hall of the Palace, Love. He wants to know if his orders involve the man who is apparently on trial."

Once again Dorian saw Nassari's expression and knew that the Rider was in silent communication. It wasn't obvious to all present, but the King had learned to read such subtleties as a matter of course. He sat and simply regarded the prisoner as if considering his next words carefully to buy the Rider the time he needed.

"Relay this," Nassari said, *"I know that this man will be guarded, but I want Will to follow him where ever he goes while he is still in the city. I want to know who he talks to and what is said. If he passes any notes, I want to know who gets them, and if it is possible to learn the*

contents of those notes without being detected, I want him to do that also. However, he is not to endanger himself in any way. These people already proved earlier today that they are deadly, I would rather have him alive with less information than have him take chances." Nassari looked around and then added, *"One last thing, Love. Tell Will that while he can't be seen, his footprints will be obvious if he tracks wet snow into a room."*

Even though he couldn't see Will standing there, he looked right at him because he was looking at the spot where the wet footprints stopped.

"Will says that he is sorry and it won't happen again. He forgot that he might leave a visible trail in his haste to get here," Wanda relayed.

Nassari once again signaled the King that he was finished.

"Enough of this nonsense!" Dorian spoke so harshly that quite a few people besides just Lowell jumped. "Whether you will surrender the ring is not in question," he said motioning to the guards who advanced on the prisoner. "The decision you need to make is from which end of your finger it will be taken. Decide now!"

Lowell looked at the King as if he hoped to see some way out of giving it up. Then, realizing that it would be removed from him one way or another, he hung his head and pulled it off of his left hand and let it fall to the floor. It clanged with a finality that left even Nassari feeling a small measure or compassion for the man, though it was a very small measure.

CHAPTER 13

"**Y**OU SHOULDN'T HAVE sent him," Nadia said for the third time in the last hour. "Will is good, but these people are obviously dangerous. One of them nearly killed you, and you're a better swordsman than he is."

Will had been an integral part of Nassari's team with her during the war, and they had all become close in a way that only those who have shared such an experience can understand. While she was in love with Nassari, she loved Will as much as any of her flesh and blood brothers.

"Will is fine, Nadia," Delno responded before Nassari could defend his decision. "If he had any problems, Saadia would have alerted us, and as for Will's skill with a blade, I've sparred with both of them, and Nassari is only marginally better. Will can take care of himself, especially since he also carries Corolan's blade. That saber may not have been made specifically for him, but he is a Dragon Rider, and the blade responds even more because he is of its original owner's blood. With it, he is almost equal to me or Brock in a fight."

"Well, I don't see why he can't stay in contact," she replied.

"Because," Nassari spoke up, "he has told us to wait so that he isn't distracted by trying to hold a relayed conversation while he is doing his job. Besides, he is at the jailhouse, surrounded by Corisian guards. Even if he inadvertently allowed himself to be seen, they all know him, and they know that he is a Rider and the King's nephew. The worst that could happen would be that the man he is watching would then know that he is being watched and Will would return to us with no more information than we already have. I told him specifically not to endanger himself. I wouldn't have sent him if I thought that he would be in any real peril."

"I know, darling," Nadia responded, "I didn't mean to imply otherwise. I just worry that he might go beyond your orders and get himself into trouble. He is a full-grown man, and as brave as any, but whether he will admit it or not, he still feels as though he walks in his brother's shadow." Before Delno or anyone else could argue, she added, "Don't think that carrying Corolan's blade does anything to offset that, either. While he's proud to own something that belonged to his grandfather, on some level, he still sees even that as nothing more than another hand-me-down from his big brother. He is still prone to taking chances to prove himself."

Rita put her hand on Nadia's shoulder and said, "Saadia has promised to tell us the minute that Will finishes and heads back. Until then, even though they aren't relaying communication, she is staying in contact with him. If there is any trouble, we will know instantly."

"The snow's fallin' again," Elom said, as he stood and looked out the window. "How are we supposed to keep watch if we can't see more than two feet outside?"

"Wanda has placed a ward around the building," Nassari responded. "Nothing bigger than an alley cat could get within fifteen feet of the outer wall without her knowing it."

"I just don't understand all of this," Elom replied. "I thought you said it was the riders that did the magic, and the dragons that did the flyin'."

Even though his books had been packed, Craig had been going over the basics with Elom since he, Adamus, and the smith had arrived at the house.

"That," Craig said, "is the usual case. However, that doesn't mean that the dragons aren't capable of working magic independently of us. When Riders are fighting on dragon back, they usually work the magic, so the dragon can then concentrate on flying and using her natural weapons, whether it is her flame or claws. Working like that as a team allows the Rider to add the dragon's magical strength to his through the bond they share, and saves the dragon from the distraction of working magic while trying to handle the complex maneuvers of flight during battle. If both partners were trying to use magic at the same time, then neither would gain any more than a small benefit from the partnership and they would not be significantly stronger separately than any other single magic user. Even the Elves, who often work well together, cannot match the power of the bonded Dragon and Rider because, while they do cooperate, they don't have that bond that allows the magic to flow so easily between them. However, that doesn't mean that a dragon isn't able to work strong magic. A female dragon is as strong in that respect as any human or Elven mage, providing that she devotes time to study and practice."

"That is why," Delno said, "when I plunged my blade into Hella's flame bladder and then pushed off her back, Geneva was able to use magic to keep me alive after she caught me. She wasn't able to heal me completely because I still had Corolan's saber stuck through my leg, but she kept me from bleeding to death until she could set me on the ground so that Nat could remove the blade and finish what she had started."

"So, how does this ward thing that Wanda is doin' work then?" Elom asked.

"That's a good question, and is a good example of what we've been doing," Craig answered. "We've been working on simple shields. What Wanda is doing is an extension of that. Instead of erecting a solid barrier, like I've been teaching you to do, she erects a very weak shield, known as a ward; then she maintains a strong connection to it. The shield is so weak that something, or someone, coming in contact with it wouldn't even know he had done so, but his passage through it would be instantly transmitted to Wanda through the connection she is keeping with the ward. It won't keep anyone out, but it will alert us to their presence no matter how stealthy they are: even if they were invisible and completely silent Wanda will still feel them there."

"How is that done, then?" Elom pressed. He was like a sponge, ready to soak up any information that was available. Craig had been quite impressed with the man's mind and how quickly he was catching on, considering that he had just bonded that afternoon.

"Wards are more complex to erect and maintain," Craig replied. "Let's stick with shields and healing for now, and save wards for a little later on in your training."

Elom shrugged and sat back down across from Craig and nodded to signal that he was ready to get back to his practice.

"For someone who didn't initially want anything to do with magic," Nadia whispered to Nassari, "Elom sure is taking these lessons seriously."

"He's always been like that, dear. Once he sets his mind to a task he puts everything he has into it. As far as he's concerned, it's either worth doing right, or it's not worth doing at all. Elom has never been happy settling for the middle ground."

"*Saadia has reported that Will is on his way to you, Love,*" Wanda broke into his thoughts. "*He says that you and Delno should be ready to move when he gets here.*"

"*What has he found out?*" Nassari asked.

"*I have told you all that he has relayed through Saadia; He is approaching the house now. You can ask him that question yourself in a few moments.*"

Nassari had just finished telling the others what Wanda had said when the door opened and Will stepped inside. He had obviously run all the way.

"I waited for hours," Will told Nassari and Delno. "I was beginning to think that I would have to leave before they locked down the jail for the night when two men came in to visit the prisoner. When the guards told them that the man wasn't allowed visitors, they claimed that they just wanted to give him a few personal effects before he went into exile. While the guards were distracted going through the bundle the men had brought, and rejecting everything in it, one of the two managed to get close enough for Lowell to pass him a note. The guards noticed that the man was near the prisoner's cell door and told him to move away, but they hadn't seen the note get passed, so they didn't search him. I figured that this was what we had been waiting for, so I followed them when they left the jail."

He paused and Nassari said, "Well, where did they go?"

Will gestured toward the stairs with his head, and Nassari turned to find several of the girls standing there. They weren't necessarily eavesdropping, but this was beyond what they needed to concern themselves with. He motioned to Nadia, and she and Rita herded the girls back to their room.

When they returned, they found that Delno, Nassari, and Elom had all donned jackets, and Will hadn't removed his. The men were heading for the door intent on their business.

"Where are you going?" Nadia called to them from the stairs.

It was Delno who answered, "We are going to the Palace to see the King. I know that both you and Rita are fully capable, but you are also two of our best leaders. I need you both here to maintain discipline and help keep the youngsters out of harm's way if things get out of hand. We'll explain it all when we get back."

The four of them filed out the door before either of the women could say anything else.

CHAPTER 14

THE GUARDSMAN POUNDED on the door of the large house. "Marvin Landry, open the door in the name of the Crown!"

The little access panel of a square peephole was pulled opened and Landry looked through it. "What is this all about? Why are you banging on my door in the dead of the night?"

"Marvin Landry," the guardsman said, "I have a warrant signed by King Dorian of Corice to take anyone within this house into custody and search the dwelling for any evidence that those apprehended might be engaging in acts of treason. Open this door at once or we will break it down."

The peephole closed and faint footsteps could be heard receding down a hallway. Another guardsman stepped up and the two men put their shoulders to the door. There was a heavy thud but the thick wood held.

"Move!" said a deep voice from the darkness.

Elom stepped up and elbowed the guardsmen out of the way. Then he hit the door with his open hand at the level of the latch. The door cracked around the latch but still held. Elom set his jaw and drew his hand back. The crashing blow he dealt to the door finished the job and it swung in so hard that it hit the wall and rebounded. Elom hit it again as it swung back at him and the upper hinge broke, leaving it hanging askew. The big smith then stepped quickly through the portal.

As four guardsmen vied with the remaining three Riders to follow Elom, someone much farther inside the house swore loudly and the sound of more members of the city watch trying to break down the back door was clearly audible.

Elom moved extremely fast despite his damaged legs. There were two doorways offset from each other in the hall. As Elom reached the first, a man inside the room tried to thrust a short spear into him. The big man reacted easily; his quick reflexes belying his huge size. He simply leaned back out of the way and grabbed the weapon with his left hand, and the front of his assailant's shirt with the other. He disarmed the man and pulled him off of his feet right up against his own chest. Then he just extended his arm, with the man still dangling from his clenched fist, back toward the door jamb. The would-be killer hit the wall so hard the force of the impact rattled the heavy timbers of the house.

As he dropped the now unconscious man to the floor, he said to the closest guardsman, "He was tryin' to burn some papers; see if you can save any of it." Then, not waiting to see if his order would be obeyed, he turned to continue down the hall.

"Elom," Delno called out. When Elom turned to see what he wanted, he added, "We need to stay together. Wait for the rest of us."

Elom stopped walking and drew his blade while he waited for them to move up. The other three guardsmen let the Riders pass them. After seeing Elom force the door, then nearly kill a man with an almost casual shrug of his arms, they were now content to follow rather than lead. As Delno passed the first door, he saw that the guardsman had managed to pull a mass of papers out of the fireplace and that most of the pile looked no more than slightly charred.

Delno, followed by Nassari and Will, moved quickly to catch up with the big man. Suddenly, two rebels wielding swords rushed out of the second doorway. Even though they were somewhat surprised, both Elom and Delno easily managed to turn the blades of their attackers. Then Elom, with his blade locked on that of his opponent, quickly raised his left arm and used his greater reach to slam the side of his fist down on top of the man's head, knocking him to the floor.

At the same time, Delno caught his man's sword with his *main gauche* and then used his Dragon Blade to incapacitate his assailant by slashing at his left knee. When the man fell, Delno twisted his offhand weapon and neatly disarmed his opponent.

He looked at Elom's adversary. The man wasn't breathing. A quick examination with his magical senses told him that the blow to the head had forced the man's skull down so hard that the top vertebra of his neck had been forced up into his skull and severed his brain stem. He was quite dead.

"Easy, Elom," Delno said, "We need to keep them alive if possible."

"Sorry," Elom replied, "I guess I got overexcited. I'll try and be more careful."

They stepped into the room as Delno motioned for Will and Nassari to continue on. There was a crash as the back door finally gave way under the efforts of the men of the city watch who had been sent to cover that exit.

Inside the second room, they found an assortment of weapons, and several jars marked with the skeletal hand that signified poison. Some of the weapons were miniature crossbows and the bolts for them were designed to be filled with liquid.

Elom looked at the crossbows and bolts and said, with disgust, "Assassins' weapons, made to be used by cowards."

Nassari and Will were moving down the hall towards the sound of a scuffle. When they reached the doorway at the end they found that the rest of the guardsmen had captured Landry, his wife, and two other men in the large kitchen as the group had been trying to flee and had been stopped at the back door when the men of the city watch broke it down. The body of another conspirator who had tried to fight the guardsmen was on the floor.

Nassari sent four of the six guardsmen in the kitchen to meet up with their fellows in the hall, and help search the upstairs of the house.

Delno and Elom left the one conscious prisoner from the second room in the care of one of the remaining guards and joined Nassari and Will in the kitchen.

"Well, Landry," Elom said as he walked through the doorway, "not so haughty now, are you?"

"You have no right to break into my home like this," Landry said. His voice had a high pitched, nearly hysterical quality to it. "I'll see you all jailed for this. You have murdered this man, and for all I know, three others. I'll see that you all hang, and those colossal beasts of yours will be turned into boot leather and dog food."

Everyone expected Elom to have choice words for the man, but all he did was shake his head before softly saying, "You're pathetic, Landry." Then he turned away from the councilman and said, "Delno, if you need me, I'll be back there making sure those murder tools are properly cataloged and packed off to the palace as evidence."

As Elom left the room, Delno leaned over and whispered to Nassari, "Since when has he started calling me 'Delno' again? I'm not complaining, but he usually calls me 'Corporal.'"

It was Will who answered first, "I've noticed a change about him since he bonded with Nora. He seems to have more confidence in himself now. Before, on the rare occasions I saw him away from his shop, he looked a little lost; like a kid who can't find his mother in the plaza. Now he seems to be more at ease with himself even outside his shop."

"Nora has a lot to do with it, that's for sure," Nassari said, as he looked thoughtfully in the direction the smith had gone. "But, I think it actually started when he decided that he needed to get out of the shop and come with us. I told Nadia earlier that Elom doesn't do anything unless he does it all the way. Just making that decision was only the first step, but now that he's started on the path, he's totally committed, and that puts him, in his mind, back on equal footing with you, Del. He's finally going to be completely healed spiritually."

Despite everything else that was going on around him, Delno had to take a moment and wipe his eyes. Then he said, "It's good to see. He's a good friend, and seeing him finally come to terms with himself is something I've wanted for a long time."

The three Riders then turned back to the prisoners.

"Looks like you three will be spending the night with an old friend," Nassari said in a casual tone. "Tell me, Marvin, how long have you and Clarence known each other?"

CHAPTER 15

"I'M NOT SURE I understand any of this," Nora said shaking her head. I would talk more with my bond-mate but he is both physically and mentally exhausted from all that he has been through, and I felt it best to let him dream normally rather than pull him in tonight."

"Yes," Geneva replied, "Normally I have trouble keeping Delno from coming here, but tonight he is sleeping so deeply he hasn't maintained enough awareness to manifest. Even we can succumb to the fatigue caused by too much time spent in the Dream State. Most of us in Corice will be leaving for Horne soon; it's best if we let our bond-mates rest normally while they can."

"What exactly don't you understand, Nora?" Wanda asked.

"Although I have fought small bands of them in the past, I didn't participate in the war against our ancestral enemies. Consequently, I was not in the group that came north to settle matters in the land humans call Borne. As I understand it, that group helped the humans remove a tyrant and save the people who lived there. However, now those people are trying to undo the good that was done and go back to a way of life that brought about only death and destruction for generations of their people."

"That is because you are trying to apply reasonable thought processes to an unreasonable species," Karina, an unbonded dragon who had joined them interjected. "Human civilization, and I use that term loosely since their society can only barely be considered civilized, is full of such contradictions."

"You have spent too much time talking with my mother," Saadia responded with obvious disdain for the speaker. "You should not pass judgment where you have no compassion."

"You forget, Saadia, that I flew with your mother in Horne. I watched those men we were assigned to guard. I learned enough during that time to know that I want nothing more to do with them."

"Then you should have nothing to do with them," Pina stated hotly enough to cause a ripple in the Dream State. "You have joined a discussion among a group of bonded dragons as if you are simply looking for companionship, but your words are obviously meant to be inflammatory. Either keep your comments concerning our bond-mates civil or keep them to yourself. We've all had more than enough of this type of nonsense lately."

"Enough," Geneva said sharply as she glared at the un-bonded dragon. "Karina, Pina is right. You were allowed to join us because we are open to showing un-bonded members of our species how our relationship with humans has enriched our lives, not to defend ourselves. If you cannot behave you will be excluded from our group."

"I was merely making an observation, but I will hold further comments, for the time being," Karina replied.

"To answer your question to the best of my knowledge, Nora," Wanda spoke as though she had not been interrupted, "humans see the world differently than dragons do. They are physically weaker, so they must congregate for safety. Any society needs leaders, and the humans are no exception to that rule. Those who were ousted from such positions in Bourne wish to regain their authority and privilege. The commoners don't really care who is in power so long as their own needs are taken into consideration. Because of how the country was ruled, there are many shortages, and some of the former ruling class are using those shortages of food and medical supplies to incite a few of the commoners to action."

"But why is it that these people our bond-mates captured to-night think that all of their fellow 'countrymen," the word, since it had no meaning in dragon society, was a bit strange for her, "are in open rebellion against Corice?" Nora asked.

"The leaders of any rebellion like to think just as these people do. It is one way to justify their cause not only to themselves but to those who might be swayed to their line of thinking. Remember, most of the people involved in this are either former nobles or those who were once in their service, not the farmers and honest crafts-men of Bourne. It is easy for the people who never worked to pro-vide sustenance for themselves to forget who is truly responsible for their empty bellies when they have someone promising food for them if they join the cause. Most of the folks in Bourne are reason-able and understand that such shortages are the direct result of the former king's ambition and the willingness of his nobility to go along with him. The vast majority of the Bournese know that all will once again be well when the snows let up and sufficient goods can be shipped. Do not mistake the ambitions of the few to be the will of the many," Wanda answered.

"Then how do they expect to win such an unpopular rebellion?" Nora asked. "Surely they must know that even if they eliminated the Dragon Riders and all of the people sent from Corice, they would still need the cooperation of the population at large?"

"Once again you try to use logic to understand a species that has no basis in such concepts," Karina spoke up before Wanda could reply.

"Karina, I have heard enough and do not wish to have further contact with you this night," Geneva said without showing the emo-tion she felt. "Go and find your companionship elsewhere."

The other bonded dragons in the group all nodded in agreement, and before Karina could voice any protest, she faded from view.

"Now, then," Geneva said as if there had been no interruption in the conversation, "You must remember Nora, that many humans have no more ambition than the most unassuming members of our own species. Dragons like that never raise objections to anything the Council puts forth. They are quite content to let their leaders make the decisions and abide by them. There have been instances when certain Lineage Holders have sided against such a person in our own society in favor of a friend concerning territory and hunting rights, and the actual 'injured party' has meekly accepted the 'ruling' rather than seeking help from other leaders to avoid getting involved in a confrontation."

"Geneva," Pina said, almost shocked by such a revelation, "are you accusing some Lineage Holders of impropriety?"

"No one specifically at this time," Geneva responded. "However, it does illustrate my point."

"It's not just an accusation," Saadia added, "Why do you think Karina was here sounding off just like she who is my mother?"

"I knew your mother had an agenda concerning adult dragons seeking bond-mates, but to practice such open maneuvering as to favor one dragon over another?" Wanda asked.

"Oh, yes, she has done so in the past, and is most likely doing so again," Saadia answered. "Sheila has never sought to bond, but she has never been so outspoken against it as she is now. That has prompted me to investigate her motives in the matter since that abysmal meeting we all attended. I was going to speak to both Lineage Holders present about my findings when we became distracted with Nora's questions."

Saadia paused to see if anyone objected to her change of subject before continuing, "She and Karina both have territories that almost border each other off to the northeast. There is another dragon whose range does border Karina's and that person is favorable to dragons finding bond-mates if they choose; in fact, she is thinking about seeking out a companion among humans, but she is simply waiting until after spring mating flights to see if she conceives this year. If she quickens, she will raise her daughter or daughters independently of humans so that they may decide for themselves when the time comes."

"Very sensible of her," Geneva responded. "I assume that your mother is trying to curry some favor with Karina in response to all of this?"

"Yes," Saadia replied flatly. "Karina is looking to mate this year as well. If she can add Farrah's territory to her own, she won't have to move far to find suitable range to feed her own hatchlings if she conceives. If she doesn't mate successfully, then having the extra range will simply improve her future chances. You see, those territories are near the home ranges of three mature and highly desirable males." She paused to let that sink in before adding, "Stepping back to our earlier topic, Farrah isn't that worried about losing her own territory, because she knows that many will petition the Council for ownership of those lands once she is bonded and moves away. It is very likely that such a space, situated so close to a prime mating area, will be given over to a more mature dragon, since Farrah's hatchling will be concerned with little more than food and privacy for several years, if not a whole decade."

"You think Sheila is willing to help Karina acquire that land if Karina speaks out in favor of Sheila's ramblings?" Pina asked. "Why on earth is she so obsessed with this crazy notion?"

Saadia was quiet for several moments. She looked around as if someone might be eavesdropping before replying. "The issue for Sheila isn't really about 'slavery'; it's about her standing on the Council. Since the war in the south, her authority has been limited much more than it ever was. She has worked hard for nearly three millennia to get to the position of authority she carried at the beginning of the war. Then two bonded Lineage holders, one not much more than a hatchling, and the other a person whose lineage has become scattered over the generations, have taken the wind right out from beneath her wings. It galls her no end that Geneva and Wanda carry as much, if not more, weight in Council than she does."

"But that's preposterous," Wanda said as if she were biting into something that had spoiled. "Each member of our ruling class gets one vote, and each of the six cells gets seven votes amongst themselves. Major decisions are then voted on by each cell casting one ballot, and the lone, most mature Lineage Holder casts the tiebreaker if such is needed. No one dragon can hold any real sway over another. Also, Geneva and I are in the same cell, and Sheila is in another group altogether."

"In theory, you are right," Geneva noted, "however, in practice, as you should know, with your bond-mate being who he is, a better politician can often gain an advantage and get others go along with her. What I don't understand is why, with sensible dragons like Kalah in such positions of power on the council, Sheila would think that her schemes would amount to much."

"Well, I don't claim to know all of the particulars, since I, myself, am no Lineage Holder, but Kalah and her line have long since given up on the idea of retaking our first homeland," Saadia replied. "That idea has been kept alive primarily by your line, Geneva. And forgive me for saying so, but some of your line, your own grandmother, in particular, were as obsessed with retaking the high mountains east of Horne as Sheila is with eventually gaining control of the Council. It wasn't until your mother, though, that the Geneva line's great plan to eliminate the beast-men entirely and resettle those territories was moved to a lesser concern. However, even she worked in that direction whenever she could while helping Corolan move towards his grand plan for establishing new human settlements in the fertile ranges of the rest of the world. That is why she and her bond-mate spent so much time in Horne rather than occupying themselves more with eliminating all of the obstacles to settling the northeast. Not only did they both feel that the beast men presented a threat to everything if not kept in check, but, as I know from her talks with Sheila and other non-bonded dragons, she never completely turned away from the old fort and mountains just east of Horne."

"I am not totally versed on this subject, since she who was my mother chose not to obsess on the issue the way her own mother had done, but I realize that many of my ancestors were set on that goal," Geneva agreed, "and it was that obsession that blinded my grandmother and her bond-mate to most other concerns, and nearly got them both killed. In fact, truth be told, my grandmother's devotion to that end helped, in part, to lay the foundation for the human expansions of Horne. Her help, given so freely to the ruling clans of that human territory in the hope of securing those lands, helped to strengthen Horne's iron grip on the area. That eventually lead to the clan wars, and it took those horrific events which led to the deaths of so many dragons to convince my mother to put her commitment to those lands second to Corolan's vision for the future." She paused for several moments and the others waited patiently for her to gather her thoughts.

"Much that is difficult for men to see becomes quite apparent to those who live for thousands of years," she said finally. "Because of that, I will take no real offense at your words. However, you are right; my family risked everything to get control of those mountains, and I have not missed the fact that we could be poised to do just that in the foreseeable future, but I am not blinded by some ancestral commitment."

She looked around and held each of the other dragons' gazes briefly before continuing her train of thought. "I see that territory as belonging to bonded dragons and their human partners. The first dragons to bond with humans came from that area and remained in those mountains when all other dragons moved off to find more hospitable lands. With the help of their human partners, those who stayed formed the first unified resistance to the Rorack's instinctual need for expansion. That territory belongs to bonded dragons by right of prior claim, not to mention our continuing fight for it."

They were all silent for several minutes, each deep in her own thoughts.

Finally, Geneva added, "For more than twenty thousand years, we have been forced to live on the fringes of two completely different cultures, with no territory to truly call our own. I would like nothing more than to establish a place we can call home where we will no longer be a 'country in exile', and not really a part of any society."

They all simply sat looking at her for a few moments, until Saadia spoke up, "I understand your motivation, Geneva, and I believe your cause is righteous. However, Sheila only has her eye on being the top-ranked dragon on the Council. She was well on her way to achieving that goal when Delno persuaded her to get the other dragons to join his cause.

She paused and chuckled a little, "How could she not answer that call? So many of our people think of those mountains as home even after thousands of years, despite the fact that many don't come from the same seven families as the original bonded dragons who fought the first-ever war against the Roracks." She snorted contemptuously, "Getting those lands back, or at least making a positive move in that direction, should have consolidated her power. That was why she so readily agreed to aid the humans. By going along with Delno's plea for assistance she could then hold herself out as the guiding force among the dragons in retaking our ancestral home."

She shrugged her shoulders in a very human-like gesture. "I now believe that the only reason she didn't try to stop me from seeking a bond-mate was that she believed I could be used to sway the bonded dragons to support her as well." Then she laughed outright before adding, "She didn't plan on you and Wanda emerging as strong leaders. Many now look to you two instead of the older, 'wiser' dragon she presents herself to be. It seems she was laid low by her own scheming; that meeting she called is a clear example of how much she has lost. Even Kalah, the oldest and wisest dragon on earth, wouldn't have censured her like that before the war; too many others would have spoken up and supported her cause."

Saadia stopped for a minute and took time to draw a couple of deep breaths as if what she was about to say disturbed her greatly. "Sheila will not accept you and Wanda securing those mountains for bonded dragons, especially since she considers you both to be nothing more than young upstarts. Doing so, under any circumstances, will only increase your reputation, and in her eyes, hinder her plans. She will use her ranting about slavery to strengthen any claim she has that bonded dragons retaking those lands is nothing more than removing the Roracks only to hand that territory over to men!"

All five dragons were quiet for some time, Nora's lessons in human politics completely forgotten.

Finally, Geneva spoke up. "To hell with Sheila's schemes! If she causes us any real trouble to hell with her, too! We will continue just as we have been doing, and if she actively stands against us, she will find more trouble than she can handle. Her political ambitions are simply petty concerns that really have little bearing on our situation. We will help our bond-mates as we have always done, and, if in the process, we can secure a place of our own, for bonded dragons and their partners, slightly apart and independent from both human and dragon society, we will do so."

The others nodded their agreement.

"I have spoken of this with Delno," she continued, "and Wanda has talked with Nassari. Both men agree with us, but they have helped us understand the need to proceed with caution so as not to upset the balance in Horne. Regardless of any other concerns, our first loyalty is to the world at large, not to any one society, not even our own. We can not risk open confrontation with Horne if it can be avoided. Their king is ambitious, and in many ways as much of a childish tyrant as Torrance of Bourne, but he is past middle age and will only live a couple more decades at most. We've bided our time for millennia; a few more years won't make any difference, and will give us time to sway Thomas's successor to our way of thinking without open confrontation."

She paused for just a moment before adding, "For now, we have done all we can do, and I believe we should follow our bond-mates' example and get some real rest."

CHAPTER 16

THE KING WAS once again holding formal court, and this time most of the older Dragon Riders were present.

A man dressed in the uniform worn by those in direct service to the king spoke out loudly enough to be heard by all in attendance, "We have assembled this day to witness the sentencing of these people convicted of treason, the chief conspirators being Marvin Landry, his wife Clarice, and Clarence Lowell, as well as a dozen other co-conspirators who have been found since. His Majesty acknowledges that a third of those to be sentenced are women, and he regrets that, due to the seriousness of the charges, no leniency can be accorded them. Although Clarence Lowell has already been sentenced in this matter, he is in attendance because the King and his advisors have decided to alter his sentence in keeping with that of the others, since more recent evidence has proven beyond doubt that he is not only part of this conspiracy, but the main driving force behind it. In the three days since the recent raid, the evidence gathered there has been thoroughly examined, and is not only quite damning for all of the original accused, but has also provided names of other rebels, both in Corice and Bourne, who now also stand awaiting judgment. Some of those named in the conspirators' own documents have so far eluded capture, but they have been convicted in absentia, and warrants for their apprehension, either dead or alive, have been issued."

The king's crier paused for breath before continuing. "Since there were so many involved in the plot, the King has declared that Corice is still in a state of war, and the Council has agreed and granted King Dorian the emergency powers that such calls for. Therefore, in accordance with Corisian law, his Majesty has decided to use those powers to summarily rule that all of those who are involved in this unsavory business of subversion and murder are, on the basis of overwhelming evidence, guilty of treason."

After having the herald read all of the names of the prisoners and their specific parts in the crimes, the King sat silent for a moment. When he spoke, he sounded tired, and a little sad.

"We have tried, through the years, to do Our best for the people of Corice. We have even tried, during the border wars that have cropped up, to limit the death and destruction dealt to our neighbors to the north. Now that, with the aid of the Dragon Riders, both lands have finally achieved a lasting peace that will stop the cycle of death, destruction, and financial ruin that such wars have caused over the centuries, We had hoped to put all of that behind us and move on toward happier and more prosperous times. However, there will always be those who are not satisfied with the greater good, but will seek to take all that they can for themselves, whether that is to gain in money or in power."

Dorian paused for a moment. The prisoners, some standing stoically, some shifting and fidgeting nervously, could do nothing but wait until the King was ready to move on. Everyone else in the hall simply stood patiently while their monarch collected his thoughts.

"We are loath to send so many rebels into exile, but it is Our opinion that having such a large number of you executed or incarcerated might, in the short term, rally other fools to your misguided cause. However, We cannot, in good conscience, inflict such a huge group of malcontents as yourselves upon our trading partners directly to the south where you might do mischief in those lands, or take it into your minds to cause trouble for Corice from inside the borders of a country where Corisian law holds no power, but where you will be virtually on this land's doorstep. Therefore, it is Our decision that you shall be kept in prison until spring. Those of you who are members of the peerage will immediately be stricken from the roster. Once the roads are passable, you will be split into random groups of no more than four. Each group will then be taken, shackled and under guard, to separate locations as far from the borders of Corice as it is possible for Our troops to take you. Once you have reached that location, you will be released and given the barest minimum supplies: a knife, a piece of flint, a blanket, a piece of rope, three days' worth of hard rations, and a waterskin. If you should make your way back to Corisian soil, including the Duchy of Bourne, anyone who finds you is hereby charged with taking your life and then bringing proof of your death to the Palace. Upon the delivery of such proof, the person who carries out that sentence shall be rewarded with one hundred gold crowns."

"You have no right to do this!" Clarice Alton Landry shouted as Marvin Landry tried to quiet her. "I am a citizen of the Kingdom of Bourne, and you are a usurper. I do not recognize your authority over me!"

"Guards," Dorian responded, looking right at the nearest officer, "We are finished here. Have the prisoners taken to the holding facility and held in solitary confinement until the full sentence can be carried out. None of them is to have any communication with the others, or with anyone else in the meantime. Perhaps it is good that they will have plenty of time for the uninterrupted contemplation of what they have done."

Dorian rose and motioned for Delno and Nassari to join him as he walked toward the private dining hall. Nadia and Rita, as senior Dragon Riders, moved to follow. As the Duchess of Bourne, Laura Okonan also attended the meeting.

CHAPTER 17

ONCE EVERYONE WAS seated, Dorian shook his head, and said sadly, "While I knew that Lowell wasn't working alone, I had never expected to find so many people actively involved, and I would certainly have never anticipated finding so many Corisians, including a member of the Council, participating."

"I have known Marvin Landry for years," Laura stated. "He's not the type I would consider to be a revolutionary."

"His part is actually easy to explain," Dorian replied. "He was one of the first merchants to move goods to Bourne when the war before the last one ended. His wife is a member of House Alton, for which the town of Alton in Bourne is named."

Laura nodded, "That explains how he met the conspirators, but not how he could so easily be turned into a traitor."

"He claims that she fell in love with him and that once they were formally married, she moved here to help him with his business," Dorian said. "I don't think it happened all at once. Remember, this plan was originally put in place by Warrick himself, working through Torrance, to disrupt our kingdom and leave us ripe for conquest. She had more than two years between the two wars to work on swaying her husband's loyalties."

"I supposed if she were subtle enough, and worked on him for that long, it is understandable," Laura replied.

"After participating in questioning her," Dorian added, "I believe he was deluding himself about her love for anything other than power. I am convinced that she met and married him as part of a plot to get a member of their nobility highly placed in Corisian society. After all, the only thing that could have given them a better position would have been if they could have married her off to a member of the ruling family. Since I had no family that they knew of at the time, they settled for a member of the ruling Council. The only thing that still remains unclear is whether he participated covertly in helping Bourne in the last war."

"I hadn't even thought about that," Laura said angrily, "but now that you bring it up, that plague found its way into the city readily enough. If he had a hand in that, he should be tried and hung for all of the deaths that resulted from the disease."

Delno was a bit taken aback by his mother's statements. "I thought you opposed the death penalty on moral grounds, Mother?" he asked.

"There are exceptions to every rule, Delno." she replied, "and if that man had a hand in callously killing hundreds of innocent men, women, and children, I'd pull the cord on the trap door myself, and hope his neck didn't snap so he'd suffer for his crimes."

Delno stared wide-eyed at his mother for a second and then simply nodded without responding.

"If there were any evidence of such, he has long since seen it destroyed, Niece," Dorian said.

He turned back to the group. "When the Riders stopped the plague, defeated Warrick, then returned and removed Torrance, this group had to shift their plans from outright military conquest, so they felt compelled to try and instigate a rebellion."

"But why the assassination attempt on Nassari?" Nadia spoke up. Then she realized she was addressing the King and gave a sheepish smile of apology. Being so young, and common born, she was still unused to being on par with royalty, despite her many hours of dealing with the council.

Dorian smiled at her, "It's all right, my dear. If we didn't want you to be part of this discussion, you wouldn't have been allowed in the room. As a Rider, you are the equal of anyone here. Speak your mind."

"Well, I know that Nassari is Delno's right-hand man, but Delno is the actual leader of the Riders that are here in Corice. Not that I would wish him harm, but why didn't they try to assassinate him? Why go for Nassari so blatantly here in Larimar, when they could have gone after Delno more easily in Karne?"

"I can answer that, also," Dorian said. "This group had seen the Riders remove two of their leaders, one of whom, Warrick, they actually believed to be invincible."

Nadia still looked a little confused but waited for the king to finish his thought.

"After their defeats, first here, and then again at Stone Bridge in the last war, they had a better understanding of the devastating power of the dragons. Since the Riders would come to the aid of the government, the revolutionaries felt they had to remove that threat completely before they could move ahead with their attempt at a coup."

The King paused to sip his wine, and Nassari said, "May I?"

Dorian nodded for him to take over the explanation.

"You see, Nadia, these people couldn't imagine that we would actually go to all of the trouble to remove both Warrick and Torrance just to hand the whole country over to Corisian rule and move on. They truly believed that, like Warrick, we planned to rule these lands, as well as set ourselves up to do the same in Horne. They saw all of our work to supply the Riders and the Legion headquarters as little more than a ruse to put a strain on the coffers of Corice, and to keep people from realizing that we were going to take up where Warrick had failed. Since I am the one who is most versed in Corisian politics, it is I who have been dealing with the politicians. The chief conspirators felt that as long as I could continue to wrangle supplies out of the Council, the Riders would simply stay camped on their doorstep, and prevent them from moving ahead with their plans."

"That would also explain why Landry was so dead set against supplying the new Riders even though he wanted them gone," Nadia said, almost surprised at the revelation.

Nassari nodded and said "Delno, the obvious leader, is too well-liked by the commoners of both kingdoms; indeed, many of the Bournese see him as their savior. So killing him not only would not remove the most politically savvy of us, the act might also cause their own countrymen to rise up against them. They felt that they would eventually have to deal with the Riders and the dragons, but they also believed that if I was gone, not only would the supplies stop flowing, but Delno would then still be forced to leave Bourne to deal with matters in Horne. So killing me, even though the assassin wouldn't survive, would kill two birds with one stone, so to speak."

"Fortunately that didn't succeed, and it brought about the exposure of their whole scheme," Rita observed.

Also, by killing me so publicly," Nassari continued, "they could prove to their followers that Riders weren't invulnerable. Their next step, once Delno and the more experienced Riders were gone, would have been to send more assassins out with those small crossbows and poison darts we confiscated to kill not only the loyal members of the Council but any Riders who remained in either city."

"Surely they had to know that killing any Dragon Rider would be a suicide mission?" Nadia asked. "Even if they succeeded in murdering the human, the dragon would hunt them down."

"That," Nassari replied, "is why the men in the outer rooms of Landry's house attacked us, but two of those in the kitchen gave up without a fight. The aggressors were zealots to the cause. They knew and accepted that any assassination attempt on a Rider was a one-way trip. If they weren't killed in the initial attempt, then the dragon would be driven to seek revenge and kill the assassin before she flew off to mourn her bond-mate and die. In fact, they believed that if the dragon became maddened and destroyed property or harmed innocents in her search for such revenge, it would only strengthen their cause and bring more people around to their way of thinking. That is why the men we met in the hall didn't flee or surrender. When presented with the opportunity to kill four Riders, they were willing to try it."

"The more I hear of these people," Rita said, "the more convinced I am that they are all insane."

"Well, Rita," Dorian responded, "the three Houses of Bourne, House Bourne itself, House Alton, and House Lowell, have practiced extensive inbreeding to keep their noble lines "purer" than any other Houses either here in the north, or even in the south. Over the centuries, we have learned that such inbreeding is likely to manifest in one or more of three ways: crippling disease, mental retardation, or insanity. I have come to believe that the aggression that is so apparent among the noble houses of Bourne is just another manifestation of the insanity that has been bred into those family lines, and Torrance, while not completely stupid, wasn't exactly a genius."

"In a way," Delno put in, "we're lucky they made that attempt on Nassari at the docks. If they had waited another week, the bulk of the Riders would have been gone, and they could have moved directly against the rulers of the country. Then, after assassinating the King, as many Council members as possible, and the Duchess of Bourne, they would have been able to use the ensuing chaos to move in and take over. Not only would we have lost many family and dear friends, we would have played bloody hell digging the rebels out of here later."

He paused for a moment before saying, "This type of thing is one of the reasons I gave my grandfather's blade to Will."

Everyone looked at him expectantly.

"He is a Rider and at least as brave as any," Delno continued, "and also a direct blood relative, so, since it's important not only to me, but to Geneva as well, to keep it in Corolan's family, he was the logical choice. However, it was the sight of that blade in my hands that caused such utter despair in Torrance that it drove him to suicide. Many of the more superstitious citizens of both countries might be easily swayed to follow any who held such a prize."

"I have to agree in this case, Nephew," King Dorian spoke up. "Such symbols of dragon power should remain in the hands of Riders, not held out as talismans by those who hold political power."

Delno nodded, "I know my mother would never seek power for herself, but I was loath to leave it with her because it would have become a symbol of power in the Duchy of Bourne, and it could have been used to rally disenfranchised nobles who might have wanted to depose her now since many of those same aristocrats have been laboring under the false belief that the blade belonged to Warrick, whose family had blood ties to Torrance. It's some of the same reasoning behind the Queen of Palamore's decision to give Brock the Dragon Blade of Palamore; get the thing out of the hands of politicians and back where it rightfully belongs, in the hands of a Rider and under the protection of the dragons."

"I can certainly agree with your reasoning," Rita replied.

He paused and drew a breath before adding, "I just didn't realize that such a rebellion was already in the works so soon after the end of the last conflict. I knew that if the blade should be stolen, it would then be in the hands of someone who would use it as a symbol in the cause of overthrowing Corice, the way Simcha had tried to use the blade he stole from Palamore. I was not only ensuring that the blade remained in my own family, but I was also trying to remove such a symbol and possibly head off a civil war generations from now. I never thought it would be this year."

They all sat for a moment and then Dorian looked directly at Nassari and said, "I know that you have already delayed leaving Larimar for one day because I asked you to stay and attend this court; however, before you go, there is one last favor I would like to have from you."

"If it is within my power to grant that favor, I would be happy to help you in any way I can," Nassari replied.

"Before you fly off to new adventures, I want you to write down at least some of the more choice bits of information you have been using to blackmail the Council." As everyone stared in stunned silence, he continued, "The Duchess and I still have to deal with those misers. For now, they are quite agreeable because they are afraid that, with elections coming up soon, and Landry having been convicted of treason, they might be tarred with the same brush in the eyes of the voters and lose their positions. I will garner some good-will from the Council members by holding the prisoners until after the elections so that their transport doesn't influence the vote by reminding people of Landry's part in this. Still, though, I may need that information, and any other I can gather on my own, to keep them from withholding the funding of projects the Duchess and I have in mind for Bourne sometime before the next election cycle."

Nassari laughed and then saluted the King. "Everyone says that I am the master of politics, Your Majesty, but I must acknowledge that you have outmaneuvered me. I applaud you. As for the information, while I have promised not to make what I know public knowledge, I have not promised that I won't pass it on to a private individual. I believe that when I leave in the morning, you will find a letter addressed to you, accompanied by certain other incriminating documents that will contain what you seek."

CHAPTER 18

ALARGE GROUP GATHERED on the plain outside the main gates of Larimar as the family and friends of the more than thirty riders who were leaving for Horne had come to wish them all well and see them off properly. Family members had told friends and acquaintances about the departure, so not all of those in attendance actually knew any of the riders personally, but the sight of that many dragons all poised for takeoff was too spectacular a pageant to miss; a crowd of over three hundred had assembled to watch from a safe distance.

Nassari was looking over Nora's saddle. The smith had managed to get one practice flight in since it's completion, and Nassari, although he trusted Elom's judgment and attention to detail, felt compelled to double check his friend's rig.

The saddle was exquisite and easily the most ornate Nassari had ever seen on a dragon. The stitching was done in a beautiful scrollwork pattern along the edges, and there were stylized dragons in flight tooled onto the fenders. Besides the fancy work, it looked more comfortable for both man and dragon than any of the other rigs as well. If he hadn't known better, he would have sworn Rupert must have worked on the thing for weeks, not just three days; he'd certainly had every journeyman and apprentice in his shop on the project, probably around the clock. Nassari was a bit jealous and wished he had had the time to have the craftsman make one for him, also.

"Well, my friends," Delno said as he came up behind Nassari and Elom, "it looks as though you are finally going to be leaving for Horne. I take it you have a secure chain of command set up for the flight."

"Oh yes, no problem there," Nassari responded, "we have a strict squad formation with me, Nadia, Will, Adamus, and Craig each acting as a squad leader. I'd have given Elom the position over Craig, but even though Elom is better versed in military tactics, Craig is the more experienced rider, and we're not flying off into combat." Then, before Delno could say anything, he added, "I wish you didn't have to stay." He paused and shook his head, "I know we agreed. With everything that's happened, it's for the best."

"Rita and I will train the six older Riders who have agreed to stay until spring. They are all over seventeen and therefore don't need to be watched every minute. We will also train Saadia's hatchlings and their Riders, since they are too young to travel with you now. You and Nadia can bring replacements for them when you come back for Dorian's wedding. After the wedding, we should be able to leave the riders you bring without more supervision since they will be fully trained, and Rita and I will be able to finally take a much-needed rest, while you and Nadia take the teams Rita and I have trained back to Horne with you. After we have visited the Elven lands, we will return to the Fort for the meeting of the Council of Riders. Then Rita and I will stay at the headquarters and begin to make plans concerning the exploration of the unsettled lands while you and Nadia have a bit of a holiday."

"Hopefully, once your mother and the Council get Bourne divided into districts, and get representatives in place, the threat of civil war will be ended completely, and we can stop housing Riders here. I just hope in the meantime that both the Riders and the politicians remember this is only temporary." Nassari patted the dragon on the chest and said, "Thank you, Nora, the rig looks just fine."

"Of course, once the group here is trained, they may not want to leave right away," Delno replied. "After all, they are from these lands, and we will have no right to make them go if they don't want to. However, Rita and I will try to convince them to move on for a time and see more of the world. They are also all *old enough* to take the Legion Oath, as well, if we can get them to attend the meeting. It probably won't be hard with a Lineage Holder asking them to attend, but I don't really want them to feel coerced."

"So, you have noticed our tendency to take command as if the new Riders are simply underlings, also?" Nassari asked.

"Yes, but I think a large part of that is simply that these Riders are so young. Once they are ready to move out into the world, and their bond with their own partners is fully developed, they will begin to act more independently, and we won't feel so overly protective towards them." Delno responded before moving to say goodbye to the smith.

Nassari waited while Delno and Elom exchanged their goodbyes, and then he and Delno walked toward Wanda and Pina: Nadia and Rita were already standing near the two dragons.

As they got close, Nassari pulled a sealed leather pouch out of an inner jacket pocket, and, handing it to his friend, said, "Give this to your uncle. I'm sure he'll find it most helpful, and I'm equally sure he won't overuse it."

Delno looked at the satchel like it might bite, then he shrugged his shoulders and put it in his own pocket. "I am glad I never let you talk me into a career in politics."

Helen Orin and William Cutter stood a short distance away waiting to say goodbye to their respective offspring.

Nassari hugged Rita.

Nadia, after making sure none of the youngsters were watching, hugged Delno. "I have enough trouble with them not taking me seriously while they think I'm an overbearing tyrant," she said with a smile, "If they saw me hug you, they would know I have a human side, and all discipline would be lost."

While Nassari said farewell to his mother, Nadia hugged her father and said, "I will be back as soon and as often as I can."

"I know you will, Nadia; you've always been my little girl. The only thing that will console me once you are gone will be my new friendship with Helen."

"Are you sure you are doing the right thing, Papa? I know she is a wonderful woman, but giving up your property to move off to Bourne?"

"When your mother died bringing you into to this world, I thought I would never find love again," William replied, "so I gave my entire attention to raising you right. Now you are not only a strong young woman but a respected Dragon Rider. I feel free to make a new connection with someone I can love who loves me. Besides, it is not as though I am simply abandoning our family property. I have turned it over to Francis, my eldest and most stable son. If I were to find that this new position in the Dutchess's court is not something I am suited to, I will have a home to return to." He paused and said, "I believe Nassari has said his goodbyes and is ready to leave. Good fortune, my lovely child!"

He kissed her one more time, then the two embraced quickly before he turned to Helen Orin, and led her far enough away to prevent them from being pelted with debris when the dragons launched themselves into flight.

Nadia climbed into her saddle, Nassari climbed into his, and they both waved goodbye to their friends and the family members who had come to see them off. Nassari took a few seconds to smiled at his mother standing arm in arm with William Cutter, and then raised his hand high, and traced a circle with his fingers to signal for take-off.

The change in air pressure on the ground was quite obvious as more than thirty pairs of giant wings beat down nearly simultaneously. The dragons rose as a unit and stroked the air furiously to gain altitude. Nassari watched as the ground fell away and the people on the field appeared to get smaller and smaller.

Once they reached a height of about two thousand feet, Nassari signaled the large group to break off into squads, and all five teams turned east-southeast and headed towards the high mountain peaks in the distance.

CHAPTER 19

"THERE IS A *large patch of dead trees off to the south, Love,*" Wanda told Nassari. "*It looks as though the saplings died when the slope they were growing on gave way from a summer flood more than a season ago. The wood has ended up at the bottom of that sheltering rise. It also appears to be well seasoned, and I believe that the slope has had enough time to recover and is now stable. If you want a sheltered spot to make camp that has available firewood, I don't think we are going to find any better place in such barren country.*" She paused for a moment before adding, "*This land was once so full of life and beauty. I know that the high mountains are a harsh environment, but much of this condition is due to the to the beast-men running unchecked for so long in close proximity. Even though this is technically beyond their normal range, the runoff of their filth washes down and pollutes this side of the mountain.*" Then she added with even more disgust, "*What they don't destroy, they defecate on.*"

Nassari sighed both mentally and aloud, though it wasn't audible over the sound of the wind in his ears. "*It will be under the control of dragons and beautiful again, Wanda, but right now I have trouble being concerned with anything beyond getting these youngsters safely through these mountains. Once things are settled in Horne, we can begin to work on both plans: the settlement of the unclaimed lands, and regaining the dragons' ancestral home.*" He thought about the campsite for a moment before continuing. *"All right, Love, tell the other leaders to put down there. It has been a long, cold day, and I would like to get a fire going and have some hot food and drink."* As Wanda relayed his message and banked to begin her descent, he gave his squad the signal to follow him down.

Once on the ground, he quickly issued orders to the younger Riders to gather as much firewood as they could carry: the other squad leaders did the same. While the kids were collecting the wood, Nadia set Will, Adamus, and Craig to the task of laying out the camp so that, once the tents were up, there would be no confusion as to where the boys and girls would sleep.

"What do you want me to do?" Elom asked. "I can carry my weight. I am quite capable of fetching firewood or pitching a tent. You don't have to coddle me. As long as you don't ask me to run anywhere, I can keep up with most of the others."

"I'm sorry, my friend," Nassari replied. "I didn't mean to imply that you aren't fully capable of working with the rest of us. The thought just didn't occur to me. I am so used to you being one of the ones in charge that I forget that you are a novice Rider. I just don't feel right ordering you around like one of the youngsters, especially since I've known you so long, and you are as old as I am."

Elom smiled and said, "I guess that makes sense. I shouldn't be so sensitive about it. I know you don't think of me as a cripple, but I'm so used to others doing so that I've almost come to expect it."

"Well, you won't get any special treatment from me," Will said, as he joined them. "I was with you when we made that raid on Landry's house; I know just how capable you are." Then he smiled and added, "There's a stream over there, and we could use some water if you wouldn't mind helping me fetch it."

Elom smiled and nodded as he grabbed three of the six water skins that Will was carrying. Then the two of them headed off to the stream.

By the time Will and Elom returned, Nassari had a large central fire going, and Nadia was directing several of the youngsters who were preparing food for the group. Once the water had been added to various pans and set to heat, the leaders sat down near the fire to talk; their respective draconic partners sat near enough to join the conversation if they so chose, but the long flight had left them more tired than the humans.

"I thought that it only took three and half days to travel from Horne to Stone Bridge," Elom remarked. As Nassari and Will both nodded, he added, "Countin' today, we've been flyin' steady for four days, and we haven't reached the downhill side of the mountains yet. Why's it takin' so long?"

"With that saddle of yours, I wouldn't think it would be bothering you as much as the rest of us," Will retorted.

Elom smiled at the jibe. "Oh, I'm not complainin' about the flying. I never thought I would enjoy anything so much. I'm just anxious to get to Horne and see if any of my equipment has arrived. I've been talkin' with Craig quite a bit, and we think we're startin' to understand how I've been workin' the magic into the stuff I make. Now that I have an idea of what I'm doin', I'd like to see if I can improve on the skill a bit."

"Well," Nassari spoke up, "I can sympathize with that, especially since you've promised to make me two new blades. However, I believe that we are moving as fast as possible. This mountain range is wide as well as long. That, and the fact that the mountains themselves are so high and treacherous, is what creates the eastern barrier that keeps the beast-men from spreading in that direction unchecked."

"When we flew back at the beginning of fall, the prevailing winds at altitude were west to east. We pushed hard and flew until after sundown before stopping each day. On this trip, we've been flying against those same winds most of the time, and that has slowed us down," Wanda interjected.

"And don't forget," Saadia added, "the days are shorter now than when we left Horne, and we've been stopping at least an hour before dark so that we can set up camp every night."

"All in all, though, we're still making pretty good time. I figure, and Wanda agrees," Nassari spoke up, "that we will start on the downhill side of the mountains before noon tomorrow, and should nearly make the foothills before nightfall. If the weather holds on the other side of the mountains, we should be at the fort before dark the day after that."

"We'll have to be especially careful starting tomorrow, then" Will responded. "Once we cross the mountains, we will be in the heart of the beast-men's territory. So far, we're still only on the eastern-most edge of it. While they won't be gathered in large numbers, they are still dangerous, and we will have to be doubly on our guard to make sure none of the youngsters wanders too far from camp to dig a latrine pit, or for any other reason."

"That's true," Nadia replied. "I hadn't been thinking about those monsters, but now that you remind me, I realize that not only did quite a few get away, they have had about three months to get over any fear we instilled in them."

The young Riders who were preparing dinner indicated that it was done, and everyone moved to get food and a hot drink.

After all of them had eaten and everything that could be cleaned and packed was done, even the more exuberant of the Riders went to their tents without complaint. The long day's flight was tiring enough, but, despite wearing heavy jackets and gloves, the cold left them exhausted and longing to do nothing more than snuggle into their blankets.

Next morning, after the rest of their gear was packed and ready, Nassari called all of the Riders together rather than having them mount up immediately.

"Everyone listen carefully," he said in a loud, clear voice.

In the silence that followed that command, two of the boys who were still holding their own private conversation could be heard whispering. Elom grabbed one boy in each hand by the backs of their coats and carried them up to the front of the group and set them down directly in front of Nassari.

"*You should both have been paying attention to your bond-mates and helped them keep on task here,*" Wanda chided the children's draconic partners. "*Whether or not you actually flew against the beast-*

men in the last war, you, as members of our own society, know full well that crossing the lands inhabited by those fiends is dangerous. Since your partners are so young, it is up to each of you to watch them and make sure they stay out of trouble until they mature enough to develop some common sense."

Nassari nodded once to Elom, and then said sternly, "Now then, if no one else has any more important business to deal with while I am trying to speak, I suggest that you listen to what I have to say, since it may very well save your lives."

Even the two boys Elom had interrupted realized that this wasn't a joke and paid close attention.

"We will be crossing the midway point of the mountains this morning," Nassari continued. "Those mountains," he pointed to the nearly sheer rock cliffs and jagged peaks to the west, "are the last barrier between us and the home range of the Roracks."

"I thought there were no more Roracks," one of the girls said. Then realizing she had spoken out loud, she smiled and turned a little pink.

"We may have killed close to nine thousand beast-men the day we defeated Warrick's army," Will spoke up, "but a conservative estimate of how many ran off into the hills was twelve to fifteen hundred. I saw them flee, and I would have put their numbers easily at two thousand, and there are still more that weren't under Warrick's control out there."

"Our course has us flying directly toward the area they fled into," Nassari said, regaining control of the briefing. "It is unlikely we will be able to pass beyond the Rorack's territory before we have to stop again. Therefore, you are all on notice. No one will wander off from the main group for any reason. I don't care how bashful you are, if you need to dig a latrine pit, you tell your squad leader, and one or more of us, as well as one or more dragons, will accompany you. We are not telling you stories of the boogie-man to get you to behave. If the beast-men catch you alone, they will kill you and eat you, and if you are very lucky, they will do it in that order. These creatures are stronger than normal humans, so don't count on your magically-enhanced strength to save you. Also, I have seen a beast-man who had an arm lopped off redouble its efforts to kill the person who wounded it, and I have heard similar stories from others. Pain seems to give them strength to fight harder, rather than discourage them from continuing the battle. Wanda is, at this moment, giving your bond-mates the same speech I am giving you. Since almost all of your bond-mates are already familiar with the beast-men, they will help you remember this talk. We are no longer playing "see if we can get by the adults and have fun"; this is real. We are not on some children's holiday where you can play games and do as you please. You are all now Dragon Riders, and I expect you to act like it. Any nonsense before we reach the Legion Headquarters will not be tolerated, and damn little after we get there, as well."

Nassari looked over the group; no one appeared to have taken the message lightly, so he raised his hand in the signal to ready for flight, and said, "Mount up and stay in your squads."

CHAPTER 20

"WHAT IN THE blazes are you two doing so far from camp?" Elom nearly shouted. The boy, Jeremy, who had not reached his sixteenth birthday, and the girl, Sarah, who just turned seventeen a few days before, had been kissing when the smith found them well over a hundred yards away from everyone else. They almost jumped out of their skins when he startled them.

"You know damn well we are all supposed to stay close to the others, and here I find the two of you playin' show and tell in the moonlight without even your dragons watching over you. Whose bright idea was it to send your partners away? Did you think Nassari and Will were joking about the monsters that inhabit these lands?"

As if his words had conjured it from thin air, there was a harsh bark from the darkness. Elom pulled the nine-inch belt knife he carried as he turned toward the sound. Three beast-men suddenly burst out of the shadows at them. The girl screamed, and a little way off a dragon roared.

Elom stepped in front of the two youths and caught the first Rorack by the throat with his left hand. The monster's claws dug deep furrows into his arm, but the big man held fast and used its body as a shield against the second. The third creature swung around the first two, and Elom buried his knife in its chest to the hilt. He lifted the Rorack in his left hand off the ground and slammed it into the third before that one had time to do more than stare blankly at the spot where he had stabbed it. There was a loud pop as the first beast-man's neck snapped from being thrown around like a rag doll. Elom retained possession of his knife as he pushed both of them away.

The second Rorack rose to its feet, and Elom could see that several more were now coming out from between the rocks and trees to join the fray. He swung his knife up and over like a hammer and drove the blade hilt-deep into the second beast-man's skull as it tried to dive at him. He yelled, "Run!" at the two younger Riders, but had no time to turn to see if they complied with the order. Eight more of the creatures were nearly on him. Suddenly, there was a deafening roar right beside him and flame lit the night. The beast-men at the front of the charge didn't have any time to avoid the blast as Nora breathed a narrow cone of fire that engulfed them while sparing him: four more of the monsters down. The four enemies bringing up the rear rolled to one side and avoided the worst of the blast.

The impact of other dragons landing hastily was unmistakable as the remaining beast-men tried desperately to regain their feet. The whole area was suddenly alive with flames as Wanda, Pina, and Saadia came to Nora's aid. Nora breathed forth another cone of fire, but it wasn't really necessary; by this time, the last Roracks were already dying from the blasts of the other dragons.

Two more dragons arrived: the bond-mates of the two adolescents. Both were under a decade old, and neither of them had ever spent time in Rorack territory. Their concern for their Riders turned to chagrin as Wanda rounded on them angrily.

"Where were you both when the beast-men were trying to kill your bond-mates?" she demanded, loudly enough that even those still in camp heard her words. "If it hadn't been for Nora's Partner, these two youngsters would be dead, and both of you would soon follow them to shadow. I don't care that your partners wanted privacy and asked you for space. You were all given specific instruction to watch over these humans because we couldn't trust headstrong youths to control their impulses. I am extremely disappointed in both of you!"

Those were strong words from a Lineage Holder, and the two dragons looked down at the ground in a very humanlike gesture, unable to make eye contact with Wanda.

"You are both now on permanent watch until further notice! You will not sleep until we reach the old fort." She looked at the young couple and added, "You two will watch with them. While it is not possible for a human to go that long without sleep, you will stay with your Partners, and away from each other, and watch the camp. You will only be called in from watch long enough to eat and clean up all of the cooking utensils after the meals."

The two joined their bond-mates in closely examining the ground at their feet.

"I have spoken," Wanda continued, "however, you can be sure that Nassari will have more to say to you on the matter, and I'm positive Nadia will have more than a few choice words to add herself." She looked at the two dragons as well as their young partners and added, "For all of you! If Nora or her bond-mate wish to vent their frustration with you about this, they have more than earned the right, since all four of you owe them your lives."

Wanda, Saadia, and Pina then took flight to scout the area and verify that there were no more beast-men close by.

"Let's get this group back to camp," Nassari said disgustedly. "We will have to decide whether we will pack up and leave tonight, or risk staying until morning."

"I suppose that will have to wait until the dragons get finished making their sweep," Will replied.

"Mm-hmm," Nasssari replied, "Once they're back, all of the leaders will have to confer and make the decision." He looked at Elom who was still bleeding from the deep gouges on his arm, and added, "Until then, someone should see to Elom's wounds."

"C'mon, Elom," Nadia said, "I want to put some salve on those before we heal them. You haven't been bonded long enough to be sure that you are immune to disease, and there's no telling what kind of filth those foul creatures had on their claws."

"I'll be all right. I'll just wash my arm in the stream and wrap a bandage around it."

Nadia put her hands on her hips and glared at him. "Don't make me have Nora force you to behave, too. Some of those marks are deep, and you need healing. So you go ahead and wash them, but I'm going to put some of the ointment that Nat gave us on your arm, and then you will let me heal the wounds."

Elom had turned to his Partner and laid his head against hers. To everyone's surprise, he shrugged his massive shoulders and said, "All right, let me just wash up first. Nora says it's a good idea, and I have to agree. I'll meet you by the fire."

"That was easier than I expected," Nadia whispered to Nassari as they watch the big man and his bond-mate walk off toward the stream.

"Elom may be big, taciturn, and somewhat stubborn, but I'm sure Nora was already *talking* to him about letting someone take care of those wounds," Nassari responded. "For now, let's get these others," he swept the area with his arm to indicate the small crowd that had gathered, back inside our perimeter and set a better watch."

Nadia, Nassari, and Will then herded the younger Riders and the other dragons who had joined their bond-mates back to camp.

Since the dragons who had scouted reported no further signs of their ancient enemies, the leaders opted to stay the night as planned, though the number of dragons keeping watch was doubled.

The next morning another meeting was called before they mounted up.

Nassari had no trouble getting their attention this time. "You all know what happened last night. If it had been anyone besides our mastersmith who had found those two, we would probably have three dead Riders and Dragons now. As it was, it took all of Elom's great strength, as well as the flame of four dragons to deal with it. As I have said before, we are not joking or just trying to scare you into compliance with tales of those creatures. They are a very real threat, and they are cunning enough to understand that a group of dragons means that there are likely to be humans who will be vulnerable." He paused while everyone looked at the pair who had snuck away from camp the previous evening. After giving the two young Riders a few moments to be uncomfortable under the scrutiny, he went on. "I know that Dragon Riders are independent. Once you all reach the age of sixteen, you are free to make your own choices. However, on this trip, I am in command, and the other, older Riders will help me enforce my decisions. Those of you who are under the age of sixteen have no choice; we have been charged by your parents to take care of you, and you have to listen. If anyone over the age of sixteen isn't willing to accept that, he or she can simply mount up and go off alone. I will not tolerate any further nonsense on this trip; decide now!"

Nassari waited several moments to be sure that no one moved to leave before he said, "I see we have an understanding. Now let's mount up and get out of here."

CHAPTER 21

FROM A DISTANCE the old fort looked like little more than a small building in the middle of a vast open plain, however, its true size became apparent as the group glided down from the mountains toward it.

Since Nassari had pushed them so hard and had only allowed the group to land twice all day to allow the humans to relieve themselves, there'd been no need to stop and make camp since the attack. They'd seen signs of Roracks both times they'd landed, and once, while the dragons were flying, they'd noticed a group of the monsters out in the open. The dragons had wanted to flame the creatures, but Nassari kept them on course, refusing to allow them to indulge their instinct to kill the beast-men. At the time, he was more concerned with getting everyone safely to the fort than hunting Roracks while the dragons and Riders were tired and laden with the extra equipment they had brought along.

Wanda didn't like it, but she understood the reasoning. She passed on the order to the other squad leaders, and didn't give him any trouble over the decision; she was as anxious to reach the fort as he.

"I have contacted Pauline and Terra," Wanda said. *"They are waiting for us with a full report about all that has transpired since we left this place."*

"That doesn't sound so good. I wonder what's happened that they feel the need to report before we can even get off-loaded and settled."

"They have said no more to me, Love. I suppose that we will find out when we land. I have instructed them to vacate the courtyard, but they replied that it is already empty. There is only enough room inside for two dragons to be comfortable, and I have decided that Pina and I will take that space, since you and Nadia are in charge."

Nassari chuckled; that was likely to get some response from Chureny and Pauline. The pair was ready enough to bow to the authority of the Lineage Holders, but Chureny had kept quarters in the fort for almost seven hundred years: he wasn't likely to take having Pauline's position usurped lightly. "Oh well, one thing at a time," he said to himself.

"Ready to land?" Wanda asked.

"I've been ready to land since we got airborne this morning, Love. I enjoy flying with you, but I will be glad to see a hot bath and then have a meal that wasn't prepared in the great outdoors."

The pair touched down in the courtyard, and he dismounted quickly, so Wanda could move out of the way and make room for Pina. Chureny stood back, content to wait for Nadia to land, but Raymond rushed forward to report to Nassari immediately.

"The soldiers from Horne have moved back into the fort and taken over, Sir," he reported by way of greeting. "Their commander has moved into the biggest set of rooms and set up as if we were never given rights to this place at all. He tries to order us about as if we're nothing more than raw recruits in his own army."

"What?" Nadia exclaimed. She hadn't been far behind Nassari and had heard the report. "We were promised this place by the King as payment for coming to the rescue of this country. Now Thomas has rescinded that?'

Raymond saluted her but didn't turn away from Nassari as he spoke. "The King has put this popinjay in charge of the army here, and he took that as being in charge of everything. The man treats his horses better than he treats the Riders."

"Really, Raymond, don't exaggerate," Chureny spoke up. "At least he doesn't try and put bits in our mouths and use spurs on our flanks, though the halters do tend to chafe a bit."

"We left you two and six others here; how have the rest of the Riders been taking to this man?" Nassari asked.

"There are only four of us left. Four said they could get better treatment chasing bandits for Trent or Ondar and left outright. Those of us still here pretty much ignore the man. Tension is high because we don't listen to him directly, but go to the patrol commanders to coordinate our efforts with the ground troops. We would have contacted you in the Dream State before now, but there wasn't anything you could do before you arrived anyway."

"The man has driven four Riders away?" Nadia said in astonishment. "Does he know that more than fifteen hundred Roracks escaped the day Warrick was killed? Has he even stopped for a moment to consider that we have no idea how many of those monsters are out there that weren't under Warrick's control?"

"I have complete understanding of my situation, young lady."

Everyone turned to face the speaker, a portly man in his mid-fifties wearing the uniform of a military officer of Horne. The rank on his collar was full colonel, and the sash around his waist confirmed that he had at least seen one campaign where actual combat occurred. Since it wasn't slung diagonally across his chest, though, he had never been confirmed as having actually drawn steel and fought during his career.

"What are those beasts doing in the courtyard? I have given strict orders that those animals are to be housed on the plain, not here!"

Pina growled and Wanda said, "Animals? Beasts? I'll have you know that dragons are more civilized than most of the common humans in your army, and much better house-broken."

"Let me handle this, Love," Nassari said. Wanda settled down, but didn't apologize.

The colonel wasn't intimidated by the dragons and said to Nassari, "You are obviously in charge of the dragons: control those beasts!" It was an order issued by a man who was used to being obeyed.

Nadia started to make a heated reply, but Nassari spoke first. "The dragons control themselves. They are fully sentient beings capable of taking responsibility for their own actions. They are traditionally treated as royalty when it comes to social ranking, and you would do well to remember that."

"We are not in a social situation now," the colonel replied. "This is a military operation, and I have full authority here. You are all under my command, and I will issue orders as I see fit. Your only choice is to obey my orders or suffer the consequences. Now, get those animals out of my courtyard!"

This time both dragons growled menacingly. The colonel was still not impressed, but the two staff officers who had accompanied him out of the building were wide-eyed with fear.

Nadia was nearly spitting incoherently in rage.

Nassari straightened to his full height and said, "Colonel, the Riders were given this fort as a headquarters by your King. You are therefore our guest. Our Partners will come and go as they see fit while here. I am done playing this game of who can out-shout whom. If you have any doubt about this, I suggest that you send a communiqué to His Majesty in the capital and get clarification. You can bet your next month's pay that I will dispatch a Rider to do just that as soon as I can divest my bondmate of that saddle and other riding gear. Then I intend to move into the quarters that I have been informed you now occupy. Your choice is simple; you may have your own possessions moved, or I will have the stuff thrown out of the rooms and left wherever it happens to fall."

The colonel's face turned nearly as bright red as the dress sash he wore. "You are in no position to come here and dictate to me! I am in command and this fort is now, and always has been, a military command post for the protection of Horne's northern border. I have every intention of sending a message to the King, and until I receive a reply, you will either accept my command, or you can leave this country. I will not allow thieving Dragon Riders to take over this fort."

"Thieving Dragon Riders, is it?" Elom's voice boomed out from the gateway of the structure.

"Yes, thieving Dragon Riders," the man responded. "Horne has suffered nearly as much depredation from your kind as we have from the beast-men over the centuries...."

Chureny cut him off. "Up until now, Colonel, I was content to let Nassari deal with you, but as one of the Riders who has been in residence here for the past seven centuries, I take direct offense at such a statement. The Riders have patrolled this land's borders for millennia. It is because of us that the country has been allowed to expand right up to the base of the eastern and northern mountain ranges. One of the other three Riders in residence, who was also a friend of mine, was killed in the honorable pursuit of his duties. All we have ever asked for in return for our service is a room to sleep in, basic meals, and a few herd beasts for our bond-mates, and for that, your people, commoners and nobles alike, have blamed every instance of economic insecurity on us. I am sick of it; you will either watch your tongue, or you will meet me on the field of honor where we will settle this with our blades."

Chureny and Colonel Matson stood glaring at each other. Matson was overweight and on the downhill side of fifty. Chureny may have been over seven hundred years old, but he looked like he could be anywhere from his early to late thirties, and he kept himself in good shape. The staring match lasted for several more minutes.

Nadia moved to intervene, but Nassari held her back. He relayed through the dragons that this needed to run its course. Obviously, Chureny would slaughter Matson in a fight, but the Colonel felt compelled to exert his authority. If he backed down now, he clearly felt that he might as well walk away and start packing.

Matson blinked first. He turned to Nassari and almost whined, "Can't you control the Riders under your command?"

"Nadia has already sent Will and Mark to the capital, Nassari. No one wanted to send Saadia since she had just traveled so far, but we saw little choice. Mark and Lena are well rested, as well as more familiar with the direct route to Fallon. Mark is from Horne and knows the ter-

rain, but Will knows a great deal more about dealing with royalty, and being the royal nephew of Corice, he will be better received by the King," Wanda interjected.

"So, you now admit that the Riders are under my command; good, that's a start," Nassari spoke as if his own thoughts had not been interrupted. "Now then, Riders have been dispatched to the capital to get clarification as to the disposition of this fort and the surrounding plain. Until then, I believe that the last word we had from the capital placed this building in the hands of the Dragon Riders. However, darkness is upon us, and I am willing to let things stand for one more night. Nadia and I, as well as our senior Riders, will find quarters inside the fort, and the rest can bed down closer to their Bond-mates. You do not have to move your quarters until tomorrow. We will, however, need hot food and drink, as well as access to the bathing facility that was set up inside the walls before we left."

Before Matson could respond, Nassari extended his arm to Nadia, and the pair turned and walked toward the entrance of the inner building.

Matson turned to Raymond as Craig, Adamus, and Elom sauntered past. "We don't have food ready, and there isn't enough wood to heat water for that many people to bathe," he complained.

"Really, Colonel," Raymond replied, "just have your cooks stew up something palatable, and get a detail of men to fill the cisterns. These Riders are cold, hungry, dirty, and tired from their long flight. They will gladly eat almost anything that they don't have to cook themselves, and as for heating the water, we can use magic – or dragon fire." He waved dismissively as he and Chureny headed off to join the other senior Riders in the main hall.

CHAPTER 22

THE DRAGONS GLIDED silently down toward the palace. Will had them land outside the walls of the King's residence but inside the city of Fallon. He was tired, and he had no intention of waiting for hours out on the field until someone on the watch noticed them. He and Mark only stood outside for a few moments before a group of soldiers came out. The captain in charge extended an invitation from the King to join him inside.

"Your Majesty," Will extended his hand to shake but didn't bow, and instructed Mark not to show such deferential treatment, either.

Thomas was obviously insulted by the perceived slight, but he extended his hand and shook. "What may We do for you, Rider?"

The use of the royal plural wasn't lost on Will. He had made good use of the time spent under the tutelage of his uncle in Corice, and he knew that Thomas was trying to treat him as a subordinate. He was determined to neither acknowledge subordination nor give outright insult. By all traditions, he was on equal footing with this man, and he needed that to be clear.

"We are here to discuss what has occurred at the old fort since we departed from your lands several months ago."

Mark had been born in Horne. He was actually the only one of Warrick's Riders who had decided to stay on and try to put the country right. Even though his part in the war had been limited to scouting, he felt remorse and wished to do all he could to make amends. He also had some understanding of court etiquette, and visibly flinched at the possible insult to his King.

Thomas reddened slightly, but since it could be argued that Will was simply speaking of Dragon Riders collectively and not using the royal pronoun, he couldn't take offense. With two fully mature dragons on his doorstep, Thomas decided to stop the game. "I sent a military contingent to ensure that the Riders had all the help they needed to keep the beast-men from regrouping. What has happened that requires you to fly all this way in the darkness to get clarification of that?"

"It seems that the commander you put in charge misinterpreted your orders and has taken possession of the old fort as his headquarters. Since it was you who signed the original order that the fort and surrounding plain were to be under Dragon Rider control, we thought it best to come and get confirmation that those orders still stand."

Will's eye was continually drawn to a mural that had been roughly drawn on the wall of the audience hall. It was obviously the preliminary sketch for a depiction of the last battle of the war, but the size and proportions of the dragons were wrong. The dragons were goose-necked and too slender, and the riders looked much too large in relation to them.

"I see you have an interest in the wall decoration," Thomas said. "I thought that since this Kingdom might no longer stand if it weren't for the Dragons and their Riders, I would honor them in some small way."

"It's very good," Will responded, "but, as an artist, I can see some flaws in proportion and scale"

"Really?" Thomas asked. "The man who is doing the job is quite good and has done numerous portraits for the nobility. He comes highly recommended."

"The artist has done a fine job, and I don't fault him, but it would be obvious to anyone who is truly familiar with dragons that he has worked from descriptions, not first-hand knowledge. If you would like, once we have settled this other matter, I can return and help get the flaws ironed out. I can also provide live dragons as models. After all, this is your main reception area; I'm sure you want the mural to be accurate as well as eye-catching."

"Well, the artist is scheduled to return in the morning," the King said thoughtfully. I'd hate to have to repaint this after it is finished. If this young Rider would be so kind as to take a letter back after breakfast," he indicated Mark, "you could simply stay here and help the man get this sketch redone before any pigment is applied."

"I think that is a good solution to both problems, Your Majesty. Now if I could trouble you for one last thing." At the King's nod, he continued, "I have ridden far and been sleeping in the wild. I'm sure that I am offensive to anyone who is close to me. If I could trouble your servants for quarters and a bath...."

Chapter 23

THE NEXT MORNING, after having a night to sleep on his situation, Matson was back in full bluster. "I'll be damned if I will give up my quarters for you and this pack of strays." Elom started to move toward the man, but Nassari placed his hand on his friend's arm and stopped him.

"The orders I have, signed by the King himself," Matson continued completely oblivious to the dangerous looks that Elom and Chureny were both giving him, "give me the authority to establish a command here and guard the border from any beast-men who remain in the wilds. Therefore, I refuse to move either myself or my staff officers to make room for you and your Riders. If you want better quarters, I suggest that you begin building them as soon as you can procure your own materials to do so."

"Oh, you'll make room," Nadia said in a tone of voice that dripped honey. Nassari knew that tone as Nadia at her most dangerous. "I've stationed six dragons outside the gates, and we have Wanda and Pina inside. As far as your soldiers are concerned, that portal is now one way. You may leave, but you will not come back in! Your cooks and other servants have already vacated the building, and the junior staff officers you sent on errands are now milling about just outside unable to come back to get further orders. What Nassari said last night still holds true: your only choice is whether you move your possessions in an orderly fashion, or whether we throw them out onto the plain as we lay hands on them."

Nassari held up both hands to forestall further argument. "Our messengers arrived at the capital early enough last night to actually speak with the King, and Mark will be back in less than two hours. Once we have Thomas's written words on the matter, this will be settled. For now, I have listened to all of the arguing I can stand before breakfast."

Again he extended his arm to Nadia and the two of them walked toward the main hall where the tables were laid out with food. Matson ordered them to stop and come back, but they ignored him.

"Put a sock in it, Matson," Elom growled as the man turned on him. Then he too, walked away to join Nassari and Nadia at breakfast.

Matson sat in his office and refused to go out and deal with his soldiers. He ordered his senior officers still in the building to do the same because he knew that the dragons would not let them back inside: he was a self-imposed prisoner in the fort. If he went out, he wouldn't be allowed back in, and his claim on the building would be weakened. He sat alone in his office like a petulant child until Mark returned with the King's written orders.

To: Colonel William Pritchart Matson
Subsection to: Lt. Colonel Jonathan Sellers

While We find it admirable that you have taken your duty so seriously, that duty was never meant to place the Dragon Riders under your direct command. Neither did We intend for you to take possession of the old fort, or of the surrounding plain. That property and any responsibilities for its upkeep were ceded to the Riders at the close of the War Against the Roracks. In consideration for that property, the Dragon Riders have agreed to coordinate with our ground troops in guarding Our borders against further incursions by the beast-men. You are therefore ordered to relinquish the entire fort to our allies.

Since the Kingdom of Iondar has recently elected to stop all trade relations with Horne, you are further ordered to take one-third of the men under your command and return to the capital, where you will meet up with the rest of the troops We have assigned to you, and you will then move to ensure that no trade goods either come or go across the Horne/Iondar border.

Subsection:

It is Our decision that Lt. Colonel Sellers is to take command of the troops remaining and establish a new fort as close to the nearest village or town as possible. Materials for any needed construction will be sent for that purpose as soon as such are available. Until then, the officers will find quarters in the local village, and the men can erect tents for their comfort and protection while they fell any local trees they need for timbers with which to build a stockade. Local procurement of goods and supplies is authorized and writs for payment will be issued.

Lt. Colonel Sellers is also hereby promoted to the rank of Colonel in accordance with his new duties, and We send Our congratulations to Colonel Sellers.

Signed and Royal Seal affixed by
Thomas Richard Fallon Horne,
Royal Sovereign of the Kingdom of Horne.

"Well, I'd say that the King's orders are quite clear on the situation," Nassari said genially. "I suppose we can tell the dragons to allow your soldiers to come and go now, since you will need to move your things out."

"This must be a forgery. The King would neither order me out of quarters in favor of your group nor recall me for such a menial border patrol. Why, that's little more than a punishment detail. I will not take this seriously until I can send my own trusted messengers to the King to confirm this document."

"Give it up, William: you and I both know the King's signature and the royal seal well enough to know this is no forgery." Sellers turned to Nassari and Nadia and continued in a conversational tone. "I'll get a detail up here to move our things out of the fort. Now if you'll excuse me, I have to make arrangements for my officers in the local village."

As he turned to leave, Nassari said, "Colonel Sellers, before you run off," the Colonel turned back to face him, "first, let me congratulate you on your promotion. Second, if it will be of any help to you, I will put several of the young Riders and their bond-mates at your disposal to ferry you or your procurement officer to and from the village: it may not be that far, but flying is still much faster than riding a horse." He turned to Matson and added, "I'm not slighting you, Colonel Matson. I would happily assign a Rider to take you to the capital, but I don't have enough dragons to take the men you must lead. I will, however, be sending several dragons as an escort, since your straightest path puts you traveling along the road nearest to the mountains. I bear no grudge in this matter. We really are here to work with the armies of Horne."

"What you and your Riders do is your business," he replied with obvious disdain. "I don't believe that my force will need an escort since I will be taking over two hundred men. You may conserve your strength and keep your dragons here." Apparently, Matson did still hold some resentment.

"William, the Riders are not against us. You were told early on that this fort was given to them, but you insisted on headquartering here. Now the matter is completely settled: let it go," Sellers responded. He turned back to Nassari. "As for myself, I gratefully accept your offer, Sir. Even though the village is close to the plain, it is still an hour's ride there and back. Being able to fly will not only save time, but I won't be bounced along on horseback either. The beast men killed so much livestock that I was unable to procure a

personal mount before I left the capital, and none of the military-is-
sued horses are gaited, so I thank you heartily for the consideration."

Later that night, Nassari stood watching the changing hues of
the Dream State while Wanda searched for Geneva.

"I have found her. She and Delno are coming now."

Geneva and Delno seemed to materialize from out of nothing.
Interestingly, Nassari would have said that the small ledge they had
perched on wasn't big enough for two dragons, but the space just
expanded to accommodate Geneva as she appeared.

Delno greeted his old friend and second-in-command with a
question. "Getting settled in all right?"

"We had some initial trouble, but it's been handled."

"What kind of trouble?"

Nassari filled him in on the goings-on since the group had left
Larimar. He told every detail, including the attack where Elom was
injured.

"I trust our good mastersmith has suffered no permanent hurt?"
At Nassari's nod, Delno continued. "It disturbs me that you were
attacked, but we knew we hadn't gotten all of those monsters. I had
hoped, however, that they would be several years in hiding before
they became brave enough to strike at any sizable targets again."

"It could be that is the case, Dear One," Geneva interjected.
"You may have noticed that Nassari said nothing about attacks in
Horne, just the one attack against Dragon Riders inside the beast-
men's territory. They may have gotten a bloody beating on the
plain, but that only reinforces their racial hatred for my kind. It
may still be several years before those abominations get brave
enough to leave the boundaries of their home range and again
hunt in human lands."

"True enough, Dear Heart," Delno replied. "I hadn't thought
about it that way. It's one thing to be beaten and driven out like they
were, but it's quite another to suddenly find your most hated enemies encamped in your front yard. It's entirely possible that the
beast-men felt compelled to attack your group on some instinctive
territorial level."

Nassari nodded. "We saw signs of beast-men everywhere we stopped. I'm not sure, but I think there were a lot more of the monsters out there that weren't under Warrick's control than even he suspected. As you were fond of telling him, his control wasn't nearly as absolute as he thought."

"I believe, at least until we can assess their numbers better, it's best if Dragon Riders avoid travel routes that will force them to camp in Rorack lands. It will take longer to go around the mountains, but flying straight over them might be too dangerous. You and your group most likely got through relatively unscathed because there were just too many of you to take on openly." Delno paused for a moment. "This other news has me disturbed, though."

"I told you we handled it, Del."

"Not the nonsense with Matson. I've met the man and he's a conceited idiot. I half expected something like that from him. What disturbs me is the news about Iondar. Cutting off trade relations is often the first step in a process that leads to war. They were obviously more upset about Thomas's snub concerning the troops they sent than I thought. Damn the man, he was so impressed with the force of dragons that he all but forgot the ground troops who fought in that conflict. He even told Brock's cousin that he was displeased that Iondar had opted to send such a small force."

"If I recall," Nassari interrupted, "King Thomas referred to the Iondarians as an insignificant force, and he didn't stop there. He pointed out that Corice, which had no direct trade relations with Horne, sent over half a thousand men despite the fact they were embroiled in a war of their own. He actually made it feel as if the Iondarians were lucky that he didn't take offense at their gesture."

"You're right; Thomas was rather insulting, especially since the King of Iondar sent his best men. That force was only two hundred strong, but they were the King's own personal elite guard. Not only that, the King of Iondar was the one who sent word to the elves and convinced them to send Walker and his Hunters. That was not an insignificant gesture, and I personally told Thomas that. Is the man trying to start another war he can't afford?"

Nassari shook his head and shrugged his shoulders in puzzlement. "I don't claim to understand his motivations, but I've been told that Iondar only threatened an embargo; he was so put out he ordered troops to be sure no goods travel across the border in either direction. Apparently, he thinks he can force Iondar to back down by ensuring that nothing gets through."

It was Delno's turn to shake his head wondering. "He just spent a good deal of his available treasury securing his lands from Warrick's madness. That last war disrupted trade and badly hurt his Kingdom financially, and he still owes a great deal of monetary compensation to the other nations that answered his call for help. If he simply returned to business as usual, he'd be a decade paying off Ondar alone, much less Palamore, to name the chief creditors, and that doesn't even count the debt to Trent, and to a much lesser degree Tyler and Llorne. He's damn lucky that Corice was so anxious to get those Bournese defectors off of refugee status that Dorian hasn't presented Horne with a bill for services rendered. Now that the war is over, he should be embracing his allies, not alienating them. We'll have to watch this situation closely. I don't want the Riders directly involved if it can be avoided. We have an obligation to guard against the Roracks in the north, but we have no such mission in the south, especially since Trent will most likely side with Iondar if this goes badly. Several Riders will want to side with Trent, and at least one will feel compelled to help Iondar."

"Do you think Brock would move directly against Horne if his homeland goes to war?"

"I don't know for sure," Delno replied, "but if it happens, I don't want this war to put the Dragon Riders on opposite sides of the conflict. The Riders must remain neutral in such struggles if possible. Not doing so is what brought about the original decline in the riders during the clan wars over two thousand years ago: we are just now beginning to recover our numbers, and only because so many unbonded dragons have sought out human companionship since the war against Warrick. Also, if war breaks out in the south, we could find ourselves alone guarding our position against the Roracks in the north."

"If worse comes to worst we can always move back to Corice, though I am loath to have to deal with those politicians again any time soon."

"We have no option but to hold that fort, Nassari. Jhren has been doing some research in the Elven Libraries, and it seems that the beast-men have attacked in a more ordered manner than normal in the distant past, and the few times the beast-men have been organized, that place has been involved to one degree or another. The old man thinks it has to do with the nature of the magic surrounding the fort itself. It is definitely where the Roracks and other magically constructed creatures were made, as well as where the compelling stone originated, and now that the stone has been fused back into the mother rock by Warrick and Hella's energy, it could be even more dangerous. Even Jhren isn't sure how it was used to control the beast-men, but he does say that he sees no way to further limit the possibility of using it again short of destroying it entirely, if that's even possible. Besides that, we've put too much into it to let it go so easily."

CHAPTER 24

"I JUST WANTED TO let you know that the last of the wagons I sent out from Larimar has arrived," Elom reported. "I'll have the metal works set up before long: it took the Riders and that detail of men Colonel Sellers lent us more than two weeks to get the main building built outside the Fort due to the lack of materials, and it's nothing more than a big barn at this point, but it'll be a proper working shop soon enough. Our main problem now is getting the coal to fire the forge and the iron to work with. One dragon can't carry enough to really make a difference, and that nobleman, Bastian, damn near asks for blood to let the wagons cross his land."

"Aren't those roads maintained by the Crown?" Nassari asked.

"No," Colonel Sellers stated flatly as he maneuvered around the smith to get inside Nassari's private office. "It's expensive maintaining roads, so, since such a long stretch of it crosses Bastian's lands, the Crown has him do the maintenance, and he's allowed to charge a toll. Not that he maintains his section of the track very well. He barely keeps it passable and bleeds merchant caravans dry to let them through; he's the reason that the few trade goods we get here are so damned expensive. What he's doing isn't illegal, but it's as close as he can get without being prosecuted. Believe me, as military governor of this province, I'd put a stop to it, if I could."

"Aye, that's the rub," Elom responded. "We're close to the mines, but because of the toll, we'd pay less to have a wagon load of the stuff shipped from the southwest out of Trent using that road that runs closer to the mountain. We'd save a few coins if we paid this noble-born thief to supply the wagons and handle the shipping, but giving the man anything rubs me raw. I'd just as soon cut cross country and carry the stuff on my own back!"

"I could try and say the material is for the garrison, and it wouldn't be an outright lie since you've offered us the help of your metal shop, but Bastian knows we don't use that much for just the army. He'll bypass me and complain to the Council of Lords if I try to bring more than one wagon load of iron and maybe two loads of coal in under military seal. I might be able to call in a couple of favors and get away with it: he's a minor Lord and most of the other noblemen don't like him anyway. However, that would be one less favor I could seek if something else crops up in the future: it's political currency I'd rather not spend if we can find another way."

"No," Nassari said to Sellers, "bring in only as much of each as you can get away with, and we'll deal with the rest of our need." He turned to Elom and asked, "How far to the mines?"

"It's about a two to three-hour leisurely flight, about fifty, sixty leagues to the coal: little farther to the iron."

"Well, we've got nearly three dozen youngsters milling around looking for trouble to get into. Some of them are over the age of seventeen and can go their own way if they choose. We've no right to stop them, and if we can't find ways to keep them busy we may have to send them off to find meaningful tasks elsewhere anyway." Nassari shook his head and said softly, more to himself then to the other two men, "The Riders are supposed to be independent, but that was before we had a Legion Headquarters and two Lineage holders in charge. The meeting this summer may bring about some surprises for all." He stood staring blankly for a moment until Elom spoke up and broke his train of thought.

"What do you have in mind concerning our current situation?"

"Just this; we have to pay a toll if we use the road, but Bastian doesn't own the sky, we do! The dragons can't carry that much; about twenty stone plus their Rider won't overly fatigue them. If we have five teams go to each mine and carry back a full load, that's about a half ton of coal or iron each trip. That still leaves more than a score of dragons to fly the regular routes and keep track of the beast-men. They'll only be able to make one or two trips a week even rotating the teams, so it will take longer to get our supplies than using one big caravan, but it will give the kids something to occupy their time between patrols."

"Aye, that might just work," Elom said thoughtfully. "Best if they fly out in the afternoons and then camp near the mines overnight: that way the dragons will be rested before they have to lift off the ground with the extra weight the next morning. The dragons all say that it's easier to get airborne before the sun is too high in the sky and the heat makes the air thinner. Give me a couple of days and I can rig up carrying slings so the stuff will be suspended under the dragons where it won't interfere with their wings…" He trailed off for several moments as he turned his extremely talented mind to work on the preliminaries of the problem before he looked up and said with a smile on his face, "Maybe we can fly right over Bastian's manor house on the return trips."

Nassari smiled. "As satisfying as that might be, I'd rather not antagonize the man if it can we avoid doing so. I still have a small herd of cattle coming in from Trent, and I don't want them delayed at the southern borders of Bastian's lands because he has taken offense to us flying our goods right over his head. With the extra work the dragons will be doing, they will all need to eat again before too long, and there is almost no game large enough to sate them nearby. The adult dragons can't carry whole steers from the southern end of Bastian's land: it won't do us any good to save the money on the supplies only to spend it on procuring food for the dragons." He paused for a moment and sipped his coffee. "I'd have the drovers keep the herd off of Bastian's land nearer to the mountains and avoid as much of our local Lord's tolls as possible, but traveling too close to Rorack territory

with that much meat isn't worth the risk. After all, we can't effectively protect the cattle if the stupid beasts are stampeding because the
dragons are close enough to keep them safe. I wouldn't spend so much
on importing meat if it could be avoided, but dragon mating flights
take place mostly during the spring, and males can rise as late in the
year as early fall. None of ours have gone in search of mating flights
this year, yet, but there are already two un-bonded dragons who are
pregnant and have contacted Delno asking to clutch here so that their
daughters will be bonded. They feel that Dragon Riders will be better able to care for their children, and coming here won't put them in
direct contact with non-bonded humans. Those dragon-children who
will hatch are going to need to eat."

"Leave it to me then. I'll get those slings rigged and make sure
we get our goods with 'His Lordship' none the wiser. As soon as I
get all of that taken care of, I'll start on those new blades I promised you."

"What mischief are you men up to now?" Nadia asked. She was
wearing her flight jacket, and still had a bit of color to her cheeks
from the cold winds at altitude. "I've done a full sweep of the area
and found no signs of Roracks. That hunter who reported seeing a
large group of them near here should probably learn a bit more
about the local mushrooms before he eats them while he's out track-
ing game."

"To answer your question, Darling, we are making plans to bring
in our supplies using dragons rather than pay the extortion that the
local nobleman charges under the guise of honest tolls."

"Good," she replied, "I've dealt with that man a couple of times
and in addition to the fact that he's a middle-aged lecher, I always
feel as though I need a bath after being in his company and dealing
for goods."

"We only deal with him for supplies, such as fresh vegetables,
that are cost prohibitive to have shipped, though; if the slings that
Elom is designing for the dragons work, we may even be able to bypass Bastian on that count, also," Nassari said with a smile. "As for
that report; don't be so quick to dismiss it. We know that the beast-

men are cunning, and that they have occasionally been known in the past to work together in groups as large as one hundred and fifty strong without any compelling magic, and I've heard tales of even larger gangs of them working together. Apparently, if their leader is strong enough, and has enough loyal sub-chiefs, he can maintain them as a cohesive unit and keep infighting to a minimum. A chief that powerful is likely to be smart enough to keep his troops hidden. We'll change the patrol routes and see if the shift in direction and scheduling reveals anything."

"That brings me to the reason I came this morning," Sellers said. "I have to get a report off to the capital. We've found and eliminated one group of forty-four beast-men, but it was costly. We need more arrows, and I have to replace the two men who were killed by those monsters. The King has cut my manpower to a minimum and I can't afford the losses without replacements being sent."

"While we enjoy your company, Colonel," Nadia replied, "There's really no need for you to come all the way up here to ask for a Rider to carry a message. I will tell Adamus to dispatch someone, but in the future, if you need to send a communiqué just see him directly to avoid any delay. He can usually be found somewhere near the Riders' barracks."

"I am glad that you clarified that. I was told of your words about the Riders doing vital tasks and not available to 'anyone who was too damn lazy to sit a horse.'"

"That comment was made to the local merchants, not the military. You and your staff officers have not abused the privilege of having the dragons to carry messages. We work together with the army and have no qualms about helping you maintain communication with either your outposts or the capital."

Sellers smiled and said, "I am grateful. I only wish I could have had such allies in past campaigns. I must admit, if they pull me back and send me to border patrol, I will miss it. The ability to communicate with the capital in less than a day when it takes a week or more to get return message when we send a courier on horseback is a big advantage this far out in the field."

"What about the local merchants?" Nassari asked. "I've been so busy with getting the incoming supplies settled, and keeping track of the tensions on the southern border. I'm afraid I may have been ignoring our own local situation."

"As you know, the local village has a population of about six hundred," Sellers replied. "It was smaller before Warrick began to make himself known here, but the population swelled because the survivors of some of the other settlements close by had nowhere else to go. Since this village was so close to the Fort, Warrick let it thrive to keep his own supply lines open."

"The locals actually prospered to some extent because of their cooperation with our enemies," Nadia said angrily.

"Not everyone is a warrior, Dear," Nassari replied. "Many of the people there only did what they had to do to survive. We can't fault merchants, craftsmen, and farmers for doing what was necessary to protect their families."

"People from our homeland would have fought!"

"Yes, and they would have died at the hands of Warrick's beast-men."

"She's got a point, Rider." Sellers came to Nadia's aid. "They didn't have to give up so readily, and they certainly didn't have to cooperate so much, and Lord Bastian was chief among the collaborators! If I could prove it, I'd have the man in irons working in one of those mines."

Nassari held up both hands, palms forward, and said, "Peace, both of you. I understand your sentiment, but that war ended months ago, and we have another to avoid in the south before we start a third here. Let's stick to the subject of now. What have the local merchants been doing?"

"They have noticed that Colonel Seller's messages get prompt attention, and he has his replies no later than the next day. They feel they should have the same privilege, so they can conduct business faster and beat out the competition. They want us to carry their private communications like we have nothing better to do."

This time Nassari's smile was purely deviousness. "Correct me if I'm wrong, but isn't their chief competitor Lord Bastian himself?" Everyone else nodded, so he continued. "Then I see no problem with helping them out, for a fee...."

CHAPTER 25

"WHAT BRINGS THE commander of the Legion of Riders and the Military Governor to my humble shop?" Elom joked.

"It's been just over a week since your supplies started arriving by dragon, and I've come to check on the progress of those blades you promised me," Nassari replied with a laugh.

"I'm just tagging along to see if your skills are all that I've been told," Sellers jibed.

"You came at the right moment then; I just put these in their new scabbards and was going have Nora relay a message to you." He handed Nassari the weapons without ceremony. "With Craig's help, I was able to figure out that working the magic into the blades is pretty much just a matter of intent: now that I'm bonded, and doing it on purpose, the steel is even stronger and takes a keener edge than any others I've ever made. They're not Dragon Blades, but it will be a long time before you have to sharpen those."

Nassari examined the blades: both were exquisite. The master-smith had basically remade the blade Nassari originally carried; long, thin, and curved. It was too long to be considered a saber, but not quite a scimitar like those used in the south. The guard was fashioned like Delno's Dragon Blade. It had a similar theme; however, it was only one dragon. The tang of the blade went through the dragon's open mouth and came out of the back of the bronze animal's head, so that the blade itself looked to be held in the dragon's jaws; the body formed the main part of the guard, and the wings were partially unfurled to enclose the wielder's hand for further protection; the tail curved up and around the back of the tang to form the pommel. The whole guard was done in bronze with nickel-steel reinforcing.

The *main gauche* was pretty much a match for Delno's, but about an inch shorter the way Nassari preferred: the guard was the same in every detail. It was a dragon and the tang of the blade went directly through the center of the body while the head and tail formed the top and bottom of an S. The pommel was a simple bronze knob heavy enough to use as a small hammer if the need arose.

Colonel Sellers whistled appreciatively, and Nassari said, "My friend, your work is exemplary. I could search for centuries and not find the equal of either of these blades. Thank you!"

"Tell me, Mastersmith," Sellers asked, "what is this patterning I see on the blades?"

"That's a bit of a trade secret that my dad and I came up with. The blades are made of layers of steel twisted together and hammered flat. If it's done just right it not only makes a superior blade, it looks darn pretty, too. Once you have the hang of it, you can even control the patterning to some extent."

"I'm afraid, though, that once Nadia sees these you will find yourself with another order to fill," Nassari stated.

"She's already seen them, and I'm making her a new saber, and she'll have a targe made from shed dragon scales to go along with it," Elom replied with a laugh. "You'd have seen them before now yourself if you came out of that office once in a while."

"I do come out of the office. I do physical training before the sun rises, and Wanda and I fly together regularly every afternoon. However, I have to make sure that we have enough groceries to feed everyone."

Elom chuckled at the reference to the old joke about him eating like two men.

"I would like to stay and talk with you for hours," Nassari went on, "but I do have much to accomplish this morning. What I came out for was to commission a belt knife; it's a gift. It needs to be nice, but not as nice as either of my blades. In fact, I specifically don't want it so nice that it would be coveted by a king. Nadia and I have been invited to Lord Larad's birthday party. Since he is the head of the Council of Lords, we have to attend. I want the belt knife as a present. It needs to be better than anything he can get for himself in the capital, but it shouldn't be so great as to make the King jealous. I get the impression that the man has more than a passing knowledge of metal, so the steel must be good, but he will still appreciate something flashy when it's sheathed. We're dealing with the pettiness of ranking nobility here."

"When do you need it?"

"I'm afraid this one came up suddenly, Elom. I received the invitation yesterday eve, and the party is set for four days from now. I hope I haven't given you too tight a schedule."

"Four days is more than enough time. In fact, I've got a nice double-edged belt knife made: I just need to fashion the guard, pommel, and handle."

"He's partial to the color green, if that helps," Colonel Sellers interjected.

"Green, you say," Elom responded thoughtfully, and he suddenly brightened. "I've got just the thing. I brought a chunk of malachite along from Corice. Malachite is a beautiful stone, but I don't like working the stuff because the fumes it gives off when you grind it are poisonous. But this piece is perfect, and I know how to be careful when dealing with it. I'll get the leatherworker to make a scabbard and dye it to match the handle. I'll have the blade ready in time."

"You are a lapidary, as well?" Sellers asked.

"When the mood strikes me," Elom replied. "A man should be able to do more than just one thing; never know when a hobby will overlap into your job."

"True enough, my good Mastersmith."

"We will leave you to be about your work, Elom," Nassari said, "and we must move on to ours. Thank you again for these marvelous blades."

Elom waved off the thanks as he turned and strode back inside his shop without further comment.

"The man tends to be a bit single-minded when he gets a task going," Seller's commented.

"He's been like that ever since I've known him, and I've known him since we were both children," Nassari stated. "Now then, we have to be about our task."

"I'm sorry that I have to drag you off to town, Rider, but Bastion watches everything that goes on around here. Riders come and go from the village often, so one more dragon won't be suspicious, but bringing the merchants here would get his attention."

"Not a problem, Colonel. I don't mind getting away from my office for a while anyway. Do you want to ride your horse back, or fly with me and Wanda?"

"I want to fly, but it would be a curious sight to have both of us coming into town together on dragon back: I'd better ride the horse and meet you there," he replied as he took the animal's reins from the young staff officer who was holding them. "Besides, this animal is one I sent for and had delivered all the way from Trent as a congratulation present to myself for being promoted; he's gaited, so the ride is much more pleasant than using one of the military-issue horses like I was riding before."

"Then I will see you in the village," Nassari told him as he turned and headed back to the courtyard to meet up with Wanda.

"*I see that you have a new sword and knife,*" Wanda said when he walked up to her.

"Yes; once Elom got enough material to fire the forge, these were the first things he made."

"*He and Nora made, Darling. Never forget the draconic side of the equation.*"

"*Nora helped?*"

"*Of course. Did you think that those blades were forged in a coal fire?*"

Nassari stopped short while hefting Wanda's saddle in place. "These blades were forged in Dragon Fire?"

"Yes," she replied with a chuckle. "Don't be so surprised; your friend is, after all, bonded to a dragon."

"I didn't realize that dragons had such fine control over their flames."

"While all dragons can control their flame to some extent, Nora has much more skill at it than any other dragon I've ever met. It could have something to do to with the Rider to whom she is bonded. Any female can control her flame to a near pinpoint when etching a Dragon Blade onto a shell, but it requires strong magic to do so in order to direct the flame and protect the unhatched dragon. Nora is able to use a similar technique to regulate her flame when helping Elom. It apparently takes the equivalent of one full breath, expended in short tightly controlled blasts, to produce two blades like that. I do believe that those blades are the first ever to be made in such a manner, and, since the amount of flame Nora can produce in a single day is still limited like any other dragon's, I don't expect our good Mastersmith to start mass producing them."

"You're right, of course." Nassari looked at his new blades for a moment before continuing. "The one thing I've learned is to never underestimate a dragon, and never believe that you have everything figured out when bonded pairs are involved."

Then, getting back to the task at hand, he threw one end of the belly strap over Wanda's back and she lifted herself up and used her back foot to kick it to him so that he wouldn't have to bend underneath to retrieve it. Dragons' hands had opposable thumbs but weren't as dexterous as those of human beings because of their sheer size, and their hind feet were more like the hind feet of a cat, but they could use all four appendages with quite a bit of precision when they wanted to.

"I certainly hope this trip is worth it," he said aloud, almost absently.

"Any time we can fly together, Dear, it is worth it," she responded in kind.

Nassari switched back to purely mental communication, "Yes, but if that is all we are going to accomplish today, I would much rather

pack a picnic lunch and spend the time on a river bank in your company instead of meeting with these men."

"That does sound like a wonderful idea. Perhaps after your business
in town is concluded, we can do something like that."

"You have a point. I haven't had a break in weeks, and you have
been stuck in this courtyard because of that," he said. "If you don't mind
the extra company, you could contact Pina and have Nadia bring food
and drink after the meeting."

"Actually, while I love being alone with you, I have become quite ac-
customed to Pina's company. I will do just that. We can fly south to that
spot in the river where the other dragons have wallowed a nice bathing
pond. I'll be sure and remind Nadia to bring soap, a brush, and dry
clothing for you."

While she didn't do it out loud, the mental tone was so close to
laughter that the difference was moot.

"You do that, Love," Nassari replied indulgently and chuckled to
himself.

CHAPTER 26

"**G**ENTLEMEN!" NASSARI CALLED the merchants sharply to order. There were nearly a score of men in the room, including Nassari, Colonel Sellers, and his second-in-command.

The meeting had been going on for some time and the only thing that had been accomplished so far was that the merchants of the village of North Point had managed to convey their belief that they had a right to use the Dragon Riders as messengers, and were thoroughly unhappy about being frustrated in their efforts to do so.

"I did not put the rest of my schedule on hold and fly into town to sit here while you give voice to your asinine complaints." Several men jumped to their feet to make strong objections to Nassari's choice of words, but a dragon bellowed in rage from just outside and everyone went quiet.

Nassari silently thanked Wanda, and said out loud, "The Dragon Riders are not here as conscripts to this kingdom. We are not under the control of the military, and we are not obligated to spend any of our time on your personal business. We are an independent agency, fully autonomous, and contracted to assist with keeping you and the rest of this country safe from the beast-men. We were given the old fort and the surrounding plain as part of the payment for that service. Nowhere in our contractual agreement is there any clause about being at the beck and call of the local businessmen and politicians."

"Then why have we been summoned to this meeting in the first place?" a short fat man with a perpetually red face asked.

"You're right," Nassari responded. He got to his feet and added, "There appears to be no reason to attend. Since I cleared my entire afternoon to come here and work out a reasonable fee schedule for providing you what you want so that you will have an edge over your competition, and you are all completely unwilling to cooperate, I believe I will use the remainder of the time I have today to take a much-needed break." He turned to Colonel Sellers and said, "If you, or any of your officers, need anything from the Riders, please see the liaison; I will be unavailable for the rest of the afternoon."

Nassari turned his back on the merchants and began walking toward the door. A chorus of voices erupted behind him protesting his dismissal and demanding he turn around and deal with them at once. He completely ignored them until one voice called above the others for silence. The man who had moved to quiet the others was tall, with a deep, commanding voice. His name was Samuel Millersen.

"Please accept our apologies and stay, Rider," Millersen said.

Nassari stopped but didn't turn around.

Millersen quickly went on. "We have erred in our dealings with you. Many here had assumed that the Riders were under the control of our King, and it has been hinted by some in the capital that we would be given assistance in conducting business out here so far from the other civilized areas of Horne. Many of my fellows simply thought that, since you regularly allowed the military to use your services to transport messages, we would be given the same privilege. Again, I apologize."

Nassari turned to face the man. "The reason we so willingly work with the military is simple. They get no special treatment. We ferry their messages for them because, since we work so closely with them to keep the Roracks in check, it is in our best interest to ensure that they are well-stocked and supplied. Our dealings with them have much to do with keeping ourselves alive, and very little to do with altruism."

He stood silently letting that sink in. Several of the men began whispering to each other, and he didn't try to call them to order.

After a couple of minutes, the red-faced man spoke again. "We have been led to believe that the Roracks were completely defeated, and we are now safe from their depredations."

"Well, I don't know who led you to believe that, but if you do, I have some property in the mountains to the east I'd like to sell you," Nassari quipped. He shook his head sadly and continued, "On the last day of the war, we killed nine thousand or more of those monsters on the plain. We had more than eighty dragons in the air and three thousand troops on the ground. Even with the plain around the fort soaked with their blood and littered with their charred corpses, a good two thousand of them escaped into the hills. Of those we killed, not one appeared to be female, and none were immature. I personally have never seen a female Rorack or one of their young, but I am fairly certain they exist. After all, the beast-men don't simply spring up from the very rocks fully formed and ready to plunder the countryside. Somewhere out in those mountains are a large number of those creatures who weren't under Warrick's control. We hurt them badly, but it's only a matter of time before they return to their old ways and begin raiding in settled lands again."

"Well, I thank you for your honesty, Rider," Millersen spoke up. "It's good to have an understanding of what we're up against. However, that doesn't really have a lot to do with the reason we are all here today. North Point is either a small town or a large village, depending on how you look at such things. However, there is fertile land lying fallow, and we have plenty of raw materials available. We could have a thriving community if most of the local merchants weren't stifled in their business dealings. More prosperous businesses would mean more available goods, and that, plus the natural resources of the area, would lure more men and women to move here, especially now that we are under your protection. We all know that what is stifling our trade is the difficulty of dealing directly with those in the capital and beyond. We can't take the road to do our dealings without Lord Bastian getting involved, and he charges us more than it's worth to import most trade goods. He can't be made to see that it's in his own best interest to let some of his competition thrive. If he would loosen up and let more trade through, or we could even get where we need to go to negotiate contracts without his involvement, we'd have more people come in and that would increase everyone's profit. What we need is a way to travel without his knowledge, but for all intents and purposes, he owns the roads, and his men watch so closely that a rabbit can't scurry past his lands through the brush without his knowledge."

"What makes it worse," the red-faced man, Ben Thorne, said, "is that most of us owe him money. That gives him the right to have a say in any contract we negotiate if he finds out about it. Since we can't go to the privy without him hearing about how much paper we use, he is always able to put his hand in and make sure that enough of our profit slides into his coffers that we can't even get out from under our original debt. If we fall behind on the payments, he can legally move in and take over. Because the man cooperated with Warrick completely, he was the only one allowed to do business as he pleased before the war ended, and that left him in the position he's in now."

"Bring me proof of that, and I'll see to it that he's clapped in irons and either sent to work in the mines, or hanged outright," Sellers exclaimed.

"Colonel," Millersen replied, "if we had proof we would give it over without hesitation. Any proof there is will be hidden at his estate. He's a noble, so you have to have strong evidence before the Council of Lords will allow you to issue a warrant to search the property, and since the evidence you need for that warrant is hidden where you need to search..." He trailed off as he shook his head at the futility of the situation.

"Well," Nassari spoke up, "one thing at a time. The first thing we need to do is work out an arrangement to get you the transport you need to do business. The Riders can't just fly off willy-nilly at the drop of a hat. Also, we have our own enclave to support, so we can't do it for free." As several of the merchants attempted to speak at once, he held up his hand for silence. "I didn't say we would gouge you for our services, but you have to agree that honest work deserves honest compensation. Riders are usually not born independently wealthy. We have little means to support ourselves, especially when our main job is patrolling the borders and keeping you all safe from the beast-men. You can't expect our people to help you increase your profits and not be compensated for our time and effort. We are willing to carry your correspondence, and even your persons on occasion, but we won't do it for nothing. Such exercise puts a strain on our draconic partners, and that increases their need to eat, and meat is not cheap to import."

The merchants settled down, and several of them actually nodded in agreement. Nassari smiled; he knew he had them on the hook: now to play the line a bit.

"Also," the Dragon Rider went on, "we still have the problem of getting the goods across Bastian's lands. There is an old road that is still passable that runs along the mountains, and fords the river near the eastern edge of his Lordship's territory. Since he charges by distance, as the law allows, you will still have to pay his toll for any wagons coming across that section of his land. However, that puts your goods on his property for less than one league at the southeastern-most section of his Lordship's property. He'll make it as expensive as he can, but it will still be profitable for you even after paying the toll."

"But, no caravan has gotten through on that road unscathed in over a decade. It runs right along the foothills. With the army pulled back to the southern border, how are we supposed to get past the Roracks? Or, are you saying that you have overstated the danger of the beast-men earlier?" Thorne's voice took on an accusing tone as he asked the last question.

"I have overstated nothing," Nassari shot back. "However, you have forgotten about the dragons' primary function in this country. We are here to protect Horne from the Roracks; that includes any

caravan traveling on that road. Since we will know when those caravans are traveling, we will be able to make sure we step up patrols
accordingly. Since it is open ground, three or four dragons should
have little problem keeping the wagons safe even from large bands
of the monsters, and you can compensate us for the extra patrols
by bringing herd beasts and goods to the fort." Before anyone could
object he added, "I never said the Dragon Riders wouldn't profit
from this arrangement, Gentlemen. I am simply pointing out that
we can all do so if we work together."

CHAPTER 27

"THEY WERE QUITE agreeable once it was pointed out that it would still be more profitable to pay us as couriers than to continue as they have under the watchful eye of Lord Bastian," Nassari said as Nadia poured wine-laced fruit juice into metal cups.

"Well, anything we can legally do to ensure the prosperity of the Riders is good, and doubly so if it goes against the interests of that… 'nobleman'. She said the last word as if she were speaking about something slimy and disgusting that one might find growing near an outhouse.

The two of them sipped their drinks and watched Pina and Wanda bathing in the river.

"I'm glad you invited me here," Nadia said. "We haven't taken a bit of time for ourselves in weeks."

"Yes, and thank you for bringing the food, the sandwiches were good and that sweet cake you brought was wonderful."

She was about to reply when they were both frozen by the harsh bark of a Rorack behind them.

Nassari was the first to move. He grabbed Nadia and nearly threw her down the steep embankment to the water. Not wasting time to do more than grab the belt with his scabbards attached that he had laid aside earlier, he was right behind her.

The bank itself dropped away sharply where numerous dragons had widened and deepened the river while bathing in this spot. The drop-off was about three feet above the water level and the depth was now about wing pinion height to the largest dragons, around seven to nine feet from the surface of the water to the sandy bottom, depending on exactly where someone was standing. The river, fed by mountain streams, was still quite cold, but neither he nor Nadia noticed as they went beneath its surface. What they did know was that beast-men couldn't swim; the creatures sank like stones and would be unable to pursue them beyond the banks at this point, though they could certainly go around the dragon-made pool and ford the shallows.

Nassari looked up as he kicked off the bottom and saw bright yellow flames above him. Breaking the surface, he could feel the heat of Pina's breath as she seared the beast-men who were screaming their rage at the top of the hill above the bank at the spot the two riders had just vacated. As Pina's flame stopped, Wanda's began and the whole area where the picnic had taken place was engulfed in fire. Even with cold water up to his shoulders, the heat was uncomfortable as he backstroked while searching for Nadia.

He turned around and saw that she was already climbing out on the opposite bank, and swam hard to catch up with her. She was unarmed, since her belt and blades, as well as her targe, had been left behind with the remains of their lunch. He wanted to reach her quickly because he could also see several beast-men circling around the pool toward her. When he reached the far bank Pina was already beside her Bond-mate and Wanda had just finished another blast of flame and was now moving to join them.

Nassari drew his weapons as he tossed the belt away so it wouldn't entangle his feet. He braced himself for the attack he knew would come and handed his knife to Nadia. He stood with her back to back ready for the next wave, but the beast-men never got the chance. Just as the humans were coming to the conclusion that, even with two dragons fighting alongside them, they would be hard-pressed just to survive against so many Roracks, the air was sundered by the thunderous roars of more dragons. Reinforcements, called by either Wanda or Pina, most likely both, arrived from the fort, which was less than a mile away. Some had their riders with them, but many were alone.

About half of them swooped down as a unit, and flame erupted all around those on the ground. Nadia was mostly shielded by Nassari's body, but his exposed skin was nearly blistered by the heat before he could get a shield in place. The dragons were too big to be protected by the humans standing between them and the flames, but they were several paces farther back, and their scales were more heat resistant than unprotected skin. None of the four of them were likely to complain considering that the wall of fire had saved their lives even if it left them slightly singed.

Nassari could hear the angry screams of the frustrated Roracks even above the tumult of the fires. They were clearly frustrated because they couldn't get at their prey through the blazing barrier that separated them. Their anger quickly turned to anguish, though, as the remainder of the dragons made their strafing runs on the monsters themselves. The battle was over as quickly as it had begun, and this time not one of the beast-men escaped back into the mountains.

Even though the vegetation was somewhat sparse, it took almost a quarter of an hour for the flames to die down sufficiently to allow the other dragons to land nearby. Adamus jumped from Beth's back before she was completely down, and Craig only waited barely long enough to be sure his Bond-mate was stable before dismounting.

"Sorry if you got a little cooked," Adamus said as he approached. "We had to do something to keep the main group of them from getting too close. There was room for a small margin of error, but not much; it was near thing. If Craig and I hadn't already been in the air…" He trailed off, unable to give voice to his train of thought.

"Yes," Nassari replied, "near indeed! The dragons have been bathing in this spot for weeks, and it's so close the plain we let our guard down. If those damned creatures hadn't made some noise before attacking, we'd both be dead!"

They all walked around the pool to where he and Nadia had been, only a short time ago, just finishing a nice peaceful lunch.

Nassari spoke as he surveyed the carnage. "Apparently, the beast-men have been observing this area and waited until they thought they had a good chance to survive before striking."

"You're right, of course," Nadia replied. "The others have been coming here in larger groups of no less than four dragons at a time. With two of them bathing and two of them to keep watch, it wouldn't have been prudent to attack before now. She dug into a pile of ashes with her booted toe. "We were careless and they were able to sneak up on us. Even our bond-mates were too distracted to notice the monsters. It was foolish to think we were safe, even though we were only a couple of miles from the fort itself." She picked up what was left of her weapons. The leather belt and scabbards had been reduced to powder, the grips were burned to thick ash, and the steel of her saber and both knives was bent and twisted by the heat even though they had been somewhat shielded by her other gear. She dropped the blades in disgust. "We should both have our arses kicked and be put on extra duty for a month! I wouldn't even expect this type of negligent behavior out our greenest youngsters!"

"Well, I don't know if I'd go that far, but you're right," Nassari said while he idly kicked at the pile of ashes that was all that remained of their saddles. "We got complacent and let our guard down, and it nearly cost us our lives. From now on, no one is to take our security for granted. If any riders leave the plain for personal reasons, they are to be accompanied by at least two others. If they are simply going for a bath, fine, they can take turns with one bathing and two of them standing watch at all times. If either of our bond-mates had been alert rather than lounging in the water below the bank, the Roracks would never have gotten so close without being detected." He took Nadia by the hand and began leading her toward the dragons. "The overall smell of dragons is not only pleasant, I find it soothing; however, the stench of the chemicals from their flames is neither. I want to return to the fort and get out of these clothes so that I can wash the stink of it from my body."

CHAPTER 28

"I KNOW IT'S OUR own damn fault, Del," Nassari said after telling Delno about the battle at the river and judging his friend's reaction. "We got careless. We've had reports from some of the soldiers about signs of beast-men in the area, and even our own scouts had reported seeing one or two groups of them. We just let ourselves get lulled into a false sense of security because we were so close to home."

Both men considered each other for a moment.

"On the upside," Nassari said cheerfully, "we managed to lure at least forty of them into the open and flame them, so that's two score less of the monsters."

"From now on, I want no one to go off in groups of anything less than three, more if possible and at least one of the pairs is to be on alert at all times!" Delno retorted with such force that the landscape of the Dream State wavered.

"Careful, Love," Geneva chided. Even the other dragons might have blanched at the look he gave her, but she just shook her head and said, "I understand. You're no angrier than I am; however, we are still here at the indulgence of the other dragons, and it's only because I'm a Lineage Holder that we weren't ejected for that outburst. If you want to take these two to task properly, you will have to wait until we get to Horne."

Nadia, who normally didn't accompany Nassari into the Dream State, kept her silence. It was apparent that she felt they deserved every bit of Delno's anger and was resolved to take her punishment.

Nassari kept his smile, but the look in his eye showed that he had had enough of it. "Delno," he rarely used his friend and commander's full name except to ensure that he had the man's complete attention, "I have already accepted that I messed up. Nadia and I have been pushing ourselves hard without a break, and when we got the chance to let go for a few minutes we allowed ourselves to forget, however briefly, that we might still be in danger. You can't possibly be any more angry with me than I am with myself; however, the incident is over, and continuing to dwell on what might have happened is pointless." Delno started to open his mouth but Nassari waved him to silence. "Going on about it now and getting us thrown out of here tonight will accomplish nothing. The precautions you mentioned have already been implemented, and patrols have been increased. We are no longer just watching for signs of those foul creatures; we are now actively hunting them." Before his friend could speak up to caution him again, he added, "Those doing the hunting are our most experienced riders, and they have been given strict instruction only to engage while still in the air and not to land under any circumstances. There will be no repeat of this afternoon's incident!"

"Good," Delno said and let the matter drop, though it was clear he wanted to pursue it further. "What have you found out about the rest of the situation down there?"

Before he could answer, Nadia spoke up. "If you two don't need me anymore tonight, I'm going let myself drift back to sleep. I have to get up soon and see to the morning patrols."

She faded from view and Nassari said, "She'll probably insist on flying the patrols herself to make up for our mistake, and not just this morning. I'll be lucky if I can get her to rest before she drops from exhaustion. What we need is more help with our duties, so we can relax once in a while."

"Are you two really that pressed?" Delno asked, concern of a different sort now edging his voice.

"Well, we have some help. Craig and Adamus are good at keeping the training going and making sure the kids stay out of mischief, and Will's been a blessing when it comes to interacting with the King and his counselors, but keeping everything running and all of the bonded pairs in line requires more than just a Lineage Holder. Nadia has been a gem and is especially good at coordinating our efforts with the ground troops, and Churney is very helpful when it comes to keeping the duty roster straight."

"You're right," Delno replied, and started to say more, but was cut off.

"To be completely honest, Del," Nasssari said before his friend could say more, "with just Nadia and I actually running everything, while trying to work out trade relations, as well as head off a war between Horne and Iondar, we're stretched more than a bit thin. Add the organization of the place, and the patrols, and interacting effectively with the military, and we have all of the responsibilities we can handle at this time. Keeping up with everything often pushes us right to our limits. It's no wonder, that when we had a chance to actually relax for an hour or so, we let our guard down. Even the dragons are becoming mentally exhausted."

They both stared at the changing clouds for a moment before Nassari spoke again. "Things will get better as some of the older youths mature and can be appointed squad leaders and given more responsibility, but that takes time." He drew a deep breath and added, "I know the original riders were able to do patrols and keep up with their duties with only three of them, but they didn't have to play politics and deal with setting up the Legion while doing it, and they had three thousand soldiers taking care of ground operations, so all they really had to do then was make scouting reports."

"I hadn't realized, Nassari," Delno said softly, "I'm sorry." Then he added almost angrily, "Rita and I should be there to help, but that nonsense with those rebels in Bourne wasn't finished just because we eliminated the main players. We've been weeding out small pockets of them ever since you left. We no sooner get one group then we hear of another. I'm reluctant to leave these youngsters here to handle this without us until things are settled."

The fabric of the place didn't waver, but Geneva coughed to remind him to watch his temper.

"My apologies," Delno said to both her and Nassari, "My anger is directed at the situation and perhaps a bit at myself for not being there to help." He shook his head before continuing. "Once Bourne is economically stable, my mother and the local constabulary will be able to manage whatever crops up, but until then we're stuck here. It seems many of the common people of Bourne trust me since we ousted Torrance, and for that reason, I'm able to gather information on the dissenters. Once these people have enough food in their bellies, and their farms and jobs are back to normal, the rabble-rousers will be pretty much ignored, if not outright shunned; however, don't look for us before late spring when the first harvest is near to hand at the earliest. Dorian's wedding is scheduled to take place right after the elections in the early spring; we'll probably see you and Nadia in Corice before Rita and I can get to Horne."

"We'll manage, Del, though, with the situation here, you'll have to give your uncle our regrets. I don't see how we're going to be able to leave with so much going on, and no other Lineage Holder here to take charge if I leave."

"Dorian will be disappointed, but if I talk to him well ahead of the event, I'm sure he'll understand and not hold it against you. Your mother will be disappointed though." He chuckled a bit and added, "Of course with the amount of attention she is receiving from Nadia's father she may not be too terribly disappointed."

Nassari raised one eyebrow for a second, and then simply nodded and went on with the rest of his news. "There is a small amount of good news. I've gotten some of the local merchants to agree to pay us for carrying contracts and other messages to and from the capital, as well as carrying negotiation offers as far away as Trent. The pay isn't phenomenal, but twenty-five percent of what the riders earn goes to the legion, and that will help ensure that we stay supplied. There is some decent hunting farther east, though we have to send three dragons to make one kill because they can only carry so much weight. However, if we can't get that damnable 'nobleman' here to loosen up on either the tolls or the price of his beef, we're probably going to have to send some of the youngsters off before winter to either stay with their parents or seek gainful employ in the same manner as Connor in Orlean to ease the burden during the leanest months."

"Not my first choice," Delno said.

"Mine either," Nassari replied. "I've even thought about petitioning the King to give us the same consideration as the military concerning tolls, but I'm hesitant to do that if it can be avoided, since such an act could lead to the misconception that we are nothing more than an extension of the Army of Horne, and could be construed as making us subjects of the country. I don't want to do anything that could threaten our neutral status, but if things don't change, I may have no other choice but to send the younger Riders off and appeal to Thomas."

Delno looked very thoughtful for a moment and then replied, "Perhaps you could import a herd and start raising your own animals."

"We actually thought about that. It seemed like a good idea to buy an entire herd from Lord Johnston in Trent and raise them here at first glance, but the little that grows on this plain is mostly sparse scrub brush and a smattering of tough mountain grass. If we try to raise cattle, sheep, or even pigs in sufficient quantity to keep the dragons supplied, we'll have to import feed for them, and that doesn't even take into consideration that a herd of meat animals kept here will most likely fret so much about the dragons that they won't eat enough to keep their weight up even if we can provide sufficient fodder. If we work out the logistical problems of feed and keeping the animals from being panicked by our own partners, such a supply of ready meat will attract the attention of Roracks no matter how many dragons we have watching; we'd end up neglecting more than a few of our other duties to protect our own herd."

"Then there has to be a way to purchase what you need locally," Delno said.

"I know you wanted to keep the Dragon Riders dependent on those we have sworn to protect, Del, but that Bastian," Nassari said the name as if it were profanity he was unwilling to use in the company of others, "hasn't shown the slightest interest in such generosity; all he cares about is his own profit, and anyone and everyone else can swing in the wind."

"I'll bet he'd be mighty put out if we allowed the beast-men to run unchecked on his lands!" Delno said, and both Geneva and Wanda growled at the thought of allowing their ancestral enemies any quarter.

"It might be tempting," Nassari returned, "except doing so with his farms where it would hurt him most would also allow the creatures to prey on others who have done us no wrong because their lands border his. Unfortunately, we have to protect him as vigorously as we protect everyone else or the rest suffer even more for his greed. There is one thing we have done, though; Elom has rigged slings that allow the dragons to comfortably carry metal ore and coal from the local mines so that we don't have to pay Bastian's tolls to transport the stuff. It takes longer than shipping by the wagon load, but it gives the youngsters something real to do that keeps them out of trouble and out of harm's way. I'm also going to have those who go to either the capital or to Trent carry the rigs and bring back less perishable root vegetables, and maybe some smoked meat from Ford. We may be lacking somewhat when it comes to feeding the dragons, but the smithy is coming along nicely, and we will have enough to feed the humans here. Also, if the dragons don't have to share their kills with us, the game they do hunt east of here will stretch just a little farther."

"All right, you've done as much as you can for the time being," Delno responded. "I'm actually more worried than I am angry with you over the incident this afternoon; make sure that Nadia knows that. Rita and I think of both of you as family, and we'd be devastated if you got hurt, or worse."

Nassari smiled, "Del, the only person in my life I've known longer than you is my mother; I understand."

Delno nodded, "I'd like to get down there and help, but I can't leave. I'd send some of the younger Riders along, but they aren't leaders, and that's what you need."

"We'll figure it out," Nassari replied. "However, there is one thing you can do for us if you are willing to send a couple of the youngsters the long way around."

Delno looked at his friend expectantly.

"Nadia and I lost most of our gear this afternoon. It was only by the barest stroke of luck that I was able to grab up the two new blades Elom and Wanda just finished making for me before we dove into the river. Nadia's sword, shield, and even her belt knife were lying next to her saddle when the dragons burned those monsters, as well as our stuff, to ash." Wanda looked as though she wanted to defend the dragons' actions, especially since it was probably her who had burned the saddles, so he quickly added, "I don't fault the dragons one bit. They only did what had to be done to save our lives. That being said, however, we still need new equipment. We can put something together readily enough down here using horse saddles and some extra leather and strapping material, and Nadia probably feels as though she doesn't deserve a new saddle at this point. However, I was hoping you'd take the measurements for both dragons and have something nice made by the same man who supplied our good mastersmith."

"It so happens that I'm going to that very shop to talk to Rupert tomorrow." At Nassari's quizzical look, he added, "If you will recall, I have a small, one person rig myself that was made during the campaign in Horne. Rita and I both need saddles that can accommodate not just us, but the children as well. And since the man is favorably disposed toward Dragon Riders, not to mention being one of the best saddlers in the known lands, we felt we might as well get our rigs made here in Larimar. I'll take the extra measurements with me and see what we can do, and send yours along as soon as possible, but it will probably be at least another month before you get them."

"Oh, don't worry about that. We'll have our own leatherworkers get something put together, probably like that rig of yours, to keep us from slipping off at altitude." Then he smiled and added, "I've just been a bit jealous of Elom ever since I saw that saddle of his, and I want something as comfortable and well made."

Delno actually laughed a little. Then he sobered and said, "As for the rest of it, I know that you and Nadia won't repeat a mistake, and you'll make sure everyone else is safe. Do what you feel is right to supply the Legion even if it means petitioning for the use of a government seal: after all, you took the job for good reasons and I trust you completely. However, don't get too embroiled in the politics of Horne. We're there to keep the Roracks from becoming a real threat, and to get our own place in the world secure, not solve their problems, especially since the King seems insistent on bringing such troubles down on his own head. Unless the situation with Iondar threatens the security of the Legion itself, don't get involved. If that means that Horne goes bankrupt fighting an insane war for asinine reasons, so be it. Hell, it might not even be a bad idea if Thomas gets taken down a notch or two. Dragon Riders getting directly involved in such a conflict, however, could put Dragon against Dragon again. What happened with Warrick had to run its course, but this conflict doesn't actually involve us and could easily bring about another situation like what happened to the Riders during the Clan Wars. We will stay neutral if it is possible to do so without destabilizing the area."

"Agreed," Nassari replied, "I'm just glad only two of our Riders come from Horne. Churney isn't the biggest fan of the local nobility anyway, and the one youngster who was born in this country should be easy enough for a Lineage Holder to influence even if he is tempted to get involved." Then he bid Delno a good night and faded from view.

Delno sat for many minutes just gathering his thoughts before wishing Geneva good night and fading off to sleep.

CHAPTER 29

"WELCOME, RIDER," LORD Laran said as he extended his hand to Nassari. Then, taking notice of Nadia who was wearing tight black pants and a form-fitting green silk tunic that sported an even deeper green dragon exquisitely embroidered as though the creature were perched on her upper chest with the tail curling not quite provocatively down around her right breast, he took her hand and kissed it. "Dragon Riders," he amended, apparently unable to tear his gaze away from the beautiful, petite young woman.

Nadia smiled sweetly, and Nassari nodded, though he didn't bow to the Lord of the manor. The man stiffened so slightly that another person, not so acutely aware of such subtle nuances, might not have noticed, but it wasn't lost on Nassari that the man thought himself to be better than Dragon Riders.

Nassari said "Happy Birthday, Lord Laran," as Nadia presented the gift.

"We took the liberty of commissioning this for you," Nadia added pleasantly, using the exact words that Nassari had instructed her before they arrived, as she handed their host a small but weighty package.

By mentioning that the gift was indeed specially ordered rather than bought 'off the shelf', she made it quite clear that the Riders had gone to some effort to make sure proper respect for the man and the occasion were observed.

The noble, again almost imperceptibly, relaxed from his previous demeanor. He took the package, unwrapped the silk covering and opened the wooden box. He sighed appreciatively as he lifted the belt dagger out and drew it from its sheath. The steel was finely wrought, and the handle was a solid piece of deep green malachite, round and carved in a spiral pattern. The guard and cap were both polished nickel. The sheath itself was dyed to match the handle and finely tooled with the Lord's house emblem on it.

"We agonized over whether or not to have the guard and cap made of silver, but it was pointed out that you would appreciate a fine blade and actually use it, so we opted for the more durable nickel," Nassari remarked. "It will hold a nice luster, and not scratch and wear so easily. The blade is, of course, made of fine steel and will hold a superb edge." The statement itself, on the surface, appeared to be simple, polite conversation, but the implication was that every detail was carefully thought out, and great care was taken to ensure that the gift was truly fit for its recipient.

"The blade is beautiful," Laran replied with a smile, "and quite unexpected. You shouldn't have gone to the trouble."

"Oh, it was little trouble," Nassari replied, by using the word "little" instead of the customary "no" he subtly pointed out that there was indeed a bit of effort involved on the part of the Riders. "You may have heard that we have set up a smithy at the Fort, but you probably haven't heard that we brought one of the finest metalsmiths in the world with us from Larimar, and since he didn't trust an apprentice with a gift for such an important man, he made the blade himself." Almost as an afterthought, he pointed to the malachite and added, "He's also quite good with stone when he puts his mind to it."

While Nassari's statements showed respect for the man and his title, they also emphasized how much time and effort the Riders had put into procuring such a present, and implied that Lord Laran should be equally grateful.

The nobleman unfastened his belt and slid the open end through the sheath. He then buckled it back into place with the new knife prominently displayed just above his right hip. He smiled and extended his arm to Nadia and said, "If you will both allow me, I would like to introduce you to the rest of my friends at the party," implying that such friendship now extended to the Riders as well.

Nassari smiled and nodded while Nadia took Laran's arm, and the two of them allowed themselves to be led into the main hall of the Lord's estate. Everyone turned to see the Riders being escorted by their host. The Riders understood that the man was trying to convey the message that they were subordinates, but, to Laran's annoyance (though the man hid it well), Nassari stepped up swiftly and walked proudly beside the Lord as an equal. It took more than half an hour for Laran to introduce them to every noble in attendance.

The two Dragon Riders politely refused the invitation to stay the night at the estate after the party, giving the very real excuse that there was still much to be done to set the Legion in order and they were needed at the Fort. It was almost dawn before Wanda made room in the courtyard to allow Pina to land.

Once inside with a cup of coffee in her hand, Nadia said, "I'm common born, so I have very little experience with affairs such as the one we just attended, but I know that there was more meat in what you and Laran didn't say to each other than there was in what you did; however, I thought the whole purpose of that was to try and get more goods and services without going through that local thief who owns the bulk of the land around here. Why didn't you at least bring up the possibility of trade?"

"You can't just walk into nobleman's birthday party and start talking business in front of guests," Nassari replied tersely. "These things have to be handled gently to keep from giving insult or appearing subservient. Everything we did, from giving him the gift in just the way we gave it, and saying just what we said about the blade, right down to the way we accompanied him into the room and interacted with his other guests was designed to show him that, while we are interested in being on good terms with him, we are his equals. By maintaining that posture while he showed off his 'new Dragon Rider friends' to the lesser nobles, we have also proven to those in attendance that we are equal to any of the nobility in Horne. Even politely refusing Lord Laran's invitation to stay the rest of the night because of our own pressing business showed that our concerns take precedence over anything having to do with him. Believe me, I would have loved to have simply stayed and slept in a big feather bed and dined on finely prepared food in the capital this morning. However, not only did we actually need to be here, staying would not only have made up for having the dagger commissioned, it would have put us somewhat in his debt in his mind, which is a situation that cannot be allowed to happen."

They sat looking at each other for a moment.

Before she could respond, he said more softly, "I'm sorry, Nadia. I am very tired and that came out more harshly than I meant. Such parties are trying at the best of times. Going to a soiree like that is not a pleasant trip, and you can never relax while you are in attendance at such an event. You must maintain constant awareness to avoid either giving insult or allowing yourself to become indebted to your host, especially when the purpose is to put the host in debt to you. That party, coming so close on the heels of almost getting killed, did nothing to ease my tension or help me relax. I would have preferred to avoid going altogether, but we could not do so without a damned good excuse, and believe me, in Lord Laran's eyes, our troubles wouldn't have been enough of a reason to refuse. If we had declined, he would have taken it as a direct insult, since he went to the trouble and expense of sending that invitation by special courier. I actually don't like him very much - something about those shifty eyes and that nasal whine of his puts me in the mind of Marvin Landry - but he is a powerful lord, and I'd rather have him as an ally than an enemy. You can be assured that our next communication with him will be all business."

Nadia smiled. "I'll bow to your expertise in this matter, my love." Then she downed the last of her coffee and added, "Since you are handling the affairs of state, I will be off to ensure that the patrols are in order."

She didn't stop to change before heading out to see that the riders assigned to morning duty were coordinating well with the soldiers who would be in the area.

"Well, the officers will be in for a treat for their sore eyes when she walks in wearing that outfit," he thought wistfully as she disappeared through the doorway. Then he went to his desk and looked to see if any correspondence had piled up since he had left for the capital at noon the previous day.

CHAPTER 30

"WE BURNED NEARLY fifty of them, Sir, but at least twenty more slipped into the rocks where our dragons' flame couldn't reach. They were after that caravan of goods: it's almost as if they knew something would be coming down that road. Is it possible they are working with some human agency again?" Jeremy asked. He had celebrated his sixteenth birthday almost a month after arriving in Horne, but while he was one of the newer Riders from Corice, he was also more mature and more quick-witted than some of the older "novices". Not only that, he felt embarrassed about his part in the incident on the trip to the fort and was anxious to make up for it.

"Good report, and work well done," Nassari replied. "As to your question: I seriously doubt it. The only people, other than the Vanners doing the hauling, who knew where that shipment was going and when, were the Riders assigned to protect it and the two merchants who stand to profit from it. We purposely keep that information a closely guarded secret to prevent Lord Bastian from finding out until it's much too late for him to get involved. We don't even tell the military, so Bastian can't complain to anyone in the capital that the local Governor is involved in hindering his trade. However, the secrecy also precludes anyone else finding out as well."

"I'm afraid that what happened with the caravan is simply a result of our doing our jobs so well in other areas," Nadia added. "Since the incident at the bathing spot three weeks ago, we have stepped up patrols so much around the plain and the occupied areas surrounding us that the monsters have had to find easier pickings to try and avoid the dragons. What happened today, especially since this is the first caravan to use that stretch of road in about ten years, is most likely coincidence, though we will keep an even tighter watch on that area from now on just in case."

"It might be a good idea to increase our patrols over that stretch of road anyway," Nassari said thoughtfully. "Bastian may be a lot of bad things rolled into one package, but he isn't stupid, not completely at least. He's clever enough to take note of patrol patterns and act accordingly if the day or so before each caravan comes through there are suddenly more dragons in the sky. Best if we keep him guessing by acting as though we have stepped up our presence in the area simply as part of our overall duties in Horne."

"I'll adjust the schedules," Nadia responded, "but we may have to pull a couple of people from areas more heavily defended by ground troops to do it. We have a lot of dragons here, but with so many of them running other errands for both the smith and the local merchants, not to mention bringing in foodstuff for the Legion itself, we're starting to get stretched pretty thin."

"We'll have to rotate our forces and rely on the soldiers to do their jobs on the ground. We've just started getting our supply lines sorted out, and I intend to keep that stretch of road open in spite of Roracks and grasping noblemen!"

Realizing that his two commanders might be about to get into an argument, and not wishing to be in the middle of it, Jeremy spoke up, "Since my report is done, and I'm off duty, I'll go and tend to Dina. She wants a bath, which means we need to catch up to the others who flew patrol with us before they are done." He quickly saluted and left the office before either of them could think of a reason to call him back.

"I know we need to use that road, Nassari, but if this doesn't pay off soon, and I mean more than one wagon out of six, we will need to send more of the youngsters off to fend for themselves, and that will leave fewer dragons to fly patrols than we have now."

"I understand, Dear. I have already made arrangements to meet with Laran two days from now." Before she could complain about the timing, he added, "I know, it's been nearly a month since we attended that party, and there has been no real communication between us and that particular noble, but he's not only one of the chief players on the Council of Nobles, he's also a businessman himself. He's been working hard trying to get the king to back down on his stand concerning Iondar. Even if Thomas is too pig-headed to realize that he's bankrupting the country, the business owners who had dealings in the south aren't. Lucrative contracts that have been in place for generations have been lost because, despite the posturing of kings, the people of Iondar still need those goods, and there are plenty of tradesmen in Trent and other countries who are more than happy to suddenly find new avenues into that market. Iondar is a desert, but with rich gem and precious metal deposits. They have contracts with the Elves to help harvest and manage products from the rainforest to the east, but the Elves are very careful about how much of those resources are taken each year, and they aren't as interested in pretty rocks or shiny metal as humans are. Iondar can't simply take up the slack by further exploiting the forests without risking making enemies out of their close friends and creating conflict on their eastern front as well. The Iondarians must procure what they need from somewhere, and most of the people in that desert kingdom couldn't care less where they get the stuff so long as they don't go without. Once Thomas stops posturing and opens trade again, the businessmen of Horne will find themselves competing in venues where they previously held a monopoly, so Laran is actually doing all that he can at the moment to help us."

"You've explained this to me and I understand it, but we still need meat for the dragons. The only way we are going to get that is to ensure that we can either bring it up from Trent or force Bastian to sell to us at a more reasonable price."

"That very issue will be one of the first things on the agenda when I meet with Laran, my love, you can bet on it. These stingy, stubborn, thick-witted nobles are going to either help us with this problem, or we will bring in our own herds and use dragon fire on anyone who gets in our way. I originally didn't want to force Bastian to sell to us at government rates, but we now have two eggs and possibly as many as three more on the way, and no other animal alive eats like a dragon hatchling. I have accepted that I have to tighten my own belt, but I'll be damned if I'll continue to ask the dragons to do the same!"

CHAPTER 31

"WE'RE COMING UP *on the farm now, Jeremy; we should see the battle in a few seconds,*" Dina *told* her bond-mate.

Jeremy looked back over his shoulder at the other riders following. "*Tell Trina and Allan to move off a bit when we strafe; we need to overlap our runs, not burn the same ground twice.*"

"*Done,*" Dina replied as she began angling her flight downward toward a group of about fourscore Roracks that was moving to engage about sixty soldiers who had formed a shield wall formation around their wounded comrades.

Jeremy wanted to take a moment to make more corrections to his formation, but the men on the ground didn't have any more time. If he and the other riders didn't do something in next few seconds to slow down the beast-men's charge, those soldiers would be overwhelmed.

The squad had been scouting when the desperate call had come in from one of the single teams on patrol. He had purposely not flown over this district because they had done so the day before and it was clear, and he had been instructed to increase his patrol area.

Not wanting to believe the numbers of those monsters reported, Jeremy had hoped it was an exaggeration by the young, less-experienced rider. Now that he could see for himself, he realized she

might have actually underestimated. He could tell that two separate farms were under what appeared to be coordinated attacks
by at least two hundred Roracks split into two groups. The soldiers he and Dina were desperately trying to save had been moving in to help the people of the farms and found themselves facing
a superior force. He wasn't sure how many men were dead, but it
looked as though more than a score of the human troops were on
the ground, while those still on their feet were getting ready to try
and stop a determined charge. That was all he had time to take in
as he erected his shields to protect himself and his partner while
she dipped her head to blast a path of destruction right in front
of the formation of men and continue directly into the advancing
enemies.

Jeremy could hear the screams of the beast-men that started out
in rage and ended in hideous pain as they met their deaths by Dina's breath. He had little compassion for the monsters, but even so,
he still wished he could block out that terrible noise. As Dina pulled
up, her flame bladder temporarily empty, he looked back again. The
others, two on either side of the lead run, were doing the same. They
had used a V-shaped attack. The two on his immediate left and
right were just pulling up and the last two, farther out but still overlapping, were just running out of flame. Most of the monsters never reached the men, but some, still smoldering and half blinded,
made it through the flames and hit the shield wall with every ounce
of strength they still possessed. More than a score of them made it
through to their goal.

Jeremy's heart fell. He and the other riders were under strict orders not to land so long as there was any threat, no matter what.
He knew that none of the dragons in his squad would disobey com-
mands that had come from a Lineage Holder and that were designed
to keep him and the other young riders alive. He also knew that
two of his squad members hadn't yet reached their sixteenth birth-
days and shouldn't be doing more than scouting. He hadn't waited
around for permission before answering the call for help; there
would probably be hell to pay when he got back to the fort.

"*Damn it, we have to do something!*" he mentally shouted to his bond-mate.

"*We can't use flame now, or we'll burn our own allies,*" Dina replied. "*If we landed, you'd only add one more sword to the fight, and two of our group shouldn't even be here. The only thing we can do now is hope we got enough of them to give those soldiers a chance while we hit that large group on the next farm over before they decide to come and help their own. After we scatter those, we can swing back and run down any of these who are still alive and trying to make it back into the hills.*"

"*I know that's our only option, but I don' have to like it,*" Jeremy responded. "*Those are men down there, and I know many of them from the garrison. It goes against my instincts to leave them like this.*"

He shook his head at the futility of the situation. Even though Dina couldn't see the gesture she could feel his frustrated rage. Finally, he said, "*Let's do it!*" as he mentally indicated the direction of the next target.

After scattering the Roracks on the second farm, they returned to the men who had retreated from the site where the dragons had strafed the beast-men. With none of the living creatures in evidence, Jeremy told Dina to land and to have Trina and Allan join them on the ground. He and Allan were both fair healers and could possibly save the lives of the more severely wounded men.

"*The other three want to land and help as well,*" Dina reported.

"*They can help most by staying in the air and making damn sure those we sent into the hills at the other farm don't realize they're not seriously hurt and come back!*" Jeremy replied angrily. "*Keep them circling overhead and tell them to stay on high alert. We aren't out of this yet. Also, find out where those other teams we called for are. The fort isn't that far off; we should have had help by now.*"

An officer limped up to them as Jeremy dismounted.

"I can't say I wasn't glad to see you, Rider, but I had hoped there would be more of you," the man said by way of greeting.

Jeremy was acquainted with most of the soldiers who supported the Legion; this man's name was Lieutenant Grayson.

"We're stretched pretty thin at the fort," Jeremy replied. "Do you have any immediate medical needs you can't meet yourselves?"

The officer nodded, "We've got supplies for basic first aid, but a few of the lads are hurt worse than our medics can handle."

As Allan joined them, Jeremy said, "Show us to the men hurt the worst, we'll try and help them, but if those Roracks regroup and come back, we'll have to get into the air quickly." At the man's look of despair, he added, "Don't worry, we have no intention of leaving you to your own devices. We'll do everything we can to keep those monsters off of you, and I've called for help. Now, let's see to those wounded men.

An hour later, the worst of the wounded had been stabilized and the soldiers were set to move out to safer ground.

"You saved a lot of lives today, Rider," the young officer said, "first by flaming those fiends, then healing those who were beyond our skills. Some of them still need more attention, but we can move them safely now. I'd like to stay and secure these farms, but my unit is just too torn up. We've made litters, and we're moving out."

"The Roracks haven't completely withdrawn," Jeremy replied. "Those we haven't killed outright have retreated into the rocks where the dragons can't flame them. They won't come into the open and engage, but we can't dig them out either. We'll escort you to safety in case they are just waiting for us to leave so they can attack you again. Keep your men as far away from cover as possible. If those beast-men attack while you're retreating, I want them on open ground so we can burn them to ash long before they get to you." Then he added, "Did anyone make it off of those farms?"

"We managed to protect the civilians from the first farm where you found us. They were hightailing it to Northpoint last time I saw them, but no one made it from the other stead."

Jeremy only nodded and walked to Dina to mount up.

"Keep a protective formation over those soldiers until we're absolutely sure they're safe," he *said* to Dina as she launched skyward.

CHAPTER 32

"LORD LARAN, I have sources in the capital of Iondar to which you are not privy," Nassari said tiredly.

He had been speaking with the nobleman for less than half an hour, and already he was feeling tense and drawn out.

King Thomas might be pig-headed, and ultimately the cause of the current problems, but the high-born businessmen sitting on the council were not nearly as cooperative as he had been lead to believe they would be.

"I have had highly placed spies in the businesses of Iondar since before you ever arrived here in the south, Rider; don't be so quick to dismiss what I bring to this meeting," Laran shot back almost angrily.

"I am not dismissing you; however, my sources are placed directly in the royal palace, and the only way they could be closer to the king would be to sleep with the man. The Iondarians are extremely put out by Horne's lack of gratitude concerning the help they sent during the last crisis. All it would take to get trade flowing again isn't even a direct apology, but a simple acknowledgment of Iondar's gesture of not only sending their own King's elite guards, but also the fact that they sought out and brought aid from the Elves. Both instances not only provided us with Iondar's most capable fighters, but the foresight of sending for the Elven Hunters supplied us with highly trained soldiers who brought necessary experience gained from centuries of hunting and fighting the Roracks in their own territory. Because of those two groups, working in unison with the forces the Riders brought from Corice, we were able to spearhead the operation and gather valuable intelligence without our enemy's knowledge. If Thomas would simply draft a letter recognizing that, we will be able to not only reestablish trade but stop a war that Horne simply cannot afford to fight."

"While you do have a point, Rider, you obviously don't know King Thomas. He is stubborn under the best of circumstances, and he has never given in to what he sees as coercion through threats against the might of the armies of Horne."

Nassari hung his head and shook it slowly from side to side. "Lord Laran, it is the lack of military might, coupled to your king's current posturing that has put you all in this situation. Horne's army lost over half its men fighting against Warrick's beast-men, and that is only part of the problem. The Kingdom is nearly bankrupt from fighting the last war; another would deplete the coffers completely. Even without another conflict, Horne will be years, perhaps decades, paying its current debts."

Nassari rose to his feet and paced while he spoke, "Your soldiers are already on reduced rations due to drafting so many of your farmers, as well as lack of funding. While Horne puffs its chest and makes rude gestures at its neighbors, the beast-men, who are still a very real threat, are once again beginning to come down out of their mountains in numbers sufficient to threaten the commoners who provide the food and goods for everyone, not to mention the economic havoc the foul creatures create when they destroy anything they can't carry off."

"The King tells us that the Riders have the Roracks in check; are you saying he is lying to us?"

"While I am not calling the man a liar, I have noticed that he tends to put a brave face on events in the north. What you must remember is that dragons are quite effective against large numbers of Roracks on open ground. The monsters don't engage on such terrain unless we happen to catch them off guard, which doesn't happen often. Mostly, they have returned to their old ways of raiding in small groups, either from ambush or using cover right up to the point of an attack. The dragons help spot them and burn them when we can, but we must have ground troops to hunt them down and finish them off, and Thomas has twice pulled more men back from the northern front to reinforce the south. If something isn't done to ensure that we have infantry to support our efforts, the most fertile lands of Horne will be ravaged by the beast-men long before anything decisive happens on the southeastern borders."

"He's pulled more troops away from the north? I wasn't aware of that." For the first time, Laran appeared shaken by the news Nassari had brought.

"Yes," Nassari replied, "yesterday nearly a third of the remaining troops were formed up and marched south. Colonel Sellers has repeatedly sent for badly needed reinforcements and supplies, and instead of giving what is asked for a large portion of his remaining men have been pulled away. He and his troopers are making do with what they can scavenge and hunt, and the little we are able to provide for them at our own smithy. If this situation doesn't change in the very near future, the soldiers will be forced to pack up and escort the residents of the area to the capital as refugees."

Nassari overstated the urgency, but not by much, and he added, "The Roracks seemed to sense the loss of another two hundred troops and have increased their raiding proportionately. Since yesterday afternoon, two groups of the creatures have hit farms in what could be coordinated raids, one of which was less than two miles from Northpoint itself, nearly right under the watch of the newly established fortifications. The second farm, though slightly farther out, was still close enough to see what went on. The Riders managed to kill about half of the group at the closer farm and drive off the remainder before they could cause damage or harm any humans, but the other raid resulted in the deaths of everyone on the farm, and all buildings, and thus all stored grains, destroyed."

"I see," Laran began but Nassari cut him off.

"That's definitely not all, Lord Laran. Our dragons are working as hard, and in many cases harder, than any human in the area. They bear the brunt of patrol as well as doing much of the fighting. Normally, a dragon will eat about the equivalent of one steer and one or two pigs three to four times a year. With the amount of work our dragons are doing, that need increases to at least double that. We cannot afford to feed all of them because we simply cannot afford to pay what the local cattle breeder charges for his animals, and since he owns the lands, we cannot afford to pay his tolls to import cattle from Trent. We have considered raising our own, but that would require that we neglect the rest of Horne to watch over our own herds so close to Rorack territory. If something isn't done to help us get food for the dragons at a reasonable cost, we will have to send more than half our Riders off to other lands to seek gainful employment. If we cut back the number of dragons patrolling, the depredations will increase drastically, and there will be little that we or the soldiers can do about it."

"Tell me Rider," Lord Collins, who had been a fly on the wall until now, asked, "how is it that only three Riders were all that was needed to keep the beast-men in check before now?"

Nassari gave Collins his most winning smile; he was actually ready for such an asinine question. "Before the war, Horne kept more than three thousand troops along her northern border. The beast-men seldom raided in groups of more than fifty strong, and the role of the Dragon Riders was, for the most part, scouting. When Warrick's advance Riders moved into the Fort and displaced the three Riders who had been in residence there, no one took notice, because, initially, Rorack incursions tapered off to almost nothing. Some even accused the original Riders of having neglected their duties. However, it was actually because the only three trustworthy Riders had moved to the capital and Warrick moved in and began controlling the beast-men that raiding diminished. He was very subtle as he went about his schemes, and indeed his own identity was kept a closely guarded secret. He didn't actually move into the fort himself until the army had vacated the area. He first kept his

Roracks in check in the north to lull everyone into believing the threat was gone. Simultaneously, he had his beast-men begin raiding heavily farther south. Then, once the local ground troops had been pulled back to more "meaningful duties" protecting the southern lands, he had the monsters under his control invade by the hundreds and seize entire towns. By the time everyone figured out that they had been fooled into complacency, he and his Roracks, not to mention the young Riders he had swayed to his way of thinking, were firmly entrenched, and it took our combined forces to dig them out."

Nassari paused for a moment to give both nobles time to digest the lesson in recent history before adding, "As for your question, Lord Collins, we need more dragons because we have fewer than four hundred ground troops trying their best to do the work of more than three thousand. Without the dragons, those soldiers will be overwhelmed, and without replacements, they will soon perish and leave the northern border completely undefended. Since the bulk of Horne's arable land is in the north, leaving it open to the Roracks in such a way will eventually starve the entire country."

Lord Laran cleared his throat. "I see your point Rider. Lord Collins and I do not constitute a majority of the council and therefore can't speak with such authority. I do, however, intend to call a meeting of the council this very day and bring your observations before them. I will also see that the local cattleman you spoke of is ordered by the council to sell his stock to the Fort at the same price charged to the military. You have convinced me of the great need to heed your warnings, but we will most likely require assistance convincing the King. If you could keep a Rider stationed in or near the palace for the time being to facilitate communication, it would be helpful."

"Actually, one of our most experienced Riders is already staying there now. He is not only a veteran of the Rorack war but is the royal nephew of the King of Corice and well-versed in court etiquette. His name is Will Okonan, and he is the brother of Delno Okonan; if there are developments that require me to come to the capital, you need only contact him. In the meantime, I will have my contacts in Iondar try and sway the King there to keep the lines of communication open." Nassari only paused for a moment before adding, "With that, gentlemen, I bid you farewell; my duties in the north can only be put off for so long."

CHAPTER 33

"**H**ASSIR, YOU NEED to listen."

"I am the ruler of Iondar, as was my father before me. I have allowed you a great deal of privilege here because you are my relative and a respected Dragon Rider; however, don't think that you can talk to me like I am some petulant child!"

"If you don't want to be spoken to in such a manner, then perhaps you should act more like an adult and listen to reason, Cousin," the Rider answered to the implied threat that he would be asked to leave the palace.

Hassir simply shook his head and replied, "The king of Horne has directly insulted not only me, but our finest warriors, and he has since compounded that insult with injury by cutting off all trade relations. I have every right to respond accordingly and send troops to our borders as he has done on his own side."

"You have every right to ensure that the soldiers of Horne stay on their side of the border, but you also have an obligation to your own people to get trade flowing again. It was you who first threatened an embargo," Brock retorted. "This nation is fixed on land that is mostly desert. While some of that land is mineral rich, those mines cannot supply the other goods that our citizens need. Many of the commodities that we use have to be imported. We have begun to get more goods from merchants in Trent who are anxious to open new markets, but that is a small country and what is coming in does not meet the needs of our people. Like it or not, Horne is large and has more agriculture and industry than Trent can hope to compete with. We must seek a way to end this embargo and get trade moving across their border, even if that means accepting some insult from that pompous ass who sits on their throne."

Hassir sat for a long moment simply looking at his cousin before he spoke. "I understand all of that, Brock, and I agree to some extent. But Thomas has taken this beyond his initial insult and moved soldiers to lands that are, by past treaty, supposed to be left open by both sides. That treaty was signed at the end of the last war between our two countries almost four centuries ago."

"I remember that, Hassir. I was there and helped Corolan get the kings to sign the agreement. It came at the end of a war that nearly ruined both countries. What makes you think that there would be a drastically different outcome if war breaks out now?"

"Thomas might be moved to be more reasonable since his forces and his coffers were so depleted by the war they just went through. His armies stand, according to our best estimates, at about fifty percent of prewar strength, and he is hard-pressed to even offer apologies to other nations for not paying any interest on the debts Horne incurred when the call for help went out. We sent two hundred of our best fighters, but I was wise enough to keep my armies intact in case any other problems cropped up."

"Do you honestly think that Thomas isn't aware that you could have sent a much larger force?" Brock nearly shouted. "Hasn't it occurred to you that such knowledge is the reason he gave insult at your gesture in the first place? The man may be a self-centered egotist, but he isn't completely stupid. While I agree with you in principle, I can also see his point. If he had simply kept his mouth shut and not given direct insult, I would even be more understanding of his actions."

"You go too far, Cousin!" Hassir said angrily. "Yes, I sent far fewer men than I could have, but I must look to the preservation of my own before I can help my neighbors. You and the other Riders handled Warrick quite well, but with Horne's manpower and money so depleted, and only the elves as allies, I must still maintain enough force to ensure that others who have long coveted our mineral wealth aren't given the opportunity they have looked for over the years. Without a strong military presence of our own, the very countries who have become our new trading partners, but more importantly, and certainly more immediately, Tyler, might get it into their minds to move against us."

"Tyler?" Brock asked incredulously. "The nobility in that tiny kingdom haven't been inclined to military action in at least three generations, and even that was nothing more than a border skirmish with Trent over mining rights in a small section of the western mountains that are the natural barrier to the Rorack lands. Why has that kingdom suddenly become such a threat?"

"As to why, well, that is anyone's guess, though I suspect that it has much to do with the greed of the young king who took the throne less than three years ago. Tyler has minerals in the western mountains, yes. They mine mostly iron, copper, and tin, but very few precious metals. It is suspected that there is great wealth hidden away under the rocks that the beast-men squat on; however, the cost of extracting that wealth is more than more even the mighty nation of Horne is willing to pay in money and manpower to get it. So the men of Tyler look to our desert because they would love to get their fingers into our gold and silver production, not to mention the gems and other minerals we find here in the south. They made attempts to get us to deal directly with them and allow their mining cartel to 'manage' our resources shortly after King Ronald took the throne. When we said no, they got insistent and implied the use of military force. We sent their ambassadors back home after giving them a good look at our own armies, but the situation has deteriorated since then."

Brock rubbed his jaw thoughtfully. "I had no idea there was trouble of that kind brewing. I was so caught up in what was happening in Horne that the thought never occurred to me that trouble could come from such a small country, although with what has taken place in the far north recently, I shouldn't be so surprised. After all, much of the fighting we did in the last war actually took place in what is now the Duchy of Bourne. Do you think that Warrick's influence could have anything to do with this?"

The king shook his head. "I seriously doubt it. Tyler never had any real affiliations with the Riders in the first place; something about some slight to their king or some nobles, or both made by dragon riders long before I was born, perhaps before you were born as well. That line is one of the few that never had any kinsmen chosen as suitable candidates to be presented at a hatching, and that might have something to do with it." Hassir replied before returning to the original subject.

"After we sent the ambassadors packing, the authorities in Tyler started arresting Iondarians from caravans on the flimsiest of charges," he continued. "Rather than fine them or put them in jail, they turned them over to slavers and allowed them to be taken off and sold in Llorne, the only other country that allows the outright ownership of human beings. It has become such an issue that our own caravans heading for Corice have taken to using routes that send them directly through Ondar, which lengthens their travel time to trading partners in the far north, but avoids Tyler completely, and caravans from other nations won't hire Iondarian guards to travel farther north than the town of Ford in Trent. Of course, changing the caravan routes has hurt the merchants of Tyler and further angered Ronald to the point that he has made implied threats that his army, which he has been steadily building in numbers since he was crowned, will force 'trade' if we don't relent and at least resume normal caravan routes again. He is as stubborn as Thomas on this point, and he refuses to deal with the damned slavers and make them leave our people alone."

Hassir paused for a moment and then shook his head as he returned to Brock's question, "No, the trouble from Tyler appears to be a completely local phenomenon in response to being frustrated in their efforts to obtain our mineral wealth. However, it has escalated, especially since Tyler sent so little in aid to Horne. The only things they sent were weapons and other goods for the military, not men. Therefore, Tyler isn't now suffering the shortages, especially in manpower, that the other nations are experiencing. We may eventually see this turn to war. If that happens, we will need to keep our borders clear and hope that our neighbors in Trent will remain neutral if they cannot be persuaded to take our side. Otherwise, we could find ourselves with only our Elven allies against whatever comes from both directions."

Brock was silent for a moment before saying, "Trent is now openly trading more goods than ever before with Iondar; they will probably stay neutral at the very least. Still, with all of that, it is very much in the best interest of Iondar to get trade relations with Horne back to normal. Horne's armies may be depleted, but they are fierce fighters, and well trained. If we have a war on that front, it could distract and weaken us enough for Tyler to walk in nearly unopposed. However, with Horne as allies once again, Tyler would not dare to move against us."

Hassir suddenly looked as though he was weighed down by more than the fifty years of life he had seen, and he said, "I know that, Cousin, but I have my pride as well. If we can at least get Thomas to admit that we sent aid as asked, and pull his troops back from those positions where he has stationed them, I would be willing to give in and open trade again, but Thomas is an exceptionally stubborn man."

He closed his eyes and sighed. Then looked at the rider and added, "We will see what your northern friend with the Iondarian name can do on his end. In the meantime, you have my word that as long as the soldiers of Horne stay on their side of the border, our troops will do the same."

CHAPTER 34

"THEY ARE MOVING *toward the soldiers, Jeremy; here we go*," Dina said to her Bond-mate before angling her flight in preparation for making a strafing run against a large group of Roracks. As planned, she and the other four dragons flew down with the rising sun behind them. To further avoid alerting their foes until it would be too late for the beast-men to run into the sheltering rocks, all of the dragons quelled their urge to roar out a challenge to their ancestral enemies.

Jeremy, the leader of this squad, was keenly aware that he was the youngest Rider to be given a position of real authority at the fort, and, while proud of himself, his responsibility weighed heavily on him. He understood full well that he was answerable if anything went wrong. He and the others in his squad hadn't acquitted themselves so well their first time in a real fight. They had mostly been relegated to keeping the monsters at bay so that the soldiers and a handful of farm laborers could escape from a group of over two hundred beast men.

He checked and rechecked the formation to ensure that it stayed tight and on target. One dragon—her Rider's name was Terresa, or Terri as she preferred to be called—was out of position, and he had Dina relay orders to get her where she would do the most damage without causing harm to the other dragons or the soldiers on the ground. He had just enough time to be sure she had complied before becoming lost in the thrill of riding a flaming dragon.

There were about seventy beast men in the raiding party moving into position to attack a small farmhouse just north of Lord Bastian's lands. The ground troops patrolling the area numbered about half that. Without the aid of the dragons, it would be a slaughter in favor of the Roracks; with the dragons tipping the scales, they should be able to pull off a victory with few casualties, and hopefully no deaths.

The dragons hit the monsters from behind in perfect formation, overlapping their fire so that as one dragon pulled up another was already in place continuing the run. Jeremy was pleased to note that no more than two score escaped the flames and the soldiers didn't even get singed. He had his squad circle around and strafe from north to south running parallel to the line of men who had taken defensive positions. This time, the men felt the heat, but none were likely to complain, since that run killed more than another score of the enemies before any human had to get into the fight.

The beast men left alive redoubled their effort to reach the men. They weren't particularly smart, but they were clever enough to realize that their only chance to escape the dragons' fire was to close as quickly as possible with the soldiers. Jeremy called all of his squad off and had them circle the area. They would run down any lone Rorack who tried to get away, but they couldn't help the men on the field without landing, and Nassari and Nadia had again made it quite clear that no Dragon or Rider was to engage those monsters on the ground. If the soldiers couldn't handle it, one or two more swords probably wouldn't make that much difference, anyway. They could do the men more good by watching for Rorack reinforcements coming out of the rocks, and then, once the area was secure, landing and using magic to heal any injuries.

CHAPTER 35

"THE RIDERS DID their best, Colonel," Nassari said as the military governor gave him a full report about the morning's raid.

"I don't fault your riders," Sellers replied, "especially since so many of them are so young. I understand the lad who commanded that group this morning is barely sixteen, and was the same boy who led the squad that swooped down with enough daring and skill to allow my men to retreat from that fiasco just south of here a couple of weeks back. I don't know any grown men who could have handled either situation better." He paused for a long moment before continuing. "No, Sir, I don't fault your Dragons or Riders at all, and neither do any of those who were out there. I am simply stating facts; we lost three men who died outright, and five more will be recuperating for at least a week, even with the magical healing they received after the battle."

"I understand, Colonel, but what would you have us do? We aren't much more effective on the ground than your own men. The Dragons are powerful, but much of their fighting strength has more to do with airborne tactics and flame than prowess as ground fighters. They may be large and strong, but they can be overrun and killed just like anyone else, and their fire is harder to use and more likely to cause harm to friendly targets once they have landed."

Sellers shook his head tiredly. "I had almost forty men in that patrol, and only about half that number of beast men got past your people. Outnumbered two to one they still managed to kill three men and wound more than a dozen more. They fight hard and give no quarter under the best of conditions, but they will run away when they are obviously outnumbered. It goes against the grain to suggest it, but, perhaps, in the future, your dragons should leave them a small escape corridor so they don't fight like cornered animals."

"The Dragons won't like that at all," Nadia said as she entered the room.

Both Nassari and Sellers bowed to her as she came through the door.

"The Dragons may not like it, My Lady," Sellers intoned, "but we can't afford to take the casualties. I don't like to lose men at all – no commander does – but during conflicts such as these, losses are to be expected. However, being stretched so thin, even the loss of three men makes a difference. If we could get reinforcements from the capital, I wouldn't even suggest that we give those monsters the chance to slip away and cause trouble later. As it is, though, I have less than four hundred men to patrol an area normally watched over by more than seven times that many. Having so many Dragons available is good, but even with the eyes in the sky and the help of air support, we are losing ground, and every lost man who can't be replaced puts us a little closer to not being able to do our jobs at all."

"Will is at the palace, and he seems to have the King's ear to some extent," Nassari said. "Also, Lord Laran has been fully apprised of the situation here in the north and intends to speak to the king about sending more soldiers. Perhaps between the two of them, they can convince Thomas of the need and get him to pull some men back from southern border patrol."

"In the meantime," Nadia interjected, "I will inform the squad commanders to change their tactics. We will no longer hit the beast men from behind and cut off their escape routes. I don't know if the creatures are actually capable of coherent communication as we think of it, but they can still relay their feelings to others about how dangerous it is to raid in human lands if we send a portion of them running back into the hills with the hair on their arses still smoldering."

CHAPTER 36

"NO, NO, NO" Thomas intoned loudly. "I told you specifically that I wanted Will Okonan's bond mate Saadia to be prominently featured, and her color must be right!"

"Sire, I am trying to comply with your instructions, but there isn't enough of the blue pigment I need to render that particular dragon in her exact shade. The mineral needed to make the pigment is expensive, and…"

As the man hesitated, Thomas replied hotly, "This Kingdom may have suffered some shortages recently after such a costly war, but we are not completely bankrupt yet. There should still be enough in the treasury to buy some rocks to make paint!"

"It isn't just the expense, Your Majesty." Will stepped up to come to the artist's aid. "The mineral itself comes out of the gold and silver mines of Iondar."

Everyone held their breath as the Dragon Rider put that specific name to Thomas's current frustration. The last thing anyone wanted to do was antagonize their liege by telling him that something he wanted was out of reach in that particular place.

Thomas's face went red, but he didn't fly into an explosive fit. He calmed himself and said, "Surely we can get some of this pigment from a country that is still dealing with our stubborn neighbors.

Send off to Trent and see if you can find what you need there."

"The problem with that," Will spoke up as though the subject hadn't drifted into dangerous waters, "is that the pigment is usually only bought in small quantities. We couldn't find enough for our needs if we scoured the whole of Trent and Ondar. The amount of this pigment that we need will have to be bought directly from Iondar. In fact, it's most likely that we will have to go straight to the mines and purchase from them before what they have on hand can be divided up and sent off in smaller shipments."

"So," the king's voice took on a treacherously conversational tone, as though he were barely keeping himself in check, "are you telling me that the mural I've been planning for nearly a year can't be finished the way I want it because the Iondarians are again slighting this country?"

"Not at all," Will replied without emotion. "The pigment is there, and the miners would most likely welcome any buyer who wants to purchase a large quantity of the stuff, but with the trade embargo in effect, no one from Horne can make such a purchase without also making himself a criminal. That particular crime is now, by your own order, punishable by death."

Thomas leaned close and whispered, "Careful Rider, you edge on going too far. Don't throw my own words back at me."

"It is because I am a Rider that I do go so far, Your Majesty. I do not look at this issue as a loyal citizen of Horne, but as a sworn Legion Rider whose interest is in keeping the peace all the way around. This embargo is hurting your country very badly, and now it is thwarting you personally. All it would take to lift the trade ban would be to pull the bulk of your troops back from the south and send them north where they are truly needed and rescind the order making such trade a crime. The Iondarians want some kind of an apology, but even that won't stand in the way of goods moving once the merchants are free to deal with each other again. After all, Iondar and Horne need trade goods flowing, and ultimately Horne needs Iondar's money that comes from the goods sold to them."

Thomas showed so little sign that Will's words had an effect that anyone not carefully schooled in such political practices would have missed it. Will, however, saw the man's whole demeanor soften slightly and knew he had made his point. It would still take some time, but the situation could be brought back from the brink of war; it just had to be handled carefully. For at least the thousandth time, Will wished that his brother were in charge of the Fort and Nassari could be here in the capital playing politics. Will's uncle had taught him well, but Nassari could feel the subtle nuances of such situations on an instinctual level, and his magical ability to influence others with his words would be invaluable.

"Perhaps, Rider, perhaps," Thomas whispered back. "However," he raised his voice to a more conversational pitch, "for the time being, we will work around that particular color. If you would be so kind as to continue to help the artist, We would appreciate it."

Will recognized the use of the royal pronoun as a dismissal and simply returned to the sketches laid out on a nearby table.

CHAPTER 37

THE SMALL BLUE dragon landed nearly midway between the soldiers of Iondar and the heavily armed "trade mission" from Tyler. Her Rider remained mounted but waited patiently. After about a quarter of an hour, since it was plain that he would neither get closer nor leave the field, a group of fifteen men from the Tyler mission approached him slowly. Many of them were armed and carried their weapons as if they meant business. As they got within about twenty-five yards, Leera sent a burst of intensely hot flames that reached nearly two-thirds the distance between them. Brock yelled for them to lower their weapons and proceed, or the next blast would not miss. He was playing a dangerous game, but he was also confident that he could shield his bond-mate until she could get airborne if this "negotiation" didn't go well.

The men from Tyler hesitated for a few moments until Leera spread her wings as if to take flight. Then one man began barking orders and weapons were hastily lowered. The man in charge pulled a small white cloth from one of his pockets and began waving it madly. Leera relaxed and he, along with three others from his company, walked forward. When they were close enough to be heard without shouting, he spoke.

"What is this about, Rider? We have no quarrel with you. Why have you led this force," he waved his hand to indicate the more than two hundred Iondarian troops who stood waiting for the outcome of this parlay, "here and hindered our progress?"

"Hindered your progress? I am not the one trespassing on Iondarian soil," Brock replied in a tone that made it clear he was in no mood for playing politics. "Why have you brought this force of armed men into my homeland?"

"As we have stated in the letter we sent two days ago, this is merely a trade mission from Tyler charged with reopening commerce between our two kingdoms."

Leera snorted her contempt at the statement, "A trade mission that requires three hundred men, all armed to the teeth, on a road that is patrolled and kept safe by our own forces?"

The men from Tyler were taken aback at being spoken to directly by the dragon.

Brock saw no reason to stop her, so she continued, "I read that letter myself. It was a barely veiled threat of dire consequences if your 'trade envoys' were not allowed into the capital. Did you expect that the men of this country would simply allow you to march heavily armed soldiers across these lands and enter the capital city, and even the palace, like a conquering army? Have your leaders all taken leave of their senses?"

The man in charge got over his shock at being openly addressed by the dragon and stated, "We have been given orders to open trade between our two countries by whatever means necessary. Our leaders understand full well that we are suffering because your king has allowed his caravans to use alternate routes to the north as well as refusing to allow our traders to travel south. This situation must come to an end, and we have come to make sure that such an ending is favorable to us. We are but the first group sent; there are more to follow if we cannot bring a satisfactory conclusion to this business."

This time Brock responded, "The trade caravans you speak of are independent agents; the routes they choose are their own affair. If your king didn't openly sanction the illegal taking of Iondarian men to be sold as slaves, our caravan masters wouldn't have to take routes that lengthen their trips and cut into their profits. As for why this situation has gotten to this point, that can also be laid squarely on your own doorstep, with your failed attempts to force Iondar to all but hand over its mines to your king." The man from Tyler started to object, but Brock raised his voice and continued, "However, we are not here to hammer out trade agreements; we are here to send you back to your masters with a clear message. This country is well able to defend both its citizens and its wealth. If you, or anyone else, have the audacity to return with such a force, or even one that is larger and more well-equipped, they will be met with greater strength and stopped. You are three leagues inside our borders, and it is almost noon; you have until the sun sets to get back across that border. Any who have not done so by then will be killed without mercy."

Before they could protest, Leera shouted loud enough to get everyone's attention, "This negotiation is over, and you will be issued no further warnings. The next time you deal with me, you will regret it for as long as it takes to burn to death."

Then she spread her wings and launched herself skyward. Before she was two hundred feet in the air, she turned and angled her flight properly and made a strafing run, flaming a long line between the Iondarians and the leaders from Tyler. The men were in no real danger, but she made sure they felt the heat of her flames.

Later, in the Dream State, Brock spoke, "Leera and I sent them packing, Delno, but one dragon won't be enough to keep them out if they are determined, and my cousin's forces are now split between two fronts."

Delno watched the swirling red clouds for a moment before saying, "I've barely got Bourne settled. The crops are planted and doing well, and it should be a plentiful harvest. We can't be sure we've weeded out all of the dissidents, but my mother has been accepted by the population at large. The rebels were never popular with the commoners in the first place, so that means that Rita and I will be able to leave here with at least four of the Riders we were training. I'll leave the oldest two to continue training the children who bonded with Saadia's hatchlings, and the six of us will travel right after my uncle's wedding at week's end. We would have been able to leave before now, but the wedding was postponed until late spring for political reasons. With so much happening down there, I'd like to send my regrets, but Dorian and Corice have done so much for us that it wouldn't be right. Besides, with everything else going on we may need the allies in the near future." He paused before returning to the subject directly at hand. "Rita, though she is more familiar with Trent, knows many of the nobles in Tyler. We'll stop there on our way south and see if this Ronald can be reasoned with."

"Are you sure that's wise? The man has already proven that there is little he won't stoop to in order to get what he wants. You may be a bonded Rider, but you aren't immune to poison."

"We won't be staying for dinner, Brock. I intend to take your and Leera's example and state my case in plain terms the man can't ignore. I am going to make it clear to him that the Riders have a vested interest in what is happening to the South, and that we will tolerate no interference from Tyler. There are no Riders who come from that country, and none who bother to stay in residence there since they are not treated as well as they would be by the royalty of Tyler's neighbors. If Ronald moves to take on the South, his forces will be met by dragon fire! We can't allow this young man to cause further instability in the area. He will either see reason, or we will instill enough fear in him to guarantee his capitulation."

"Well, my cousin will be glad of this news. I will tell him tomorrow; perhaps it will allow him to turn his full attention to getting his differences with Horne sorted out before violence erupts on that front."

Again, Delno was thoughtful for a few moments before speaking. "Tell him that we will not let Tyler become a problem. However, we will not get involved in a war between Iondar and Horne. We have too much interest in remaining neutral to take sides. If push comes to shove, he and Thomas could be moving toward a bloody conflict that will not only cost many lives but could easily bankrupt both countries." Brock looked like he wanted to come to his kinsman's defense and Delno held up a restraining hand. "I know that Thomas has provoked your cousin, and if there weren't so much riding on all of this, I might even be tempted to back Iondar, but it's not just the Legion headquarters that worries me. Horne is now, and has always been, the buffer force between the rest of the civilized lands and the beast-men. Unless Hassir is ready to move in and take on that responsibility, he needs to think twice before he does anything to escalate this situation."

This time it was Brock's turn to be contemplative. Finally, he said, "I don't believe anyone has put it that bluntly before just now. I will apprise him of the full repercussions of a war with Horne tomorrow after I let him know that the Dragon Riders will be dealing directly with Tyler. Hopefully, the assurance concerning Tyler will make him more open to a diplomatic solution with Horne."

When Brock had faded from view, Geneva said, "I have found him, Delno. He isn't happy about being used as a messenger, but he has come."

"What do you want, Delno?" the Rider asked tersely, as he and his bond-mate coalesced into view.

"Hello to you, too, Kern." Delno responded and turned to the dragon, "How are doing, Serrin?"

"Much better, Delno Okonan." Serrin possessed one of the finest female voices Delno had ever heard. "My wings aren't fully functional, and there is no surety that I will ever be able to successfully fly in a mating competition again, but I can now hunt on my own and carry back what I catch. I have even started taking Kern on short flights, though getting off the ground is still difficult."

"Skip the pleasantries, Delno," Kern interjected.

"Kern!" Serrin said sharply, "You may not like this man, but there is no reason to be antagonistic toward him either. He was simply asking about my condition out of polite concern."

"No reason? Polite concern? He and Brock are responsible for you being crippled in the first place."

"My injuries were the direct result of our actions when we flew against these people. The crippling was caused because I threatened to flame anyone who got close enough to heal me until the full effect of that compelling stone had worn off. By that time, the natural healing powers of my kind had caused my injuries to set in such a way that my flight has been hindered. If I had to hold someone besides ourselves responsible, it would be Warrick and Hella, but they are dead. It is past time to put this behind us."

"It's hard to put it behind us when we are imprisoned here."

"It could have been much worse. It was Delno Okonan who came up with the solution that is giving me the opportunity to heal my injuries. If we hadn't accepted this fate, instead of being free to wander the forests of the elven lands I would be unable to fly at all, and you would be staring at the damp walls of a small stone cell."

Kern shook his head slowly, but he held his tongue as he stared at his bond-mate.

Finally, Serrin nodded and said, "Now, be nice," before turning to commune with Geneva and leaving the two men to their business.

"I have important news concerning Iondar, and I need you to take a message to the Elf King. He will most likely have a reply and you can contact me here tomorrow night."

"Aren't you afraid that I might distort the message to cause you trouble?"

"I thought of that. I understand that you and I will most likely never be friends." Delno paused for a moment. "You have your faults Kern, but you are bonded to Serrin, and I believe that such a good person as she couldn't possibly have connected magically to someone who is wholly without virtue. I think that if you agree to this, you will deliver the message undistorted. You may be a pain in the backside, but you're not a liar."

"So why should I help you?"

"Because doing so will not only be in the best interest of all concerned, it will directly aid the Elves who have done so much for you and Serrin."

Kern stood silently for a moment watching the clouds. Then he nodded once and said, "Give me the message, I'll see that it's delivered and contact you with a reply

CHAPTER 38

"I DON'T KNOW HOW you did it Rider, but those reinforcements who just arrived will certainly help, though I had hoped for more than three hundred," Colonel Sellers said as he entered Nassari's office. "I've been sending requests for weeks and you have one meeting with Lord Laran and an entire company of troopers marches into my post carrying all of their own equipment and almost half of what I've been begging the capital to send."

"It was no great feat Colonel, I assure you. I simply pointed out that the Roracks don't give tinker's damn about embargos, or who might have insulted whom. Then Lord Laran and the rest of the council were able to make the king understand that he needs to protect his richest farmland if he wishes to keep the rest of his army, and even himself, fed through the winter."

"We had actually hoped for more men than that," Nadia interjected.

"I had hoped for at least four times that number, My Lady," Sellers replied, "but I'll take any I can get. With another full company added to those troops I already have, we can now not only keep those monsters from advancing in many areas, we will be able, with the help of the dragons, to take back some of what we've lost. It's just unfortunate that one of the main reasons we can recover that territory is that the beast-men are doing what they have always done, spoiling the land and moving on. If they were truly interested in holding that ground, we'd still be hard-pressed to retake it even with the reinforcements."

"I wouldn't start any major offensives in next few days, Colonel," Nassari replied. "We need to get that farmland back, but I have only just gotten word that Lord Bastian has been ordered by the council to sell us beef at the same price he sells to the army. That has been so long in coming that even more of our Riders have gone off in search of employment, or at least fertile hunting grounds for their bond-mates. While the army's numbers may have nearly doubled, the number of Riders here at the fort has dwindled to just over twenty. With the new supplies we will be getting, we can recall most of those who left, but it will take several more weeks before they can all be found and brought back. I don't look for them to arrive before summer solstice at the earliest."

The military man was quiet for a few moments before nodding his head to show that he understood the full ramifications of what Nassari had just said. Then he spoke, "Still, there are four fairly large farms clustered almost due south of this very place that were taken. Most of the farmers and many of their hired hands were killed, and I lost some good men, but the crops have been sown and we've had regular rain. My scouts tell me that the beast-men are still there, but haven't bothered with the newly sprouted plants because they have been slaughtering and eating the livestock and using the place as a staging ground for further raiding. If we can retake and hold those farms, we will not only kill the largest group of these monsters we've seen since Warrick was defeated and stop the raids coming from there, we'll have more than two hundred acres of food come first harvest, and we'll still be able to get men in to replant. Even if it isn't enough to send any food on to the capital, those crops will go a long way toward keeping all of us fed in this area when the growing season is over."

"I'm familiar with that land," Nassari replied, "it's pretty much open ground. I'll ask Wanda to reinforce Jeremy's squad to work with the men you send to secure those farms." Nassari was quiet for a moment while he communicated with his bond-mate. "There, eight dragons should be enough for what you have in mind. However, for now at least, the other areas we pulled back from are much too close to the mountains, and therefore too close to cover for the dragons to be effective, so once those farms are back in human hands, we should concentrate on not losing more territory rather than re-taking what we've had to give up."

"I don't really like it," Sellers replied, "but I understand the reasoning behind it. You're right; three hundred new soldiers aren't enough to go on the offensive. At least you're giving me one of your best squad leaders; the men who've worked with that young man before will be heartened to hear that."

Again Nassari was silent for a moment. "Speaking of whom, Jeremy is at the front gate. I understand that retaking those farms must be a carefully planned operation. It stands to reason that he should fly you back now so that he can help with the logistics to make sure this is a fully coordinated effort. While your officers and he plan the attack, the other riders can get their own gear in order. With luck, those farms will be back in human hands shortly after sun-up tomorrow."

Sellers didn't say anything, but he was taken aback. That was as close as he was likely to get to an outright dismissal from the leader of the Dragon Riders, and it puzzled him. It only took him a second to recover his composure though; he bid Nadia farewell and took his leave.

Nadia waited just long enough to be sure the Sellers was out of earshot before rounding on her husband. "What the hell was that about? You all but gave him the bum's rush out of here. Since when do we treat our friends like that?"

"We treat our friends like that when those friends might get us involved in extensive military campaigns we are not prepared to fight."

For a long moment, neither said anything as they stood staring at each other.

"Look, Nadia, we've lost more than a dozen bonded pairs who went in search of greener pastures since we arrived. We have two dozen pairs ready to work with the armies of Horne, not including Will and Saadia, since they are required to remain in the capital. Many of them are just children. If Rita finds out how much actual combat flying those kids are doing, she will come down here and take them away from us as well, especially if we allow them to get dragged into a protracted campaign without sufficient ground troops." He paused and shook his head before continuing. "I'm just glad that Jeremy had a birthday shortly after we arrived, or we'd be in danger of losing our best squad leader. Not only is he more fit for the job than most of the older riders, he's been really anxious to prove himself since he and Sarah got into trouble for sneaking off on the trip from Corice. That's made him just daring enough to be effective, but still cautious enough to keep his squad safe. He cannot, however, do it alone!"

"We keep the younger ones in the air, and their bond-mates are fully mature and have fought Roracks before," she retorted angrily, "I don't put children in harm's way." She drew several deep breaths to calm herself. "Do you think I haven't thought about simply sending the older dragons out without their riders? They won't do it, and the kids refuse to let them go, and even Wanda has been unsuccessful when she ordered them to relent. The dragons and their riders simply will not work independently of one another. We did manage initially to get a couple of them to try it, and the kids were so upset that the dragons were ineffective because they were worried about their bond-mates who had been left behind."

"I understand all of that, Nadia, but you know damn well that Rita won't see it that way." He quickly switched back to the original subject, "Which brings us back to the main reason I got Sellers out of here so quickly. He is anxious to use his reinforcements to retake all that we've lost." She started to make a reply, but he held up his hand to forestall her comment and went on. "You heard him yourself. He asked for at least twelve hundred men. He only got a fourth of that number, and now he's thinking of going on the offensive. I agree that we need to retake those farms before the Roracks realize what they are trodding on and destroy the lot of it, but the rest of the territory they have pushed us from is simply grassland, and most of it is used by Bastian to graze his herds. He uses that land to fatten his cattle, and I am loath to risk the lives of good men simply to increase his profit."

"You should have pointed that out to Colonel Sellers; he has no more love for our local nobleman than we do."

"That's true, but Bastian is already complaining to the Council of Lords that we and the army are not protecting his interests. His complaints are falling on deaf ears for the moment, because the rest of the council members are in dire straits as well, due to the embargo. When that changes, our military commander may have to explain why he didn't protect the Lord's interests, and I want him to be able to say that the Riders were unable at the time to provide air support. A large part of the reason I dismissed the man was so that he isn't complicit in intentionally leaving those lands to the mercy of the beast-men."

Nadia was thoughtful for a moment before saying, "We'll have to run those creatures out of there eventually; the longer we wait the harder that might be."

"I know that, but for now those were Bastian's prime pastures. Without them, his herds have begun to lose weight and his profit is threatened because of it. He will be forced to sell a good many steers at lower prices so the rest of his herds will have more food and remain heavier. Otherwise, he will lose even more overall when he has to sell his entire herd for less profit. He has no qualms about increasing his interests at the expense of others, and I don't mind turning the tables on him. He is coming to town to negotiate the price of those very beasts with both us and the military. I intend to get our money's worth."

"I don't know if I like the way this is going, my love, but you are better at such dealings than I am. However, that doesn't do a thing to resolve our situation in the long run. We still need more soldiers, and the merchants of this country still need to be able to ship their goods to Iondar. Fallon isn't the only city in this country that produces goods, and the others are suffering as well."

"Will has found an angle that might get Thomas to relent even if he doesn't actually issue an apology, and Brock has placated his cousin enough that open warfare won't be initiated from the Iondarian side. Delno is on his way south now, and after a few necessary stops, including one to speak with Hassir, he will come here, and we'll get this sorted out if it isn't resolved before he arrives. Until much of what is planned bears fruit, we need to continue to handle the day-to-day operations as best we can."

CHAPTER 39

"**I** WILL NOT MISS *the signal*," Dina *said* as Jeremy twisted from side to side, straining against the leg straps that held him in place. He was trying to keep the ground troops in his field of vision while the dragons circled high waiting for the men to indicate that they were in position so that he and the others could begin the aerial assault and drive the enemy into a waiting ambush. It had taken the whole day to get this coordinated effort planned, and he was anxious to see it through.

"*I know you won't, Dear, but I don't want to take any chances. These monsters took control of this land on my watch, and I intend to exact a full measure of pay-back.*"

"*They took control because there are so many of them, and we had too few dragons and soldiers to keep them from doing so. No one faults you for what happened on these farms.*"

"*Tell that to the families of the people who died here.*" His anger was turned inward at himself, not outward at his bond-mate, but the words still stung.

"*The leader of those soldiers said, and both Nassari and Nadia agreed, that all of the dragons present did everything they could that day. Over half of the common people down there during the battle were able to flee because we covered their retreat.*"

"*I understand that intellectually, Dina, but in my gut, I still feel responsible for those who didn't make it. I hear their dying screams every night in my sleep, and I suspect that I will for some time to come, even after we've put paid to this account today."*

"*Jeremy, this is the largest and most organized group of beast-men to gather since the war. They were over two hundred and fifty strong. We had five bonded pairs in the air, and just over a hundred soldiers on the ground. Short of putting down and fighting with your blade, you did everything you could. If we had landed, we would be dead now and unable to take back this territory. You have been beating yourself up over this for nearly a month, I suggest you put that away for time being and stay focused!"*

"I am focused," he replied. "I have no purpose in this world right now other than what is going on here. That is why I am trying so hard to keep the soldiers in sight."

"*You can't keep the soldiers in sight because there is a dragon in the way directly below you; now, sit still and let me watch for the signal.*"

"Very well, you watch." As he spoke, he looked back over his shoulder at the other seven dragons who were under his direct command. "*Sarah and Jewel have dropped back; tell them to tighten up the formation.*" He wished again that Sarah hadn't been added to his squad at the last minute. He had distanced himself from her since they arrived in Horne, and he wasn't keen on re-establishing the relationship. He quashed that entire train of thought and added, "*I want overlapping runs with no breaks. Our orders are to see that none of these abominations gets away today, so no mistakes.*"

"*I have relayed your instructions,*" Dina said flatly after a long moment of 'silence'.

Jeremy watched Jewel correct her position in relation to the rest of the formation.

Suddenly, a flashing light in the far field caught Dina's attention. One of the men was using a mirror to indicate that all of the ground troops were in place.

"*There's the signal; the men are as ready as they can be for this. Keep my wings and eyes shielded just in case!*"

The reminder about shielding wasn't necessary; Jeremy, though very young, knew his job better than some Riders twice his age. He glanced back again long enough to make sure the other dragons were maintaining their assigned positions.

One of the farmhouses was a large log cabin. The leaders of the beast-men had most likely taken control of it because the thick wooden walls kept them safer than the thin boards of the barn that was the only other structure still standing on any of the four farms. The log walls would certainly stop any arrow or sling bullet; however, against dragon fire, they were only temporary shelter against the first attack. Dragon fire could turn hardened steel to a molten puddle; the logs of the cabin caught readily, and the roof was near collapse by the time Dina finished her attack.

The dragon didn't make a typical strafing run. She pulled up and hovered in front of the cabin about forty-five feet off the ground, her wings barely twenty feet over the heads of the Roracks outside the structure, and slowly swung her head back and forth, bathing the whole cabin in a cone of fire for the full eleven seconds it took to empty her flame bladder. The beast-men who ran outside during the attack caught the full brunt of it as they emerged through the front door that was the only exit.

From their encounters with Rorack raiding parties, the Riders and some of the officers in the army of Horne had begun to piece together the typical organization and behavior of the raiders. The Roracks didn't appear to have a command structure like human soldiers. They seemed to follow chiefs who delegated to sub-chiefs. The lower status members tended to stay close to their leaders in a somewhat organized circle when they were not on the move. The closer to the leaders a given Rorack was, the higher his social standing in the pack, with the lowest ranking individuals making up the outermost ring.

As Dina attacked the cabin, the rest of the beast-men moved toward the center, tightening their circle formation, and getting as close to the flames as they could stand. They barked what Jeremy assumed to be challenges while hurling any object they could lay hands on. Some carried crude spears, but rocks made up the vast majority of the weapons thrown. Thanks to Jeremy's shield and her own natural armor, Dina wasn't hurt by any of it, but the heat from the fire was so intense that Jeremy instinctively covered his face with his arms.

As Dina's flame ended, she flapped hard to gain altitude. It would take her a moment to refill her flame bladder. As she moved out of the way, another dragon took her place and repeated the performance. The fire from two dragons destroyed the cabin completely; any beast-men who didn't make it out to perish directly in dragon breath died when the burning roof fell inward during the second blast. By the time the second dragon pulled up and gained altitude, there was nothing left of the building but a few burning timbers, glowing coals, and a lot of ash.

The monsters were clever, but not overly intelligent. The concentric rings of Roracks grouped tighter and tighter, with all of them trying their best to do something to bring their ancestral enemies to the ground so they could overwhelm them. The dragons had other plans, though.

The farm, the largest of the four taken, had a small rutted track leading from the cabin to the planted fields. On one side of the pathway was a grass field where dairy cows and milk goats had been kept; on the other was a pasture for keeping sheep so that they would be near the main barn when it was time to shear them. The remaining six dragons angled their strafing runs to burn the now-tightly packed crowd of beast-men while making a clear swath of flame down either side of the path. Since it was the only way out that didn't immediately lead to certain death, the Roracks, some of them with their hair smoldering from the intense heat, ran headlong in down the open corridor toward the waiting soldiers. Just as the men on the ground began firing a hail of arrows at those out in front of the now panicked beast-men, the dragons turned and angled back to flame those Roracks running out of the open path, effectively closing the 'safe' passageway between the fires along either side the narrow track.

It was a slaughter. Any beast-men who managed to survive the heat, flames, and arrows long enough to actually reach the soldiers were cut down as the men attacked them in numbers of no less than four to one. In the end, not one Rorack survived, and there were only about a dozen soldiers wounded, though none seriously.

"That was some nice work, Rider," the captain said as Jeremy dismounted. "We got them all this time; not even one escaped back into the mountains."

Jeremy only nodded as he surveyed the scene.

"You don't seem happy, Sir," a young private standing near the captain observed, "more than two hundred of those monsters down and no major casualties; that's quite a victory for our side." The young man, one of the fresh replacements just in from the capital, was in awe of standing so close to a Dragon Rider.

Jeremy rounded on the young man with fire in his eyes. The private was no more than a year older than him. Dina growled a warning at her bond-mate, and he got hold of himself. Though his words were still harsh, he spoke softly and kept most of the recrimination out of his voice. "It would have been a bigger victory if we'd had the manpower we needed and could have beaten them the day they first attacked. As it is, we still lost more than two dozen good people here, and that's not counting the soldiers. We can't even give them a decent burial because what's left of their bones has been cracked to get the marrow out before being strewn around with the bones of the cattle and sheep."

The private just stood there with a stunned expression. The captain patted him on the shoulder and sent him off to help with the rest of the clean-up.

"I understand your feelings, Rider, but what's done is done, and no one can be faulted for the way things turned out. I was here that day, too. We did all we could for those people. We were lucky to get so many out alive and not lose most of the troops I had. If it hadn't been for you and the other dragons covering the retreat, it would have been a whole lot worse."

Jeremy looked up angrily, but before he could make a reply, the captain spoke softly. "Look, son, you're not much more than a boy, and this is the first real fighting you've seen; hopefully, it will be some of the last. However, what you need to remember is that this is war, and people sometimes die in war, and not all of those dying are hardened soldiers. Some are just plain folks who get caught in the middle. I know you want someone to blame for this, but if there is someone responsible, he isn't here. Let it go, and concentrate on what we've accomplished, not on what we've lost."

Jeremy looked down at the ground as he nodded. Dina rubbed his back tenderly with her head. He would have liked nothing better than to just sit down and cry, but there was still much to be done. The corpses of the beast-men had to be gathered in piles away from the fields so the dragons could burn them to ash. He turned without another word, and he and Dina headed off to help.

CHAPTER 40

"**I** WILL NOT BE spoken to in this manner within the walls of my own palace!" King Ronald said hotly. "Know this, Rider, Tyler has never had strong connections to your kind, therefore, you won't be allowed to continue your outright threats!"

Delno stood proudly and showed no outward sign that Ronald's words had made an impression. He shook his head and replied, "You may posture all you like, Your Majesty, but you will listen to and heed my words." His tone remained respectful, but his demeanor certainly wasn't one of subordination. "The Dragon Riders have a great interest in what transpires to the south, and we will not allow you or anyone else to take territory in that region by force of arms. If you attempt to move against Iondar, as you have threatened to do, your army will be met not only by the soldiers of that country, but by the entire Legion of Riders as well. Horne and Iondar are much too vital to allow you, or anyone else, to alter the delicate balance that exists down there."

Standing behind the leader of the Riders was a tall hooded man who had been a passenger on one of the other dragons. He had remained so still the whole time the king and Delno were having their exchange that until he moved no one else really noticed him. Now, he stepped forward and pushed his hood back to reveal slanted eyes set in the almost delicate features of his face. His platinum blonde hair was pulled back into a ponytail, which revealed his pointed ears. His overall appearance was that of a youth of no more than his early twenties, but his eyes shone with the wisdom he had earned in the two centuries he had spent traveling the world.

The king was shocked to silence. Elves were sometimes seen in Tyler as they moved to and from the Rorack territory for the annual culling hunts, but one of their kind had not stepped foot in the palace in four generations of men.

"I am Walker Longleaf," he stated without revealing any emotion. "I was contacted by my father, the king, and asked to accompany Delno Okonan on this mission."

Ronald finally found his voice, "This kingdom has no quarrel with your people, nor do we want to start such a fight. Why do you walk into Our palace in disguise and stand with those making open threats against the sovereignty of this country?"

Walker inclined his head to the king before responding, "I wore no disguise. If I had, you would not have seen me at all. I wore my hood because it has been my experience that when an elf enters a room such as this one, all attention is then turned to him, and I felt, as did my father, that you should hear this man," he pointed at Delno, "before I spoke." He paused for a moment and then continued in a soft, soothing tone, "As for your second question, it is you who threaten the sovereignty of the Elven Nation."

"That's absurd," Ronald protested, "We have made no threats against the elves. Our quarrel is with Iondar!"

"You've made no threats against my people? Are you quite sure?" he asked; his voice still neutral. "The letters that your 'trade envoys' carried specifically mentioned that not only do you have your eyes on Iondar's mineral wealth, but you intend to further exploit the rain forests to the southeast. Those forests lie squarely in Elven lands, and we are very careful of how much exotic hardwood is harvested by the men of Iondar under contracts that have been in place for centuries. According to your own words, you would have men move into those lands and clear-cut trees that take more than a century to coax into full growth. Many of the medicines that the elves make and ship to human lands to help fight infections and other ailments come from symbiotic plants that grow on those trees and nowhere else." He paused for a few seconds to let his words sink. Then with just a hint of disgust in his voice, he added, "You would simply destroy what you don't understand for the short-term profit that would come from selling that hardwood, and in the process, you would obliterate that forest and a large part of our way of life along with it. That we cannot allow."

"W-we may have acted in haste concerning the forest," Ronald stammered. "We have always believed that the forests are situated in Iondar. We had no idea that the elves had either claim or interest in the place."

Walker spoke up and cut him off, again keeping voice neutral, "Yes, you have made the mistake that so many humans seem to make concerning my people. You believe that since we live so far away and don't actively get involved with human activities that we are content to sit deep in our valleys and commune with nature rather than take part in 'more worldly affairs'. Let me assure you, Your Majesty, we watch the world carefully, and have done so for a long time. We have books in our libraries dating back to times before humans bothered with recording your history. We have seen what human greed and expansion can do when left unchecked."

"Still," Ronald regained most of his composure, "none of that gives you or these Riders t.he right to enter Our palace and make demands…"

"I am not making demands!" Walker startled everyone by raising his voice. "What Delno Okonan told you is true! There is a delicate balance in the south. Horne is the buffer between the beastmen and the rest of the world, and Trent and Iondar, but mostly Iondar, are the buffer between Horne and everything else. The rulers of Horne have always held an iron grip on their own lands, and they have looked time and again for ways to take more territory. The threat of Rorack incursion is what keeps the armies of Horne entrenched in the north rather than moving on their neighbors to the east. However, if your army weakens Iondar, Horne will, as history has taught us, once again seek to expand its borders through military might."

Ronald and his advisors were struck silent by the revelation.

Before anyone could interrupt him, though, Walker continued, though in a softer tone, "The men of Iondar reached our shores many generations ago fleeing from a war of their own somewhere over the sea. They came in five ships that were then stripped and used for building materials. We helped them establish a large settlement, and they went on to carve a nation out of a wasteland. In the many centuries since those early days, we forged an alliance with those men. When Horne began to show itself as a force to be reckoned with, the men of Iondar stood with us against that newly formed country's southeastern expansion. My people have worked hard over the years to keep our alliance with Iondar both due to our traditional friendship with that nation, and to maintain the balance of power in the south. Throughout that time, we have tried very hard to stay out of the affairs of others such as Trent and Tyler. However," again he raised his voice for emphasis, "make no mistake, we keep close tabs on the doings in the kingdoms of men, even as far off as Bourne and Llorne. Elves will do whatever it takes to keep our people safe and our way of life intact. We will, if it comes to it, march openly with Iondar, but think on what our hunter clans will be doing here while the bulk of your army is busy fighting several hundred leagues to the south."

Ronald was nearly spitting with rage, but it was Delno who spoke first. "We have said what we came to say, Ronald. As you have pointed out, this is a sovereign country, and you are the ruler. My only other parting words to you are these. We have no intention of staying perched on your city walls to force your capitulation, but neither do we make idle threats. Iondar will be defended against any force sent by you, or by any other monarch who takes to the notion of acquiring that country's mineral wealth. Now we will take our leave, and please, remember that I have six dragons in the air right now, and most of your city is constructed of wood, not stone; don't make the colossal mistake of trying to stop us."

That evening, as the dragons settled down and relaxed outside the town of Ford in Trent, Walker spoke with Delno.

"I hope that you and my father are right about this, my friend. I would have been more diplomatic with the man. He just might take insult and move against Iondar out of spite."

"That is possible, but I doubt it. Ronald may not have wanted to listen to us, but his advisors were paying close attention. He might rant, rave and threaten, and I'm certain that there will be a good many odd bits and pieces that were once furnishings in the rubbish heap tomorrow, but in the end, he will be made to see reason. His country may not have suffered the depredations endured by others during the war, but it has never fielded a large army anyway, and even now, after the build-up Ronald initiated when he was crowned, their forces are not the grand army he would like us to believe they are. The only thing that made them think they stood a chance against the military might of Iondar, some of the best fighters in the known world, was that the Iondarians were so deeply embroiled in this standoff with Horne. With reinforcements from the Elves and the Legion of Riders ready to join in, I don't believe that Tyler would dare move against the South."

"I hope you are right. Horne has only been held in check since its last expansion by the need to keep the northern territories where the bulk of their food is grown free from the beast-men. That is why the elves have been sending smaller bands of hunters year after year to cull the Roracks rather than making one massive hunt and putting an end to the cycle. While I sometimes wish the men and elves had killed all of those abominations rather than taking pity on them at the end of the Dragon-Mage war, I can see that not doing so has, to some extent, served the greater good of the world at large."

Delno had guessed that the elves could do more against those monsters, and he had always suspected that the seventy Hunters sent to help in the war were there to scout out the political ramifications of the situation as well as their stated mission of returning elven property. "It seems rather harsh to let the common people of

Horne suffer to keep their king's ambitions in check," he said.

"It is harsh, my friend, but what would you have us do? Should we directly interfere with a sovereign government and remove the king of Horne by force? That could easily lead the Elves down a perilous road toward domination of the known lands: a road that you have sworn to guard." Walker replied.

Delno was thoughtful for a moment before saying, "I don't know if there is an answer at all, Walker, and there certainly isn't an easy one that comes readily to mind. However, this current problem will eventually be resolved, and Horne will recover from the losses suffered in the war. Now that the Legion has set up in the Fort there will be more Riders to stop the incursions of the Roracks. Eventually, Horne's ambitions will again become an issue, and I am afraid the Riders and the Elves will no longer be able to sit back and manipulate affairs from a distance. We might be able to keep the status quo for a few more decades, so it may not be Thomas we have to deal with, but in a future that is foreseeable to people with our lifespans, we are going to have to get this sorted out."

CHAPTER 41

"WILL HAS INFORMED me that another two full companies of soldiers have been pulled back from the southeastern border and sent north," Nassari said without looking up as Nadia walked into his office. "With the company that was reassigned earlier this week, plus the four hundred men who were already here, we might actually have a chance to start pushing the rest of the Roracks back into the mountains and keeping them there. With a little luck, we won't lose any more farms at all, and this country will not go hungry next winter."

"Finally, we get some good news," Nadia replied. "Though I also admit that Jeremy's report about that joint operation wasn't exactly a bad thing.

"You've been driving yourself so hard these past couple of weeks we've barely had a chance to wave at each other in passing, and I've been working such late hours keeping it all organized that you've been sound asleep by the time I get to our quarters. I thought you had gotten that report but I wasn't actually sure until now."

Nadia shook her head, "Yes, I got it, but you are right; we have barely spoken lately. We have both been too exhausted to talk on the nights you actually come to bed, and often you don't even make it that far. Most mornings, one of the riders on the first shift finds you sleeping on the couch here in your office and wakes you. Then you go and do a full two hours of physical training before settling back down to your files and receipts. This time of the morning is the only chance we get to see each other at all lately. If we don't get a break soon, we won't be any good to anyone."

"Hopefully, having more soldiers will give us both more time. Now that the army can function again, we won't have to manage everything down to the finest detail."

"Well, we'd better start managing the food supply for the dragons better," she replied, changing the subject. "There are four likely candidates, three from Horne and one all the way from Trent, for the two eggs that will hatch in the next day or so. Then there are three more eggs to be laid as soon as that pregnant dragon gets here. One of those eggs is a male and he will fly off after he has eaten enough to sate his appetite rather than eat himself into a stupor like the females, but the other two will also need to be fed for several weeks at the very least." She paused and drew a deep breath before continuing. "What worries me is having enough meat for all of those hatchlings. How did you do in your negotiations with our local nobleman yesterday?"

"Hmph!" Nassari snorted. "That man is as shrewd as he is dishonest. He insisted on full price even though he presented his lowest quality stock. It wasn't until I simply informed him that we would buy our livestock from Trent and bring them in under government seal that he finally relented. He still soaked us for every last copper he could get, though. I'm afraid that nearly all of the funds we've managed to squirrel away were spent in the deal. However, we'll have enough cattle to provide for the hatchlings and all of the adult dragons here who need to eat for the next three months, at least."

"I am sorry to hear about depleting our funds, I was going to buy a new party dress for the annual meeting; it's in less than three weeks, you know?" she said sarcastically. "I don't like lining that man's pockets," she added in a normal tone, "but I'm glad we've got the meat situation sorted out. Two more riders have decided to go and look for more gainful employ. They are both over sixteen, so I had no right to stop them, but that brings our total force down to less than two dozen."

Nassari was silent and his eyes took on the distant look of a rider in communication with his bond-mate. *"Wanda, why wasn't I informed immediately when two more bonded pairs left? You are Lineage Holder here; nothing like that happens without your knowledge."*

"I saw no reason to burden you with it since it is Nadia who handles the patrols and has to adjust the schedule. You have enough to deal with already."

"No need to burden me? Wanda, I need to be kept aware if something like this happens. This affects everything, not just the patrols. With two fewer riders, we will be even more hard-pressed to keep up with everything that must be done."

"What different outcome would you have achieved? The two riders are adults and all of the dragons are fully mature. You can't stop them if they want to leave, and even I have only so much power to influence their decision. Just be glad that Jeremy looks up to you like a father figure; he's such a strong leader that he and Dina can't be easily swayed, but he stays out of the sense of duty you have helped to nurture in him. Also, Sarah, who is quite charismatic in her own right, has developed a strong attachment to our good friend Elom, though he is so preoccupied he barely notices, so those few youngsters who look to her aren't anxious to go off in search of more lucrative employ when they come of age over the next few months. If either of them were to leave, there are more than a few who would follow." She paused for a moment before saying somewhat heatedly, *"We have them all flying patrols from dawn until well after dusk, and then, instead of giving them food and comfortable rest, we send them on errands to the capital, or off to the mines to carry materials. Once they finish with those duties, if we can't find anything else for them to do, they are allowed to go and hunt in an area that is all but depleted of sufficient game. I'm amazed that only two of them left, and you can bet that we'll lose more if conditions don't change soon. I hadn't informed you before now because you drive yourself harder than anyone else, but even dragons have their limits."*

Nassari was quiet for a moment and then *said, "Thank you, Wanda, and you're right; we can't keep pushing ourselves like this. Tell the other dragons that patrol schedules and other errands will be lightened over the coming days, and the food shortage problem has been corrected for the short term."* He *started to break off communication, but added,* "I'll be out to see you soon, Love."

Nadia looked at him expectantly and said, "Interesting conversation?"

"It appears as though you, Pina, and Wanda have been keeping secrets from me."

"Only for your own good! You may be the Rider of a Lineage Holder, and the chosen favorite of our overall leader, but you are just one man. We need a break, and you need one more than most." She opened her mouth to say more but he cut her off.

"You're absolutely right! We've done a damn sight more than we contracted for, and that is at an end. We will not, at this time attempt to retake any lands lost to the Roracks since our return." Before she could object to that statement, he held up his hand and explained, "The lands in question are still mostly open grassland, and I have discovered that they are owned by Horne in general. No one, not even Lord Bastian actually holds private title to those lands, though he freely uses them as if he does, and refers to them as his own while selfishly keeping anyone else from grazing herd animals there." He paused for a moment before emphatically saying, "Until the army is back up to sufficient strength to mount an effective offensive without major air support, that land can wait! We have spent too much energy, and even put children in combat for this country; it's high time we let the soldiers of Horne do their jobs. They have enough men to protect the farms that are in direct danger, and we will provide scouts as always. I also doubt we will be able to completely curtail the dragons' natural urge to kill those monsters when they catch them out in the open, but we won't put the added strain of a combat campaign on the dragons if it can be avoided. For now, I want you to adjust patrols so that no one flies for more than four hours at a time, and all dragons and riders are to have at least two consecutive days a week with no duties, you included. Lord Laran has gone to some trouble to ensure that we can move goods under government seal, so trips to the mines and produce markets are no longer necessary; we'll move the goods by wagon and Lord Bastian can go pound salt if he doesn't like it. While the riders are still free to come and go to the capital, and they are certainly welcome to bring back anything they can comfortably carry, we will no longer need such services just to fill our larders. We'll still need to carry messages and some passengers if Bastian's competition is to stay ahead of the game, but those are cash contracts, so volunteers won't be hard to find since they will be paid." Nassari paused so long that Nadia thought he was through, but he startled her when he spoke up loudly, "From this point on, we will operate this Fort as planned. We are here to sort out the Legion of Riders. The contract to patrol the borders of the Rorack territory is secondary to that goal, and is to be treated as such."

CHAPTER 42

ENEVA, FAHWN, AND four other dragons all landed near the gates of Meer, the capital of Iondar. The Riders didn't have long to wait. There were two men dressed in court finery and a half-dozen armed men wearing tabards that clearly identified them as members of the Royal Elite Guard waiting in the shade of the arched gateway. All of the men moved toward Delno and his group as quickly as dignity allowed.

"Welcome, Riders," the taller of the two courtiers said. He then noticed Walker Longleaf and appeared a bit shocked but pleased. "Welcome, Your Highness, it is an unexpected pleasure to find a royal prince of the Elves at our gate." He bowed low to Walker. "If you will accompany us to the palace, the King has already ordered food and drink, and he extends his most courteous salutations to you all."

Walker stepped forward, and Delno, who knew him only as the down-to-earth soldier at ease among the rank and file, was a little surprised to find the elf accepting such deferential treatment as a matter of course.

There was so much to see inside the city that no one spoke for a time as they moved past stalls of vendors who were selling spices, cheeses, breads, fabrics, and so many other commodities that Delno was having trouble keeping track of it all. He made a mental note to himself that he wanted to come back when he had some leisure time and see the market properly.

Since he couldn't take it all in at the pace they were moving, he turned his attention to the elf. "You seem well-liked here, Walker; have you spent much time in Iondar?"

"I come when I can, though I don't know so much about the well-liked part."

The shorter of the two functionaries, a man who looked to be in his mid-fifties, spoke to Delno, "The prince is very modest, My Lord. He has been accompanying diplomatic envoys to this country since before my father held my position at the royal palace. He has always been pleasant to everyone, and is as well loved by the people of Iondar as is the Rider, Brock Ard, the King's own cousin."

"I simply try and treat people as I would like to be treated, Ahmar," Walker responded amiably.

Before Ahmar or anyone else could say anything, their other guide mentioned, unnecessarily, "We have arrived at the palace."

They stood at the bottom of the stairs that led to the entry of the structure. The stairway was long but shallow, rising no more than six feet from the ground at the top landing. The stair was wide enough for a dragon to walk up comfortably, though she would need to keep her wings tight against her or they would extend beyond the low marble railings on either side. At the top of the steps was a huge set of doors that, while not large enough to allow Geneva or Fahwn to enter easily, would accommodate Leera or Saadia without any real difficulty.

As Delno looked up, he noticed that the main building was about forty feet high, and topped with a dome – about another twenty feet to the top - that put him in mind of the curious round tents the Iondarians used when they traveled. The dome was made of clay or something similar and gilded so that it glistened in the late morning sun. On a spire atop the dome flew the flag of Iondar, a simple blue field with a red stripe running its length in the center. Below that flew the colors of the royal house. That flag was overall red but had a golden eagle set above a blue chevron, and a narrow blue stripe ran from the bottom point of the chevron down to the edge of the banner.

"Their flag looks simple," Walker whispered, "but it is the same as the mainsail on the largest of the ships that brought them to this land, and therefore, connects them to the earliest Iondarians who set foot in this desert. They are extremely proud of it, and rightly so. The royal banner was designed later by the first king of Iondar who was a direct ancestor to the man who now sits on the throne. These are a proud people, Delno, and their history goes back so far on these lands that living memory of such has long since passed to legend, even among the elves."

Delno smiled and replied softly, "I'll remember that in my dealings with them."

Walker smiled and nodded as they were led inside.

CHAPTER 43

"YOU DIDN'T GET any more from Hassir?" Will asked his half-brother as he Delno and Brock conferred that night in the Dream State.

"They only arrived shortly before noon, Will," Brock replied. "There are protocols that must be followed when such high-ranking dignitaries as Riders and Elven princes show up on the palace steps. Even Thomas wouldn't be so callous as to skip pleasantries and begin negotiating affairs of state with the Rider of a Lineage Holder and the son of the Elf King in his court without first wining and dining them. During the early part of the day, we were all occupied with refreshments, and then the king, though he didn't slight anyone, primarily spent the afternoon with Walker discussing mutual interests."

Will, while mostly neutral in the matters at hand, was also well acquainted with Thomas and court affairs in the capital of Horne. You don't spend that much time in the company of royalty and not develop some sympathy for your host. His older brother spoke up to relieve the tension building between the two riders.

"What news do we have from Fallon?" Delno asked as he stood watching the reddish clouds slowly swirl, while Brock and Will stared at each other.

"The king is torn between his pride in his new mural, and his feelings toward the perceived insult of Iondar instigating the embargo in the first place."

"Perceived insult to Horne? What about Horne's insult to Iondar?" Brock almost shouted.

The landscape wavered more than Delno had ever seen it do before, and Geneva said flatly, "You three need to keep your emotions under control. Brock may have been the one who spoke harshly, but the dragons who are trying to commune here tonight can feel the undercurrent from all of you. As a Lineage Holder, I am partly responsible for making sure that this place is not violated by such upheaval. The Dream State is maintained by the dragons who make up our society for their own benefit, and they have been quite indulgent of this type of human interaction up until now. Either keep your feelings in check, or I will close this meeting myself, and you can all wait until you are face-to-face in the waking world."

The three of them stood silently for several minutes getting firm control over any anger they felt.

Finally, Brock broke the silence, "Sorry, Will, I know you're doing your best, and even I've mentioned that Thomas has some real concerns in this matter. However, he needs to understand that Tyler has been harassing Iondar for some time now, and more men sent during the war against Warrick would have weakened us to the point that Ronald might have actually sent an invading army."

Will opened his mouth to speak, but then went completely silent.

"Look, I'm trying to apologize," Brock started.

Will cut him off, "I'm not angry, Brock, I'm just trying to think. Give me a minute will you?"

Delno and Brock watched as the younger man walked to his bond-mate and laid his head against her side. After about two minutes, he turned to them with a huge grin on his face.

"I was trying to think of what my uncle Dorian would do," he said. "This is how he would probably handle it. Thomas is insulted – don't get upset, I'm simply stating facts, not agreeing with the man – because Iondar didn't send more men. I am going to explain

Iondar's concerns during the war, and point out that if Tyler had moved to take hold in the south, they would also have needed to create a free corridor between their capital and the newly conquered lands, and such a corridor would have been easier to establish and maintain in Horne, since the bulk of Horne's army was occupied in the north. If Thomas chooses to infer that Iondar not only sent her best fighters to Horne, but had the foresight to protect Horne's flanks from another outside agency in the southeast, who am I to challenge the perception of a king?"

Brock looked somewhat stunned and Delno replied, "Dorian, huh? Sounds more like you've spent a great deal more time under Nassari's tutelage than our uncle's."

Still smiling, Will retorted, "While both men are masters of their craft, and Nassari has a magical gift for such things, never underestimate Dorian. You know him as the kindly king of Corice, but I have studied his ways, and much of what he projects is his public face. Because of the hard-headed and often underhanded politicians he is forced to deal with, he can be quite devious when the need arises. Remember also, that he was not only groomed for such intrigue from birth, he's had more than twice Nassari's years of actual experience."

Delno was about to come to his uncle's defense and then remembered, not only the final request that Dorian made of Nassari, but also the subtle manner in which the king had tried to wrangle Delno into permanently stationing riders under the authority of Corice before they had left to fight against Warrick in the south.

He nodded and said, "Just make sure you don't outright lie to the man, brother. A good solid argument can be made for what you've said so far, but let him come to his own conclusions; don't try to influence him to the point that he will need verification of your view of these events."

"Don't worry, Delno, I'll handle Thomas; you and Brock handle Hassir on your end, and we'll have this straightened out soon. Then maybe I'll get that damned picture painted and be able to return to actual Legion business."

"You'll get the mural done? I thought he had a famous artist from Fallon doing it."

"He did, until the man got too difficult concerning my input and argued with Thomas about how realistically the dragons should be rendered. The King finally fired him outright and asked me to finish the project." At the looks from the other two riders, he added, "It's alright; it gives me a good excuse for staying in the palace, and his majesty stays close to watch my progress, so we have time to talk when I'm not caught up in the creative aspects of the work. Also, I'm to be well paid for what I'm doing, and even though I was good before, I actually think my artistic ability has benefited from my magical bond with Saadia." Then he shrugged his shoulders and added, "Remember, too, I'm not independently wealthy, and I've always wanted to make a living as an artist."

CHAPTER 44

ELNO AND NASSARI stood watching Will applying pigment to the mural on the wall of the main audience hall of the Royal Palace of Horne. Will and Saadia had personally flown to one of the mines in Iondar and gotten the stones he needed to make the blue pigment that was an exact match for his bond-mate's color. Delno found it amusing that while the mural did depict his battle with Warrick in the background, the scene used Saadia and Will as the main focal point. Apparently, Thomas was not only impressed with the blond rider, he was quite taken with the beautiful blue dragon, as well.

Delno spoke quietly so as not to disturb his half-brother. "Rita and I had a wonderful time in the Elven lands. I'm sure that you and Nadia are going to be equally impressed by both the landscape and the hospitality of your hosts."

"I have no doubt," Nassari replied, also keeping his voice low.

"That letter of reaffirmation of friendship you carry isn't the apology that Iondar was looking for, but it does acknowledge Hassir's effort to assist Horne in the war and makes it clear that Thomas wishes to be on good terms with them. Its delivery is just a formality and can wait until after the annual meeting day after tomorrow, but I think it's important enough to be carried by a lineage holder; thank you for agreeing to do so. Some of the Iondarian nobles will still be put out, but Hassir has assured me that he will accept it and not insist on a formal apology. He has already pulled his troops back from the border now that Thomas has ordered the army of Horne back to normal duty. With the additional soldiers in the north, we should have no further problems pushing the Roracks back into the mountains and keeping them at bay. With so many dragons, we can even cut their numbers to an extent that Horne may be able to rebuild its economy before another crisis crops up."

"That is the hope, though this region of the world was forged by magic and all of the worst upheavals have come out of it. However, for now, you're right. Nadia and I will carry the letter and then visit the elves. You and Rita should find everything in order after Nadia and I leave for the south. If you have any trouble at all, see Jeremy; we're leaving him in charge of patrols since Churney is planning to accompany Raymond to Corice for a while. Before you ask, no, they aren't pair-bonded like Craig and Adamus, but they have developed a solid friendship and the two decided to travel together for a while." He paused for a just a second before adding, "Oh, yes, that reminds me; you'll have to supervise the training of the new hatchlings and their bond-mates because Craig is homesick for his libraries, and Adamus is going with him. They'll be back, but not before next spring at the earliest."

"There is one last thing I want to talk to you about while we are alone," and he glanced to make sure that Will was engrossed in his work and not paying attention to them, "and I don't know if I'll get another chance at the Fort with the entire Legion there," Delno said. "Kern assisted us in our efforts by relaying messages to allow us to coordinate with the elves. He wouldn't meet with me personally when I was there, but I still want to thank him for the effort. I'd like you to talk with him if he will see you face-to-face. Also, check with the elves who are in charge of the master stone, and get their impression of the man. I would very much like to see him reformed and returned to Dragon Rider society. Perhaps one day he will actually take the oath and join the Legion as a full member."

Nassari raised an eyebrow. "Still trying to save the world, Del?"

"Still trying to grow friends rather than harvest enemies," Delno replied. "With so much happening in so many places and with new territories to explore, we're going to need all of the allies we can get."

"I can appreciate the thought," Nassari replied, "but that one may take more time. I've spoken with Brock about Kern. The man has always been a loner. Brock can't remember ever seeing him on really friendly terms with anyone, royalty or commoner alike. The way I understand it, he wasn't even supposed to be a candidate at Serrin's hatching, but was there in the background as some sort of servant; perhaps even indentured in some way. The dragon came out of her shell and made straight for him, pushing two noble-born children out of her way pretty forcefully in the process. While nothing was hurt other than the two boys' pride, their fathers were very upset. It was all that Corolan, Simcha, and the other riders could do to keep them from having Kern flogged. The fathers of the rejected candidates actually insisted that the boy be sent away and the dragon forced to accept one of the other children. Brock wasn't sure, since he was little more than a boy himself and not as close to those engaged in the argument as the older riders, but he thought that one of the nobles actually muttered something about having both boy and dragon killed when it was pointed out that once the bond is established, it can't be broken. The whole argument ended with the King of Tyler ordering all of the Dragon Riders out of his country by day's end."

"Tyler!" Delno exclaimed so loudly that Will stopped what he was doing and looked at his brother with annoyance.

Nassari took his friend by the arm and led him out of the palace. Once on the steps outside, he said, "I'm sorry, Del, I thought you knew the whole story; you spend a lot more time talking with Brock than I do."

"No, we have been so entangled in affairs of state since we met that the subject never came up, not even when we were deciding Kern's fate at the last meeting of the Legion. Why did this take place in Tyler?"

"From what I understand, Tyler has never produced a single rider," Nassari answered, then he drew a deep breath before continuing. "Geneva – Corolan's bond-mate, obviously, not yours – agreed to allow the riders to take one of Hella's eggs there in the hopes of changing that. She wasn't particularly impressed with the candidates, but everyone reasoned that one would most likely be chosen since that was all that was available. Leera, though young, felt through her connection to her mother that Geneva was worried the young dragon would simply refuse them all and have to be raised un-bonded, but she agreed in the hopes that such a pair would allow the Riders to have more influence in Tyler in order to maintain the peace that had been so hard-won in the clan wars. It seemed that despite the fact that those wars took place about fifteen hundred years before this event, the nobility of Tyler were still miffed that close to half that country's territory had been lost to Ondar."

Nassari paused as several palace guards walked near enough to hear the conversation, then indicated that the two of them should continue closer to their bond-mates where they would not be interrupted.

With Geneva and Wanda flanking them, he picked up where he had left off. "Apparently, as I've already said, the nobles' sons were rejected, and Kern, who might have been a stable-boy or something, was chosen. In fact, it was put forth by more than one of the interested adult parties that Kern had secretly visited the egg and deliberately bonded to the dragon before the candidates could be presented. From what Brock told me, several of the men drew belt knives with the intent of killing the youth and it was only because Geneva and the other dragons interceded and threatened to slaughter anyone who got near the pair with such intentions that Kern and Serrin got out of there alive. In the end, the King of Tyler ordered all of them to leave, and Corolan had the two young bond-mates loaded onto a wagon and sent to Llorne under the protection of Simcha and a couple of others. Simcha was given the job of training the pair, and it was more than three generations of men before any rider visited Tyler again. However, even after that much time, the riders were treated no better than common beggars."

For several moments, Delno said nothing, appearing lost in thought. He finally looked up to speak, but Nassari shook his head and pointed toward the palace. Rita and Nadia were approaching. Since they were carrying their gear, the men figured that the women had seen them near the dragons and assumed they were ready to leave.

After the good-byes had been said and the women had climbed into their saddles, Delno pulled Nassari aside one last time and whispered, "What you've told me explains much, especially the part about Hella being Serrin's mother, and all of it raises other questions. I want you to check on Kern, and if possible even try and make friends with him. However, make sure you check with the elves responsible for his movements. I don't want him unleashed on the world if he isn't ready, but I don't want to lose out on five hundred years of experience if he can be salvaged. I leave it in your very capable hands." Then he spoke out loudly, "Will and Saadia will join us at the Fort in time for the Annual meeting; for now, let's get going. I want to go over the routines with you and Nadia before Rita and I have to take full control."

CHAPTER 45

JEREMY STEPPED UP onto the platform built into the rock of Rider's Mound and raised his right hand. "I solemnly swear to serve my fellow creatures to the best of my ability and to uphold the just laws of any land I find myself in. I swear that I will not participate in any attempt to usurp power from the rightful and just rulers of any sovereign nation in an effort to gain power for myself or any master I have chosen to serve, and will make every effort to protect the sovereignty of any nation that is rightfully and justly ruled. I will abide by the just edicts laid down by the Council of Riders, membership in which this oath entitles me. Lastly, I swear that I will always do my best to act in a manner that will bring honor to me, my draconic partner, our respective families, and The Legion of Riders - which I now join freely and without coercion."

The spot that had once been the compelling stone began to glow as he started speaking and continued to do so for a few moments after he finished. Once the glow faded, he stepped back and smiled at those who had gathered to watch the ceremony.

All of the Riders sixteen and older in attendance, except Mark, who was restricted from doing so for two more years, had opted to take the oath of allegiance.

Nassari had offered Jeremy the first place in the queue, but he politely declined in favor of the man who had saved his life months earlier, so Elom was given the honor of being first. To Jeremy, it was the oath itself, not his position in line, that he cared about, and he was happy to be last in line and let the others stand ahead of him so long as he did get his chance.

The next hour was taken up by all of the new members declaring openly what they intended to do over the next year; most simply avowed that they would stay in Horne and continue to help keep the country safe from Roracks, though a few opted to travel and learn more of the world and the customs of the people they were now sworn to protect. When that was done, the subject of defending Iondar from outside influences such as Tyler was formally put to a vote and overwhelmingly confirmed. Minor Legion business was discussed for a short time, but mostly only by those directly involved. Once all of that was out of the way, the entire Legion and those guests present were invited to enjoy the hospitality of the Fort. The feasting lasted well into the night.

The next morning, while most of the Riders and guests were still sleeping off the night's festivities, Delno accompanied Nassari to the main courtyard. "Look, Nassari, I know I threw that assignment about Kern at you suddenly, and we haven't had another chance to talk." Nassari started to speak but Delno cut him off. "Let me finish. I have plans, and I'm going to need every Rider I can get on board, especially the experienced ones, but that doesn't mean I want you and Nadia to spend your holiday chasing this to the exclusion of all else. See what the elves think, and talk to the man, but remember, he didn't get that angry at the world overnight, and a couple of atta-boys aren't going to make a huge difference right away. So test the waters and then let it go; when he's ready to rejoin the world, the elves will let us know. If I didn't trust them, I wouldn't have put him in their custody. The main mission you two have is to rest and enjoy yourselves."

"Thanks, Del, I will," Nassari replied. "We plan to stop over in the port city of Ma'an Azraq where my grandparents retired and see them as well as deliver the letter you brought along from my mother. Then we will finish our official business in Meer before heading on to our final destination, and a much needed holiday."

"You once told me that you would like to find your father; to make a connection with your actual roots. Southern Trent isn't really out of the way if you wanted to take a couple of days to search. Your mother has told you his name, and where he was last known to live. With Wanda to confirm his relation to you, he could no longer deny that he is your father," Delno said quietly.

"I have thought about it, Del, but I'm just not sure I even want to know anymore. He turned his back on me and my mother years ago; I can't see him doing the honorable thing now." As Delno opened his mouth to say more, Nassari cut him off and continued his train of thought, "Even at the age of sixteen, he should have had the stones to stand up and take responsibility for his part in my conception. You or I would have at that age, but he chose to risk my mother's life, and therefore mine as well, to preserve his reputation. I'm just not sure I even want to know a man who'd do such a thing to a woman he claimed to love, not to mention his unborn child."

"Men mature at different rates over their lives," Delno said. "It is possible he now regrets his decision and would welcome you with open arms. Either way, you would know for sure."

"I'll think about it on the return trip when I am rested and in a more charitable frame of mind," Nassari replied, "but for the time being, all I want is to be with my wife in pleasant surroundings, and enjoy the company of people like my good friend Walker, and forget everything else."

Nassari was about to say more, but Nadia came out just then and got his help tying their gear onto the new saddles. By the time they had finished, Delno had returned to his bed. Nassari took another look around and then mounted. Within minutes, they were high in the sky and flying in a southeasterly direction.

Chapter 46

"LOOK CAREFULLY, LOVE," Wanda *said*, as they approached a caravan at the edge of Nassari's visual range. "*It appears as though those vanners are in a standoff against a large group of bandits. Strictly speaking, this isn't our fight, but it would be unworthy of us not to help honest people against a group of marauders. I suggest we intervene, but I will accede to your wishes if you say otherwise. We are, after all, on a diplomatic mission that can only be put off for so long.*"

"I believe," Nassari replied, "*that you already know my answer, Love. I can no more overlook this than I can not breathe. We are charged with doing what is right to help the people of this world, whether they be a nation or a small group of honest merchants. Relay to Pina that we will be going down to assist those vanners.*"

"*I have already done so,*" Wanda said, "*You didn't honestly think I would actually ignore this situation, did you?*"

Nassari smiled to himself. Not even his wife knew him better than his bond-mate. "*Relay to Nadia that she and Pina are to remain in the air to cover us while I first try to reason with those brigands. I know she won't like it, however, if this goes badly, they will be more effective strafing them from behind than fighting on the ground, and doing so might give us the diversion we need to get back in the air if we have to. After all, it is damn hard to concentrate on the enemy in front of you when you are trying very hard to avoid being burned alive from behind."*

Wanda angled her flight to land between the vanners and the log roadblock that the bandits had put in place. She hastily set down close enough to flame the position, but far enough back to give her a wide enough field of view in case the bandits tried to flank them. The felled trees were piled about five feet high right at a narrow spot in the road between two low hills. Nassari was fairly sure that there were more men than just the six he had seen standing behind the blockade when coming in for a landing, and Nadia relayed through her partner that he was correct in his assumption as she and Pina surveyed the enemies from behind.

Wanda's wings had kicked up an impressive amount of dust as she set down, so the men in front of them were temporarily blinded, and didn't notice Pina circling around to a better position overhead. Wanda had filled her flame bladder while still at altitude, so she was ready for anything. She trusted her bond-mate more than any other being on the planet, either human or dragon. However, even Nassari's gift of persuasion had its limits, and she didn't think these men were in the mood to negotiate.

Nassari didn't move to dismount. Instead, he just sat there for several moments until Pina indicated that she and Nadia were in position if needed.

"Who's in charge here?" Nassari said, his demeanor calm, but his voice raised enough to be heard clearly.

"That would be me," came the confident voice of one of the bandits. That man and one other stepped up as if climbing unseen stairs behind the barricade. When the two of them reached the top of the logs, the first man said, "I am the leader of these men, and you are standing between me and my prize. Leave now, or you will be blasted out of the way!"

Nassari made no indication that he had even heard the order.

"That other man is gathering energy, Love, I am sure he is a mage!" Wanda informed him.

"I see what he is doing, Wanda, and I am not unskilled at magic

myself. If either of them makes a move, you use your flame, and I will handle the magic user," Nassari answered flatly.

Again Nassari looked at the man and called out, "**Who's** in charge here?" with a slight emphasis on the first word.

"I already told you who is in charge here, fool!" the man shouted back. Then he looked at the mage and nodded.

The mage's slight nod of acknowledgment to the bandit leader's unspoken command was nearly imperceptible. Then he motioned quickly with his outstretched hand at the dragon and rider, and a bolt of white-hot energy shot from his extended fingers.

Two things happened at once. The bolt of energy hit a small but very strong shield about ten feet in front of the mage, and Wanda breathed a cone of fire toward the two men that was so hot Nassari could feel the heat from where he was sitting behind her. The shield he'd placed between themselves and the mage was small enough that most of the dragon's flame curled around it completely unhindered.

The bandit chieftain barely had time to scream as the flesh was burned from his body, while those still crouching behind the barricade dove for the cover of the low hills to avoid the intense flame that curled up and over the structure.

The magic user managed to get a shield of his own in place, but his robes were smoldering, and all of his exposed skin was obviously blistered. The pain of the burns caused his face to contort in a grimace, and his eyes were little more than slits. He also had to hastily jump from the timbers that were now burning brightly beneath him like a huge bonfire.

The man made a motion as if to attack again, but Nassari was quicker. He released more of the energy he had gathered when he erected his shield. The mage, with his own shield forgotten when he jumped to escape the flames, flew back through the air with a gaping hole in his chest where his heart had been just seconds before. He was dead before he hit the burning logs.

Pina roared as she made a pass over the bandits, but held her flame as Wanda had instructed her to do.

Nassari raised up in the saddle as far as the leg straps allowed and once again yelled, "Who's in charge here, and you'd better get the answer right this time?"

Another bandit raised a hastily made white flag and shouted, "You are, Rider!"

"Good," Nassari shouted back, "I see I can reason with **you**. Now that we have made such a good start, I think you and the rest of your men should bring your weapons out here in the open and stack them neatly on the road before you sit down and let the men behind me tie you up for transport to the nearest constabulary." Then he added, "Keep in mind that not only are my bond-mate and I watching you, there are a fully capable dragon and her rider in the air ready to run down and kill any of you foolish enough to try to escape."

"I have always enjoyed the sight of dragons, Rider," the caravan master said as he approached Nassari, "but I've never been more pleased to see them than I was when you four showed up."

Nassari climbed down and extended his hand. The man's skin color was almost as black as jet, and he looked very familiar.

"I'm Nassari Orin, and I have the feeling we have met before."

"Wait!" the man nearly shouted, "You are little Nassari? I haven't seen you since you were ten and spent that winter staying with my mother and father. Of course, we've met! I'm Kassim, your uncle!"

Kassim grasped Nassari's wrist and pulled him into a nearly rib-crushing bear hug.

When he released him, Kassim said with a laugh, "It is so good to see you under any conditions. You have changed, but I can still see the precocious boy who used to try and give me orders when we were children." Then, with awe in his voice, he added, "and now a Dragon Rider? Such a high ranking position! Alab and `Um will be so proud of you!"

"Kassim, it has been so long I almost didn't recognize you," Nassari said. "you are only a few years older than me; the last time I saw you, you weren't much more than a boy yourself, and now you are Caravan Master. You've done well, too."

Nadia approached and Nassari said, "Kassim, this is my wife, Nadia, and Nadia, this is my uncle Kassim, son of Nassari and Mara Orin."

Kassim smiled broadly. "Your wife," he said, "and so beautiful." He bowed and kissed Nadia's hand. Then he straightened and said, "Come, we will let my men secure these prisoners and clear the road while we open a bottle of fine wine and celebrate not only the good fortune of defeating those bandits with no injuries on our side, but the return of a beloved relative."

Kassim then led them toward caravan while calling for refreshments to be brought to the main wagon.

CHAPTER 47

"WELCOME TO MA'AN Azraq," Kassim said as Nassari and Nadia joined him at the gateway to the main square of the port city. "It is a modest port, smaller than Meer by more than half, but it is still a cosmopolitan city, with much to offer."

"Not that I wish to pry, Kassim," Nassari said, "but why set up the family business here, and not closer to the larger port?"

"That is not so hard to explain," his uncle replied, "Meer is larger, but with so many ships going to Meer it can be hard just to dock. If that is the case, then the cargo on the ship must be offloaded onto a barge which raises the cost of goods. By coming to the smaller, less crowded port, the wait to actually dock is much shorter. So, by setting up our family business here, we get prime goods at a reasonable price, and increase our profit."

Nassari nodded, "That makes perfect sense. Like I said, just idle curiosity."

"Ah," Kassim exclaimed, and pointed to a dark-skinned man walking toward them. When the man was less than ten paces away, Kassim raised his voice and said, "Alab, look who I found on the road home!"

The man, Nassari Orin the elder, did a quick double-take. Then his face lit up as he smiled and said, "As I live and breathe, it is my grandson and namesake, Nassari!"

The two men embraced, then the older man held Nassari at arm's length and said, "Let me look at you!" He eyed his grandson up and down and pronounced, "You've grown into a fine, handsome young man. It is so good to see you again. How is your mother?"

Before Nassari could answer Kassim spoke up, "There is more, Alab, Nassari is a Dragon Rider now, and he is bonded to a Lineage Holder!"

Nassari held up his hand to forestall any further talk. When he had both men's attention, he said to his grandfather, "I must introduce you to my wife before anything else. Then, if you would like, we will introduce you to our bond-mates before we go and see Jida."

The older man turned to the pretty young lady, and Nassari said, "Jib, this is my wife, Nadia Cutter-Orin. Nadia, this is my grandfather whom I am named for, Nassari Orin."

Once introductions were made all around, the elder Nassari said, "It is good to hear that your mother is doing well, and Marra will be as pleased as I am about the letter from her." He smiled again and added, "Come now, my business can wait; we must go home and celebrate your arrival."

Nassari looked at him for a second before saying, "I thought you had retired, Jib."

"I only retired from running the caravan itself. I turned that over to Kassim who, by then, was already running his route to Llorne," he said as he steered them toward the gateway to the central market. "I set up an office at a warehouse. I procure the goods we ship, and Kassim has simply added more wagons to carry the extra cargo. I wanted to continue to send goods to Corrice, but your uncle Faizan decided to become a soldier instead of being a vanner. He is now a member of the king's elite guard."

Nassari nodded.

The group walked in silence for a few minutes, but Nadia was pivoting her head from stall to stall like it was too loosely attached to her shoulders trying to see everything at once. Finally, she remarked, "Before we go on to the capital to deliver that message to the king, we are coming back here so that I can do some shopping with some of the money we received as the reward for capturing those bandits!"

The elder Nassari laughed, and said, "That will work out perfectly. Tomorrow morning before it gets hot, Marra can bring Nadia to the bazaar, and I can introduce you to my business acquaintances, and show off my grandson the Dragon Rider."

He led them through several streets and finally stopped at an upscale row house in one of the more prosperous districts. As he led them into the dwelling, he called out, "Marra, come and see who has arrived for a visit."

As Marra Orin stepped in from the kitchen it was only Kassim's quick reflexes that kept the large earthenware bowl from hitting the floor when she dropped it as soon as she realized the grown man in her entryway was the grandson she had not seen since he was eleven.

The bowl completely forgotten, she threw her arms around him and said, "I had all but given up hope of ever seeing you again; welcome home!"

Later, when they finished with the evening meal, Nassari explained that he and Nadia had to move on to the capital as soon as possible, so they would only be staying one night, and any other plans would have to wait. Both he and Nadia did, however, assure them that they would stop for a longer visit on the way back from the Elven Kingdom.

CHAPTER 48

"WELCOME RIDERS," HASSIR said as the pair entered the royal court of Iondar. "My cousin Brock told us you would be coming."

"Your Majesty," Nassari spoke as he extended his hand, "it's good to meet you. May I present my life's partner, Nadia Cutter-Orrin."

The king bowed to the Rider and kissed her hand. "Your beauty makes my humble court seem pale in comparison, My Lady. I beg you to make yourself at home and brighten these halls for as long as you like."

"Thank you, Your Majesty, you are most gracious," Nadia replied.

Then, still holding Nadia's hand, the King added, "Come and sit; I have taken the liberty of having lunch prepared. I know that you have other business when we are through here, but I'm sure you can indulge the whim of a king for a little while."

He led them to a long, low table set on a slightly raised wooden stage. There were no chairs, but cushions were piled about so that those seated on the floor would be comfortable. Hassir escorted Nadia to a seat next to him on his left while politely indicating that Nassari should take the place of highest honor on his right. It took a few moments for everyone to get situated on their pillows.

Nassari broke the silence. "It's true that we are traveling to the Elven lands at the invitation of the King's son, but we are not in such a rush that we need to turn down the renowned hospitality of Iondar. I did, however, bring a royal proclamation of the reaffirmation friendship from King Thomas that I need to deliver, as well as his personal thanks for all that you and your people did during the recent crisis in Horne. I didn't know if I should simply hand it to you now, or wait in case you would like to arrange a formal ceremony."

"Oh, don't trouble yourself about that," Hassir said as he took the scroll bearing the Royal Seal of Horne. "We won't stand on formalities; Horne and Iondar have always been friends, and our most recent trouble was no more than a minor misunderstanding. That is behind us, and there are more prosperous times ahead." As the servants finished pouring wine for the king and his guests, he added, "For now, let us toast to new friendships, and simply enjoy each other's company."

Nassari was certain that part of the reason the king didn't want to make a big deal of the proclamation was that many of the nobles of Iondar wanted more, and making a show of accepting it might cause internal strife in the court.

They raised their glasses, and, smiling broadly, Nassari echoed the king's words, "To new friendships."

CHAPTER 49

"WELCOME, RIDERS," THE tall, handsome elf said as he extended his right hand to Nassari and his left to Nadia. They each accepted the offered hand, but instead of shaking, he simply held on lightly as he spoke. "I am Terrin, lead healer of the elves here at the royal enclave. The prince is busy with preparations for the feast that is being held to honor both you and the envoy from Iondar. He sends his regrets that he could not meet you himself, but did mention that you would want to speak with me since I am, to your way of thinking, in charge of Kern and Serrin, and their physical and spiritual healing."

He let go of their hands and turned around. He then took their hands in his again. "This way," he said as he guided them toward what at first looked like a huge, ancient tree. "I will take you to the feasting area, so I can enlighten you on the Rider's condition as we walk."

Nassari looked at Nadia and smiled. "Lead on," he said to Terrin.

"I have, of course, spoken with both the Prince, and with the Rider Craig about this, and that is why I know that you are to be given a progress report," the elf said casually.

"Well, we are certainly wondering when he might be ready to return to Dragon Rider society," Nassari replied.

The healer was thoughtful for a moment. "That is a tricky question. While he is keen on getting back to a meaningful life, he is not completely sure he wants to return to the Dragon Riders at this point."

"That could be problematic," Nadia said.

"Oh, how so?" Terrin asked.

"Well," Nassari said quickly, "he is a Dragon Rider and thus is a wielder of great power. We must be sure he is not going to abuse that power before he is allowed to go free."

Terrin looked perplexed. "I do believe that his rehabilitation was left up to us, and it was to be we elves who would decide when he was ready to move on. That was the original agreement; has that changed?"

The elf's voice remained calm and pleasant, but Nassari definitely got the feeling that the man was not about to give up his authority in this instance.

"No," Nassari answered, "to my knowledge, the elves, yourself, in particular, are the arbiters in this matter."

The healer smiled. "Good. I am so glad that is clear to everyone. Serrin is doing very well. She is cautious, but we expect her to make a full recovery by this time next year. As for Kern, he is healing well, too, and we expect him to be ready by early next year, late spring at the longest."

"I didn't realize he had been so badly wounded," Nadia replied. "I know he took an arrow to the shoulder, but I thought that was completely healed by Nathaniel long before he left Horne."

"Oh, I was not talking about his body. His injuries are far worse than anything physical that happened to him in Horne. It is his spirit that was damaged," the physician replied. "That is, after all, why he was placed in our care, to find the healing he needed to safely return to society at large."

Nadia simply stopped walking and looked at the elf.

Terrin inclined his head in thought for a moment and then, while gently pulling her hand to encourage her to continue walking, he said, "Normally, I would not speak of this to you about a patient, but you are entitled to know since it was your group who turned custody of him over to us. Kern was born into slavery. He was not well treated in his early years. I will not go into the abuse he suffered, but it left him with deep emotional scars that he never dealt with. That is what made him be the man he was. We have worked hard on those scars and made nearly miraculous progress. He is almost ready to have that controlling stone removed, though to be fair to his bond-mate, he will have to stay until she is fully healed."

"Well, that is good news," Nassari said. "We had hoped he would return to us, but if you say he can be trusted, and he wishes to go elsewhere, at least he will do no harm on his own."

Terrin again gave him a serene smile before speaking. "He may want to return to your group eventually, but he has great regrets for the wrongs he has committed over the centuries. He has had to examine everything in his past, right down to the slightest transgressions. Though most of his victims weren't permanently harmed, he still feels remorse. Unfortunately, most of them are long dead, and he can not make amends. So he wishes to go out and do what good he can, to 'balance the scale', as he puts it."

Nassari nodded but didn't get the chance to say anything, since they had now arrived at their destination.

As he looked at the structure, he realized that what he had thought was just a giant tree was actually a small grove of trees grown together in such a way that an interior space was formed, and he had not seen anywhere near the whole of it. As the healer led them into the enormous space, he forgot all about Kern for the time being and simply stood staring, trying to take all of it in.

The place had to be at least one hundred and fifty yards across, and pretty much circular. There were clearly defined walkways outlined by large glowing mushrooms that lit the paths. The largest fireflies he'd ever seen, at least six inches long, flew around creating a softly flickering light as they moved from person to person looking for crumbs of food to eat, or almost empty glasses to drink from. One young elf woman was delightedly dipping her finger into her glass and letting several of the fireflies take turns drinking the drops of liquid from her fingertips as others hovered in the air around her.

There were tall plants that had large glowing flowers hanging over like lamps seven to eight feet off the floor. The floor itself was covered with a thick, soft, light blue grass that interwove itself so that it only grew a couple of inches high. Straining his eyes, Nassari could see several staircases that led to upper levels near the entrance. They had been grown, not carved, into the outer walls. The place was just too big and too strange to take in all at once.

"Nae-sah-rae!" a familiar voice called out from a dozen yards away. "It is so good to see you again, my friend," Walker said as he strode up and extended his hand.

The Elf-Prince shook his friend's hand briefly and then, looking at Nadia, he said, "Where are my manners? Nadia, you look radiant as ever!" He moved closer and hugged her.

Walker turned to the physician and said, "Thank you for meeting my friends and bringing them here, Terrin."

The healer nodded once. Then, without a word, he simply turned and strolled away.

"Come, you two," Walker said, "you must be parched and hungry. I will see you fed in royal style this night. For this evening, at least, you must put all thoughts other than enjoying yourselves out of your heads, and relax in the hospitality of the elves."

Nassari smiled as Walker lead them to the banquet table. "Nothing would make me happier."

ABOUT THE AUTHOR

J.D. HALLOWELL, AUTHOR OF the popular *War of the Blades* and *Legion of Riders* series, is a 60-ish father and husband who is blessed to have lived an interesting and active life. His varied experiences include such diverse occupations as automotive mechanic, photographer, bouncer, paralegal, and massage therapist. He has been a soldier and an EMT, and has served as the chief of a volunteer ambulance squad. At one time, he was a diamond courier, and later owned a working kennel, and he has trained law enforcement dogs as well as personal protection and assistance dogs. He studied martial arts for over 30 years. Although he is now disabled  by the cumulative result of injuries sustained both in and out of the military (he has been shot, stabbed, blown up, bludgeoned, poisoned, and has even had harsh language directed toward him), he writes whenever he can, and has had four fantasy novels, *Dragon Fate*, *Dragon Blade*, *Dragon Home*, and *Dragon Justice* published, and has several other fantasy and science fiction projects underway. His other interests include but are not limited to history, archery, cooking, and making jewelry. He currently lives on the Space Coast of Florida with his wife, his son, and his Great Dane service dog.

A Portrait of the Author with Indie the Wonder Dog and a Hawk

ALSO BY J.D. HALLOWELL

War of the Blades Series
Book 1: *Dragon Fate*
Book 2: *Dragon Blade*

Legion of Riders Series
Book 2: *Dragon Justice*

JOIN THE CONVERSATION

If you enjoyed this book, please consider taking the time to leave a rating or review at the retailer where you purchased it and/or on Goodreads, Library Thing or other book discussion and review site.

www.ingramcontent.com/pod-product-compliance
Lightning Source LLC
Chambersburg PA
CBHW020349120726
47904CB00002B/516